ctober 30, 2025

's Baffled by Isle de Cairn Murders

8,934 Comments

nat Led to Isle de Cairn

encers"

Halloween

CERS MET THEIR END

THANKS FOR WATCHING

THANKS FOR WATCHING

KATE CAVANAUGH

INIMITABLE
BOOKS
UNFORGETTABLE STORIES

Published by Inimitable Books, LLC
www.inimitablebooks.com

Library of Congress Cataloguing-in-Publication Data is available.

First edition, 2026
Cover design by Christian Storm

ISBN 978-1-958607-56-5 (hardcover)
10 9 8 7 6 5 4 3 2 1

To Grandma RoRo: All my books exist because of you.
I hope this one would have made you laugh.

AUTHOR'S NOTE

Characters in this story will die in awful, strange, creative, and sometimes graphic ways.

There are also mentions of sexual assault, addiction, panic attacks, and multiple depictions of violence.

An updated list of content warnings will be kept on my website, katecavanaughwrites.com.

THE INVITATIONS

ONE

The shopping bags dangled from her wrist–Dior, Roberto Cavalli, Prada. Chanel lay in front of the others, hiding their creases, any smudges, and signs of wear and tear. An electric vehicle whirred, cutting through the background city noise as it came to a rolling stop, about to turn right. Someone smushed into her Chanel, flattening it, forcing Michelle's attention away from the Highlife penthouse and back down to the street level of 29th and 5th.

She'd been reminiscing. She'd been doing that more and more lately.

The automated, lyrical "walk sign is on" narration sounded, and she joined the growing horde in crossing the road. Still, the Highlife loomed ahead. All sleek angles, a late 2010s definition of modern, with as many fake plants as real ones.

Diego the Doorman greeted her, as did the blast of air-conditioning, the only part of the building she still welcomed without prejudice. August in the concrete jungle felt as much a prison as her own mind, both fixable if she didn't prefer the company of her complaints.

"Miss Monroe," Diego said. She pretended not to hear him as she breezed past. "Miss Monroe!"

The clear button illuminated a pale green as she stabbed it a little too hard. One of her press-ons broke off, and she hissed at the pain. Two elevators, both several stories away.

"Sorry, sir," Diego said.

Another distinct voice responded.

In a flash, Michelle dipped from her spot in front of the elevators, racing down the mailroom hall, glancing left and right, searching for the emergency exit that would spill her into the alley. Unable to find it, she heaved, taking her chance on a different door and tumbling into the stairwell.

She'd been here only once before, when someone had pulled the alarm on Halloween and she'd been forced to jog down in a panic at 2 a.m., wearing only her robe, her bonnet, and fuzzy slippers.

At the time, she'd grabbed the first bag she'd ever purchased, her prized possession she refused to let burn.

And her phone, of course. Live streaming her panic gave her a blip, a little hit of what she used to have all the time. People cared, said she was "iconic" and "so real." The next day a baby hippo was born at some zoo halfway across the world, and her fifteen minutes were up. Again.

She thought about whipping her phone out now and recording her monumental scaling of twenty-eight flights but couldn't come up with a reason–other than the truth–soon enough. So instead, she sprinted, as fast as her clogs would let her, until she reached the fourth floor. Then she slowed to a walk, then practically a crawl. That had been Donovan's voice chatting with Diego, and no doubt he'd wait her out up at her door, at least for a little while.

Michelle collapsed on the eleventh floor and decided to scroll through her phone until she reached the limit of people tagging her. It didn't take long anymore. Still, she screenshotted a few of the kinder comments–#WeMissMM–and slipped her phone back into her purse. Powered by her hit of dopamine, she swung open the stairwell door and walked to the elevator. If she ran into Donovan now, so be it.

When the elevator chimed open at her floor, her bravado vanished, and she stuck just her head out first to see what awaited her.

Instead of the towering figure of her landlord, she spotted a letter resting on her welcome mat. The faded *Home*, dotted with a heart at the end of the *e*, scrawled in her own handwriting and mass-produced for her first ever Advent Calendar, often felt like a joke now. One that was too real to quite be funny.

The elevator doors began to close, and she threw out her arm, stopping them, the alarm dinging. Out she strode, clogs clopping against the concrete "minimalist" floors, her eyes locked on the crimson envelope the entire time.

It sat upright, glittering. Impossible to miss. The fancy scrawl of her business name–*Michelle Monroe (MM)*–sparkled with gold flecks, reflecting against the warm yellow of the hallway light.

She glanced both ways before bending down to pick it up, noting its heft. For a moment, she wondered if it was a trap. As if Donovan knew she'd be like a moth to a flame, sucked in by something so aesthetic and lush. She'd open it, and inside would be an eviction notice. One last "fuck you."

Like the moth though, she couldn't help herself and blew across the paper. The sparkles of her name didn't fade, they stayed, emblazoned. With a quick flip, she spun the envelope around to see a matching crimson wax seal, stamped with a swirled *E* in the center, holding the contents treasured and safe. It, too, was dusted in gold flakes.

As if coming to her senses, Michelle quickly pulled her keys out of her purse, jammed them into the lock, and shoved her way into her penthouse loft. Her melody of bags rustled behind her as she turned around and slumped against the doorframe. With a deep breath, she let the empty shopping bags slip from her elbows, down her wrists, and fall to the floor. The now-barren loft echoed the sad sounds back to her. She reached down, fluffing and smoothing the bags before setting them upright atop her built-in entertainment cabinet, right next to her variously sized paper bags from Dolce and Gabbana, Louis Vuitton, Coach, and all the other brands she could no longer afford.

Some, like the Hermès, were from her very first purchase so long ago, back when it was still novel, still a rush. She'd kept the bag as a souvenir. Now they all sat, slightly scratched and dinged from overuse, looming over her, like the Highlife did.

As she reminisced–or "sad sacked," as she often called it to her life coach–she twirled the scarlet envelope back and forth, forth and back, and back and forth.

Normally this time of day, mid-afternoon, or just after noon, or who cared so long as there was a P.M., she'd pour herself a drink–some wine, or coffee she'd spike with whiskey, maybe a cosmo, if she felt up to the challenge of doing her makeup and recording that day.

But this afternoon she crashed onto her large, velvet green ottoman, not even making it to her couch, and used another of her press-on nails to slice through the wax seal. Inside, more gold flecks dotted the invitation.

Michelle sat upright, legs dangling off the ottoman. The invitation scraped against the envelope as she pulled it out completely, leaving several objects inside. She skimmed the large, looping letters.

You're Invited!

We've carefully curated an impressive guest list of VIPs and hope you'll join us for the most unforgettable vacation event of the decade.

"Event" was code for work. Like press or influencer events. The first time she'd learned this was at Coachella, when her management sent her out for a "pop-up event." She didn't even get to see Beyoncé because she had to take pictures at the stupid Ferris Wheel.

A handful of different sponsors she'd partnered with over the years hosted another "event" for her twenty-fifth birthday, complete with free drinks, decadent food, and people who were also working–who she mostly didn't know, and some of whom hated her guts. She'd cried in the bathroom that night, in a stall with an impossibly large ceiling and marble that echoed her sobs back to her, party of one.

But now was different. Now, work was what Michelle desperately needed.

Before reading on, Michelle tilted the heavy envelope upside down. She'd never been one for patience. Another card and several smaller envelopes spilled out. Grabbing hold of each, she felt around, the hard card stock of the envelopes crinkling. One felt like a ring, the other...maybe a memory card? Or a strange hair clip? Small ridges lined an otherwise flat object. A key?

She ripped open the one that felt like a ring, a sparkly, glittering sapphire dropping out of the bag.

There was a note, one she'd accidentally ripped in half.

But her eyes were focused only on the gemstone. It had Seraphina's telltale twisted band, only 500 made per year. Emeralds, last year's, were more her style, and she'd hoped to be back on top then, enough so she could afford one. This would have to suffice.

She gently tugged the ring onto her right middle finger–her preferred spot for all non-stackable jewelry–and grinned, holding it up to the afternoon light filtering through the window. Perfect. Someone clearly had done their research.

As the light hit it again, a thought occurred to her. *Should I be filming this?*

She turned her attention back to the remaining envelopes. The other gift wasn't as interesting–a token, representing 1,000 shares of some meme cryptocurrency–but she'd happily sell it for its supposed worth of $10,000. That would go a little way in paying back Donovan.

Or, better yet, helping her land a new loft. Maybe even a brownstone, with a nice little garden and some exposed brick. Maybe an old fire station that had been converted. Or something she could renovate! Reno shows were always a hit. She needed something evergreen like that, something to bring people back...

Glints of gold stole her attention, pulling her back to the invitation. She shouldn't get so far ahead of herself. Now was the time to see where she'd be traveling to, who she'd be working with, and to which company she owed a great deal of gratitude. On the floor, the original invitation she'd half-read sat alongside a plane ticket.

Round-trip airfare going through Miami.

She scanned the invitation again.

You're Invited!

We've carefully curated an impressive guest list of VIPs and hope you'll join us for the most unforgettable vacation event of the decade.

An oasis like no other, with sand so white and water so blue, you'll forget your troubles. Join us as we launch Excelsior: Essential Energy. Be part of the revolution.

In a different font, less loopy, less whimsical, the rest of the invitation contained specific instructions–when the car would pick her up, when she'd board from NYC to Miami, the next car that would transport her to the runway of the private jet they'd be taking to the Caribbean.

This was a week-long getaway, completely sponsored and paid for. All that Excelsior asked in return was for Michelle to share her experience with her audience.

In smaller print, it clarified this meant two or three posts a day following her arrival home, as well as one long-form video that contained at least two minutes' worth of content featuring "the product."

Michelle reached for the smaller note on her floor. It looked nearly identical to the loopy font of the invitation, but this one had indents of heavier ink, almost as if it were handwritten.

We believe in second chances. Do you?

Michelle flipped the letter around again, then scanned the floor. Surely, she must have missed something. What was "the product?" Energy? On her hands and knees, searching underneath her white sheepskin carpet, under her couch, she still found nothing. There was hardly anything left in her flat. She would have found it.

She tossed her braids over her shoulder and read the last part of the fine print again.

There's no internet access on the island, so we truly mean it when we ask that you relax. Rest. Enjoy. Let the island wash away your worries.

Michelle snorted. There was no rest for the wicked, and certainly influencers were as wicked as they came.

TWO

Sanjeev Singh lived on a farm now, so to get to the airport he had to drive the six miles past his various rescue animals and an additional two hours to get to the nearest regional airport, where he finally sat aboard his flight to reach Miami.

He kept the second crimson letter he'd received just yesterday tucked into his jacket pocket, close to his chest, and pulled his sunglasses down as the flight attendant walked by. She gathered his remaining trash as he closed his eyes, hopeful that she hadn't recognized him. If he could make it away from his own sleepy, coastal town without being stopped and asked for a picture, interrogated about his latest release or told to guess what eyeshadow someone was wearing, then it would be just his luck to get noticed on board a plane with far more famous people two rows ahead.

His phone vibrated in his palm, and he waited until he could no longer hear the flight attendant's pleasant chatter above the turbulence before peeking down at it. A DM from Sarah Pruski. His thumb hesitated over the message, but a slight rock of turbulence did what he couldn't stomach.

Their entire message chain sat before him, one that hadn't been touched in about eighteen months. The silence was louder than the all-caps accusations thrown back and forth, just millimeters above.

The new message read:

> Are you going to this oasis thing? I just realized I don't know who else to ask, and I'm worried it's just going to be me and, like, that kid who went viral for swallowing those swords.

Sanjeev bit his lip to keep from smiling. He didn't want it to feel like old times. He didn't want a repeat of all the other silly brand trips with them huddled together, joined at the hip, whispering shit about everyone else there.

Or maybe that's exactly what he wanted. What he'd wanted for months. Why he'd even accepted the invitation in the first place. He didn't need to check it again to know the words, but still he pulled the note out.

We believe there's no better time to make amends. Don't you?

He'd had a manager for years, but still remembered when he was first starting out, the sponsorship emails he'd receive where they'd spell his name wrong, where they'd copy and paste his most recent video into an otherwise generic email, when they tried to send him leather products even though he was publicly vegan. Now he had an assistant, a manager, an agent–a whole team to filter through his life.

They checked for him, confirmed with Sarah's people that she'd be there. Apparently, she hadn't done the same.

Then again…she'd messaged. A proverbial white flag, an olive branch, extended to him like the first time their friendship showed its cracks.

He'd answered the door with tear-stained cheeks to a man holding a bottle of Dom Pérignon after Sarah had been tricked into calling his first eye shadow palette "derivative."

On top of that, she released an apology video–one he still remembered, word for word. "I thought that meant like, derivative of the stars. Like the constellations. That's what he'd been *inspired* by!"

He'd wanted to believe it. He wanted to even now. Her whole schtick had always been country bumpkin, but that wasn't who she was. Not at all.

The apology worked, though. People bought his palette in droves, and the seams of their friendship had been taped over. He'd given her a second chance. And a third, a fourth, a fifth. How many was too many? He thought he'd reached his limit.

And yet...

Sanjeev typed out:

I touch down in an hour. When do you get to MIA?

Then he added:

I don't know anyone else going either.

Once again, he paused over the message, sent it off, then added another.

If it's me and you, maybe Cody or Ro, too? The old crew?

Their fight from before had nearly been wiped off the page. As the three dots appeared, his anxiety melted away. Soon he wouldn't have that as a reminder. Maybe everything really would be okay, and...

"I'm sorry," the voice came, just as Sarah sent her response. Sanjeev tore his eyes away from her message and placed his phone face down on the tray table. He'd already meticulously wiped down the area, barely content that first class might be cleaner than the coach he grew up with, but even still he cringed, trying not to show it.

"Yes, hi?" He said, blinking up to see a woman fashionably dressed, but more appropriate for beach attire than the chill of a plane.

"Hi," her voice now verged on a squeal. "Are you Sanjeev Singh?"

Sanjeev's eyes flicked to the flight attendant, sitting in her seat but with her gaze trained on the two of them.

"Um, yes, that's me," he whispered. But it needn't matter. The woman's excited claps made several nearby heads turn.

"Oh my god, oh my god, I am such a huge fan of your work. Your latest Get Ready with Me was so funny. And your rose setting spray? I swear by it now..."

"Oh, girlie, thank you!" Sanjeev said, forcing a grin on his face. "I thought I recognized my glitter effect! But I didn't want to make an ass of myself if it was, like, Selena's instead. Do you want a picture?" His voice always scaled up an octave, just like for his livestreams. He grabbed his branded psychedelic, 70s-inspired water bottle, currently full of his (also branded) blend of tea, lemon, honey, and a small pinch of laxatives, and posed with it next to his face. They both grinned for the camera, while he closed his eyes and flashed a peace sign with his other hand right next to his cheek.

"Ahh, thank you so much!" The woman said, still beaming as she moved out of the way of the flight attendant who'd come to shoo her away. "Thank you, sorry, thank you, bye!"

"No, no," he said, his voice now nearly two octaves higher than normal as he said, loud enough for her to hear as she exited First Class, "Thank *you* so much!"

If it was all a role, then he'd play it well.

THREE

Ivy hesitated as she spotted the blonde. Even with her eyes closed and mouth agape, the woman in the massage chair was unmistakably Sarah Pruski.

The voluminous hair screamed how much “closer to Jesus” she was than everyone else, and the large, gaudy cross pendant wiggled across her chest as the massage chair vibrated. Only she could manage the off-putting focus of not talking to those around her, lest she were on stage, preaching to the masses of wealthy white women who liked to pretend they were godly.

A man in a suit with a single carry-on finished checking into the lounge and whisked past Ivy, work chatter and the ordering of drinks enveloping him whole.

She could still back out now, turn around, pay for a one-way ticket home. This could be a sucky but inexpensive mistake, especially when compared with all her others.

“Ivy Strohl!” Someone behind her called. Her dark bangs fell free from her butterfly clip as she whipped around, confident she recognized the voice, but there was no way…it couldn’t be…

“Cody?” She wanted to cry. She dropped her bags to the ground and all but sprinted into his outstretched arms. He spun her around, his laugh reverberating against her chest.

"Oh my god," she laughed too, a few tears breaking free. "It's been years."

She wiped at her eyes as he set her down, and because he was so kind, so sweet, he didn't tease her for her reaction.

"Way too long," he agreed. His eyes grazed from her face down her all-black, but otherwise bohemian outfit, up to her hair. "Wow," he said, softer this time. "You've...," he trailed off.

"Changed?" She choked out. "It's been good for me. Therapy, I mean. It's helping me grow." While he continued studying her face, she grabbed the black butterfly clip and pinned the bangs she was trying to grow out. "And you...you seem exactly the same." Only a single, new wrinkle, and it made him look more rugged.

If he detected the hint of jealousy in her otherwise reverent tone, he didn't show it. He simply ran a hand through his blond curls, fluffing them up a little. Even his tiny ticks, like wiping his jaw right after, remained the same. How many times had she advised him not to do that? To keep the oils from his hair away from his skin?

It didn't matter. He was still as gorgeous as ever.

"C'mon, I'll help with your bags," he said. "We still have, what, a half hour to kill?"

As the two of them walked to the middle of the large hallway, where her oversized duffle and overturned wheelie bag lay, it was impossible not to notice the large, icy blue eyes staring at them from afar.

"Is anyone else besides Sarah here?"

"Not that I know of. I'd only just checked in when you called my name."

"If Sarah is coming, what are the odds Sanjeev is here, too?"

"You think? After their big fight in Cancun? I heard they haven't talked since."

"It's been a long time," Cody reiterated. "Maybe they've changed, too." He heaved her duffle over his broad shoulder and grinned. "Anyone else you hope shows up?"

She bit her lip. "Maybe Rowena?" She ignored the way his brows shot up. "I read her book, you know? Her latest one, I mean. The self-help one. Did you?"

He nodded, but didn't say any more, and Ivy could only guess at what the silence meant. Instead, he brought his hand up and waved. "Hey, Sarah!"

Sarah lazily lifted her palm and waggled her fingers but closed her eyes again. Message received.

"Well, now that's out of the way," he said, and Ivy snorted. "You want a drink?"

"I'll need at least one."

"Great." He plopped their bags near the floor-to-ceiling glass panels, letting them look down on the rest of the boarding gates. A neighbor in a suit seemed to recognize him, but Cody didn't notice as he took off toward the bar.

Ivy sat in one of the large, roomy chairs and tried to ignore the man's gaze flicking from her, to Cody and back again. She took a deep breath, slowly counting to ten before the telltale, "Excuse me?" came.

She turned but didn't offer more than her attention.

The businessman didn't care. "Was that Cody Planks?"

Ivy looked each of the suits in the eye, knowing that as soon as he had confirmation, he'd turn back to his friends and brag. They'd be done with her.

"Yes," she finally said.

"Knew it!" The man frat-snapped. Without so much as a thank you, he turned back to his friends and added, more quietly, "I've been doing that dude's workouts for years. His full-body-zero-equipment hotel room one is a fucking lifesaver..." and on and on and on.

Ivy glanced over her shoulder, hoping Cody was almost done at the bar. With two drinks in his hand–a white wine spritzer for her, as he correctly assumed her drink of choice was the same, and a beer–he spoke to a woman with a hat and sunglasses still on.

Squinting, taking in the woman's lean legs, her body otherwise disguised by a fur coat despite the Miami heat that no A/C could truly battle and win, Ivy wondered who she was. In her own heyday, Ivy tried to look conspicuous, never gaudy.

There'd always been two clear paths: opulence and excess, or the attempt to maintain your relatable persona for as long as possible. Eventually, you had to drift. Too much money came in, the call of multiple properties enticed, security needed to be hired, and the illusion would shatter.

People could only hold up against the deadly sins for so long, and greed was always a tempting mistress.

Ivy never quite reached that breaking point. She maintained–or thought she maintained–that clever veneer. No doubt that woman's coat ran upwards of twenty thousand, but Ivy would have bought a knock-off second-hand for several hundred. Thrifted from the best shops, of course, ones that required a parking fee and whose on-site coffee trucks charged $12 for a small juice.

No, it was a different sin that came for Ivy.

Cody turned and waved. Ivy waved back, before shifting and facing the large windows again. Below, she watched as a family wearing matching shirts snaked their way through the traffic of the terminal. She tried counting them–*8, 9, 10*–craning her neck as they found their gate, moving out of frame.

She snorted to herself. Out of frame. As if everything in the world was a photo op.

But the more she stared, the more she gritted her teeth, knowing that's exactly how she thought of things. It consumed her. If only she could turn the echo down in this room, fix the reverb, if only she could adjust the lighting like in her videos, make it not so harsh, let her gaze soften, maybe even drift to sleep for a few minutes…

She reached into her bag and patted around for her pill bottle, waiting until she grasped the telltale cool, hard plastic to breathe out. A wave of calm washed over her, knowing she'd be fine, knowing she had everything she needed.

The therapy helped.

The pills helped more.

She opened the bottle and popped three in her mouth, dry swallowing as two sets of feet came into focus.

Cody's sneakers from his own line with Nike, she recognized. She hadn't been able to see the pair of red-bottom Louboutin from across the crowded lounge. As she traced her way up the woman's legs, up her mink fur coat that hid a little black dress, and to her sunglasses, which the woman pulled over her forehead and rested in her thick honey hair, Ivy's jaw slackened. "Hi."

"Hi," Olivia Blakely said with a smile. Her voice was raspier than on-screen, yet somehow sultry, and Ivy almost felt bad for the times she'd accused her of "barely acting."

"It's nice to meet you," Ivy said. "I just started watching your new HBO show."

A lie, of course, but Olivia didn't seem to care as she bent down and kissed Ivy on both of her cheeks. "Thank you so much," she said, pulling away. "It's my biggest role yet, so I've been nervous about the reception."

"Oh no, you're great in it. Thanks," Ivy said to Cody as he handed over her spritzer. She immediately took two chugs, thankful she had something else to do with her mouth than suck-up.

"Olivia was saying she also hopes that Ro's invited."

Olivia leaned in. "I heard Paramount optioned her first series. They're going to start casting soon." She leaned back, stood upright once more, and shrugged. "I know authors don't really have much sway with casting, but…I don't know."

"It's worth a shot," Ivy heard herself say, and Cody pointed at her.

"Exactly what I was telling her. Plus, Ro loves the attention. She'll act like she doesn't, but…"

"Don't we all?" Olivia laughed.

Cody glanced to his right, to the group of men who tried to pretend they hadn't been staring. He gestured to one of the airport lounge chairs. "Mind if we borrow this?"

"Nah, man, go ahead. We don't need it."

Ivy waited. She hadn't pegged them as the type to play it cool. She figured they'd be asking for a group selfie at any moment now.

"Thanks," Cody said, pulling it over with one arm. He pointed his beer toward the other, empty seat next to Ivy. "Take a seat, Olivia."

Ivy started counting down from five. Maybe she'd been wrong. She glanced sideways, at the man hyping himself up. *4, 3…* "Actually, she can have my seat. I'm going to grab another." She stood. "You two want anything else?"

Both still had half their drinks left and waved away her offer. The fan, seeing the opportunity as Ivy shuffled past, leaned over and asked, "Hey, aren't you Olivia Blakely?"

Trust a man in a suit to think he had a chance.

Ivy slid into a new seat at the bar, requesting a glass of champagne. Spinning in her chair, so that she faced outward, across the entire lounge, she slipped her phone from her pocket and aimed the camera toward her old friend. She didn't wait for the suit to sit down. She liked having him in frame. Something about it struck a strange contrast.

Plus, Olivia was right. Didn't everyone want attention? Someone, somewhere, would tell him that he'd been featured on Whisper. He'd milk that story even longer than meeting Cody and Olivia.

Spinning back around when her champagne arrived, Ivy worked diligently on her phone, scaling and resizing, cropping and turning, until she had everything she wanted. The caption she added last. "Role of a lifetime for this porn star turned actress hoping to seduce a more famous man to up her profile."

Someone submitted a version of this blind at least once a week. It was always easy enough to fill in the blanks, reverse the genders. "Spotted at the Miami terminal. Looks like they're traveling together. New couple alert?" But now, for her own opinion, in a much smaller font, she added, "They do look cute together though..."

She adjusted her posting to go live in thirty minutes and slipped her phone back into her pocket, bringing the half-full champagne back to their seats.

"I nearly ordered that last time," Olivia said. "Decided on the gin and tonic."

"Told you it was a mistake," Cody said, in that easy, teasing tone he was known for. The man could flirt with a cactus and make it less prickly.

"Want a sip?" Ivy offered, then pulled her drink back. "Sorry if that's weird. I know we don't know each other."

"Yet," Olivia said, reaching out and taking the glass. "I think we're all about to get to know each other very well."

Cody's eyes focused on Ivy, and she returned his gaze, wondering if he was remembering the last time they all got to know each other a little too well.

"That's much better," Olivia said, handing it back. "Thanks."

As Ivy was about to take her seat, she heard her name over the intercom. "Strohl," the person said, continuing, "Pruski,

Planks, Blakely, and…Dashwood." Beside her, Olivia gasped. "Your transport has arrived. Please come to the check-in desk."

Cody laughed, but it wasn't hearty, not his usual bark of laughter, forced through him out of some genuine enjoyment. This was a chuckle, one that held a secret. "Well," he said. "Looks like the two of you both get your wish."

Ivy climbed into the backseat of the black Escalade, folding her limbs in on themselves to take up the least amount of space possible.

"No, you go ahead."

"No, sweetheart, I insist."

Ivy chewed at the inside of her cheek as Rowena Dashwood's head of black waves popped into view. She averted her gaze as Ro shuffled through the vehicle, resting her left side completely against the car as her once-friend turned and sat in the right-side seat. Olivia next, then Sarah's drawl again, "Honey, you go right on ahead."

Ivy could've sworn it didn't use to be so thick.

"I'll take the front," Cody said. "Little more room for my legs. If you don't mind, Sarah."

Sarah's pause spoke more than her flat accent could, but soon they were all situated inside the van, and on the road to the private airport.

"Have any of y'all had this Excelsior Energy thing before?"

"Never even heard of it," Cody said. He turned around, and Ivy's eyes met his. He gave her a reassuring nod and a smile, his eyes flicking over only once to the woman that occupied the seat to her right. A honk from the highway outside interrupted him, but Cody added, "Sounded to me like they're new. Figured it's worth a shot."

"And a paid vacation," Olivia said. "Did you get a ring, too, or did they spring for a watch for men or something?"

Cody held out his hand like a woman showing off an engagement ring, waggling his fingers. Ivy snorted, and she almost–almost–thought she heard a chuckle from her right. She didn't dare look though.

"You've got prettier fingers than I do," Sarah said.

"Mine too," Olivia said, holding her hands up for display. "I have Megan Fox thumbs."

"Oh, that's cute, though," Ivy said, wringing her hands. "Having something in common with Megan Fox is always good."

"Right?" Olivia's gaze shifted, focusing on the now-*New York Times* Bestselling author. "You know, I–" A jingle of messages cut through the air. The actress flipped her phone over for half a second–a move they'd all mastered, as if looking like you might ignore it but still surreptitiously checking what the messages said–but the flurry was unrelenting.

Cody pulled his phone out of his pocket next, his brows furrowing as he turned around.

Ivy licked her lips. *Had it been thirty minutes already?*

"Oh my god," Olivia laughed out, turning back in her seat and leaning forward, showing Cody her phone. "You think we should feed the rumor?"

"Never hurts," Cody said, pulling his phone upright and angling it so that only Olivia–and the smallest sliver of Ivy–was in frame.

At the last moment, Ivy ducked out of the way, hiding behind Olivia's chair.

"Wait, what's happening now?" Sarah asked. Ivy peeked around, Cody and Olivia glued to their phones again.

"Whisper posted," Cody answered as he typed. "Spotted us in the airport lounge."

"Did they post me, too?" Sarah asked, gleeful. She pulled her own phone out and began to scroll.

"No," Cody said, "Not yet."

"Damn."

"Don't worry about it. I'm not sure the caption is particularly flattering."

"It says they're rooting for us though," Olivia giggled. "Besides, any publicity is good publicity. Especially since I'm up for this role. It's with Paramount. They've made it very clear the number of followers matters."

"Traditional media isn't so traditional anymore, huh?" Cody asked.

Still biting at the inside of her cheek, Ivy managed a grin. She glanced up again, hoping, wanting–*needing*–to see their faces, their minute expressions of pleasure at being mentioned by the gossip account.

Instead, in a move her therapist would call "self-punishing," her eyes found Ro.

Big, brown eyes boring straight into hers and a scowl across her face.

Ivy averted her gaze, gulping as she turned her attention back out the window as they rolled to a stop in the large airplane hangar. It was almost time.

No turning back now.

THE FLIGHT

FOUR

The small, private charter hosted seven people max. Each seat reclined, with a leg rest. Four faced each other, in a square pod, meant for as much privacy as a metal tube could provide, and the others faced the front or side.

Refreshments included champagne and other sparkling wines, an assortment of liquors, fresh-squeezed juices, sparkling mineral water, and, of course, Excelsior: Essential Energy.

Snacks came in healthy, diet, sugar-free, carb-free, gluten-free, Paleo, and fat-free versions. Signs warned that smoking wasn't permitted aboard the aircraft, but Ivy had a hunch that rule wouldn't be enforced.

Not that she'd brought anything. She'd sworn herself to best behavior only. So far, she'd had the one hiccup, but could that even be a "hiccup" if they'd gotten a kick out of it? If anything–like Olivia said–Ivy had helped them. Relevancy was their currency, and she'd gifted them a windfall.

"Oh, and Sanjeev. He'll be here," came the Southern drawl a few seats away. Ivy tuned the rest out as easily as before.

Sanjeev Singh.

She'd always liked Sanjeev. In a strange, twisted sort of way. Like the first crush you adore so completely without ever saying a word to them, the one you build up in your head, morphing them into someone completely new and different, someone unreal.

It was a platonic crush. An admiration. But she somehow knew he had no interest in her–one, because of the woman that had always been attached to his hip, and two, because of all the people on the plane so far, once upon a time, they'd been in the most direct competition.

Sure, their styles were completely different. Ivy posed for magazine shoots where she frolicked in forests and ran naked in open plains and took close-up shots of her own slightly askew, no-makeup makeup looks.

His meteoric rise to fame–from brand deals to launching his own collections, being a guest judge to running his own Netflix shows, scoring an invite to the Met Gala–mirrored hers, though in a much tighter timeframe. What took her nearly a decade to build, took him mere months. And it hadn't been long before he overshot her wildest dreams.

One of the many reasons she'd started attending therapy, precipitated by a tiny little mental break. Her appreciation, her faraway work-crush, rapidly morphed into a bitter jealousy, so strong she could practically feel it taking years off her life as she stalked his every movement, waiting for the perfect moment to expose him. To ruin everything he'd created. To make him fall to her level, lower even. So, she wouldn't have to squint into his brightness.

But she no longer felt that way.

Not with therapy.

Though the desire to point out how men were over-represented in the beauty space, their rise to fame significantly easier, still hadn't subsided.

But as her court-mandated courses had taught her, she'd long benefited from skinny, pretty bitch privilege. (Though they wouldn't use those words.) How much had that accounted for her own success? A lot, so she was told.

As if her yearning had summoned him, Sanjeev Singh stepped up the stairs to the jet, the light around him creating a large halo. He said quiet hellos, shuffling past her and immediately falling into the seat next to Sarah. The two drew together in hushed conversation, the same way Ivy had always seen them before, and any chance she had was over. The brand trip was an entire week, but she knew her time had passed.

"Ivy," the sultry voice called. "There's a seat open here." Olivia patted the chair next to her, the one diagonal from Cody, and directly across from Ro.

Ivy hesitated for a second, feeling the weight of eyes turning toward her. Before Sanjeev could look up, she slipped away, into the seat, and settled snugly up against the window, an October heat still trickling through. "Thanks."

Olivia slipped her a quick smile before leaning forward, her warm, golden waves accidentally falling onto Ivy's forearm. "There's no chance you have any sway with casting, do you?"

Ivy and Cody exchanged quick glances before focusing on Ro, who'd already begun shaking her head apologetically. "No, sorry, I wish I did, though. You'd make an excellent Professor Partridge."

"Right!" Olivia exclaimed. Her charisma was boisterous and fun. Like how Ro used to be.

Ivy cleared her throat lightly, hoping the others couldn't hear, before she said, "Maybe she could play you? I heard your self-help book just got picked up. Something about turning it into a fictional universe?"

Rowena made a show of shrugging and rolling her eyes, but a telltale smirk tugged at her mauve-painted lips. "Well, I can't say anything for sure." She focused her attention on Olivia. "But I'll see what I can do."

"Promise?"

"Mhmm," Ro grinned.

Olivia leaned back in her chair. "Oh, sorry about that." She laughed lightly, pulling her hair off Ivy's arm, as Ivy stammered out a "No problem."

Instead of letting a silence settle, Cody asked. "Does anyone know how long this ride is?" He wiggled in the seat and spread his long limbs out into the aisle. He'd already dropped down onto the floor earlier and banged out ten push-ups and ten squats–they'd hardly been on the aircraft for ten minutes.

A chorus of "no's," rustling, and shaking heads responded. "I couldn't even find another airline that went to Isle de Cairn," Olivia said. "Can? Carn? Care-n?"

More head-shaking, more shrugging. An awkward air filled the cabin.

"It's in the Bahamas somewhere," Sarah said.

"The Bahamas is its own country," Sanjeev corrected lightly.

She scoffed. "'Aruba, Bahama, come on pretty mama' is all I need to know."

"Oh my god." Ro whipped around, but the mountain of blonde hair on the other side of her chair didn't move. "The ignorance, really, is not cute. It's a small, private island near San Juan."

"And your incessant need to be right isn't cute either," Sarah clucked.

Ro rolled her eyes, turning back in her seat, the fission between them still palpable.

Despite their own falling out, Ivy knew, in only one instance would Ro still defend her, and it would be against Sarah.

Ivy cleared her throat. "Does anyone else want a drink?" She shuffled around the outstretched legs and toward the Instagram-ready display. She grabbed her phone out of her purse, never too far away, and took a quick picture, once of the whole display, then a quick, vertical video of her outstretched hand grabbing one of the Excelsior cans and tilting it slightly. "Anyone?" she asked again.

No one replied. She glanced over her shoulder to see them all staring out the windows on the left side.

"Don't leave without me!" A woman outside the plane squealed. "Hold on, hold on!"

Ivy didn't need to hear any more, didn't need to peek out the open plane doors, to know who that voice belonged to.

Michelle Monroe clunked up the stairs before pushing her way inside the plane. Flanked on either side by designer overnight bags–not fake, Ivy immediately noticed, and from the latest season–Ivy side-stepped out of the way, energy drink in hand as she quickly returned to the twosome she planned to cling to.

Michelle spilled her belongings onto the sole remaining seat on the right side of the plane, as she continued talking into her phone. No one approached her, and for a split second, Ivy ached for her. Then the sadness morphed quickly into confusion.

Sanjeev and Rowena being invited made sense–they spanned genres of success and had "broken through" to traditional media.

In that way, maybe Olivia made sense, too. She added an air of extravagance, coming from Hollywood, being on people's TVs, even if it was HBO and even if her tits were out half the time. Cody and Sarah too, were respected–or "respected" in Sarah's case–in their own fields.

So that just left…her.

And Michelle.

Oh, how the mighty had fallen.

Ivy knew what she'd done. But as she glanced at Michelle, from her box braids, dyed lilac at the tips, down her snug bodysuit, to the tips of her sky-high boots, she couldn't conceive how it had happened to her.

Ivy knew everyone's business, but she could never explain Michelle Monroe's. People asked her–back before her mental break, before she'd stopped being invited places–"Whatever happened to that Michelle girl?" But Ivy had no answers. And she was too wrapped up in her own stresses to figure it out.

A beautiful woman, so charming, so vivacious, whose content had dropped overnight.

If Ivy believed in conspiracies, she'd think someone was blackballing her.

But Ivy knew infinite ways a reputation could be ruined without the need for conspiracies.

FIVE

Michelle kicked her feet up on the footrest, the edge of her heeled boot just barely dangling off the plush fabric. With an outstretched arm, camera in hand, she continued her livestream.

"Okay, I just got on board the plane, and I think we're all here?" She flipped the screen around, recording confused expressions that quickly morphed into smiles and waves, the chat going wild. "So many awesome people!" She said, switching to the front-facing camera before blowing a kiss. "See y'all when we touch down. Don't forget to stay marvelous!"

"I don't think they have Internet there," Ivy volunteered, likely the last thing Michelle's audience heard before she ended the stream.

"Gotta keep 'em interested, you know? 'Oh, she said she'd check in, where is she?' Besides, I stocked up on videos already. One a day until we get back."

The invitation asked if she believed in second chances, and she did. Especially for herself. She knew her assignment–get the eyes back on her. The real question was why the hell Ivy Strohl wasn't doing the exact same thing.

"Want to take a picture together?" She asked.

Ivy glanced around her group, but they were all on their phones. Only Cody the Fitfluencer sat upright, neck straight, eyes at a natural line, with his phone held out in front of him. Michelle made a mental bet with herself that posture would fall in twenty minutes.

No way he'd stay like that the entire flight.

"Um, sure," Ivy said. She walked over, none of her friends so much as glancing up, and did the old sorority squat someone must've taught her because Michelle doubted she ever went to college.

"Ready?" Michelle asked, when it seemed like Ivy was comfortable and posed.

"Yeah."

"Let's do a smile first." They beamed. "And then something sultry." Then pruned. "Oh my god, perfect. I'll airdrop them to you." Immediately Michelle pulled up an app to start fixing their flyaways and make their eyes sparkle.

A booming voice seconds later grabbed her attention. "Y'all ready to go fast as Fujii?" It came before the man himself arrived. Ian Fujii.

A broad smile wrinkled his thin cheeks in a way most often described as "rugged" on a man and "old" on a woman. His eyes gleamed, and his teeth shone unnaturally white. "We've got a little under a four-hour flight ahead of us, so you lot get comfy, get cozy, get a little crazy. But not too crazy, hey? We don't want any liabilities aboard this flight."

His wink implied he knew more about liabilities than any of them could dare dream.

SIX

Ian surveyed the band of misfit crew aboard his vessel. Superstar influencers, the lot of them, and it was a burp that interrupted his announcement. A gasp followed, as Ivy threw her hand over her mouth.

"Ha!" The raucous laughter forced its way out as he pointed at her. "Alright, you all better follow Miss Strohl's lead. Ought to try this shit out now before we gotta pawn it to the masses, am I right?"

"Here, here," Michelle Monroe said without looking up from her phone.

Before he could push through the door to the cockpit, Rowena Dashwood cleared her throat. "I'm sorry, I really don't mean to be that asshole, but..."

But she would be.

Ian knew to expect this. When he got that stupid second envelope telling him that Excelsior wanted him to actually fly the damn plane out to the island to show the world what it was like to be a pilot–and how much their energy drink could help. *We're all about redemption*, the letter said. It even waxed poetic about the brand's own failure of a first flavor and how this was their second shot. It could be Ian's too.

And, like a sucker, he bought it, despite really wanting that damn vacation. No rest for poor old Ian.

But he'd make Miss 30 Under 30 say it out loud.

"Hmm?" He tried not to show the absolute glee on his face at the discomfort on hers.

She cleared her throat. "Well…" she scanned the plane, as if hoping that someone else would jump in. The two in the front were huddled together, smirks on their faces that they tried to hide with their hands. Behind them, Ivy kept trying to control some relentless belching, and the two others–Olivia, Ian knew from afar, and Cody, he knew personally–kept glancing back and forth, as if they didn't know whether to be more concerned about the strange confrontation or poor Ivy.

That left Michelle, who hadn't once looked up from her phone since he'd stepped on the plane, hands zooming across her screen as she Facetuned photos.

"I just…I recently read an article about you and…well, your last few flights."

"What about 'em?"

"Uh, I–" Ro stammered, looking around again. "I assume you're alright now?"

"Of course!" Ian said, clapping his hands together. "Wouldn't be flying if I weren't."

Whether his answer or Rowena's own discomfort shut her up, he didn't care. "Any other concerns?" None were voiced. "Great, well I'll get us in the air in no time. Try not to walk around during the ascent, but otherwise, do whatever you want. I don't care. It's not my plane." As he swung the door open, he added, "Oh, I might need someone to film me flying a bit, anyone feel comfortable with that?"

"Oh, I've been taking flying lessons!" Michelle volunteered.

Her head popped up from her phone, expression hopeful, and Ian nodded at her.

"Maybe I'll be able to ask you some questions or something, too? We can take a video together!"

She missed the eye rolls from those who hadn't already returned to their phones, and even those who had.

Ian grinned. This was going to be a fun flight, alright. "That sounds mighty fine to me. Thanks Michelle. You come up after we've reached altitude, alright?" As if she even knew when that was. But better to have at least one person on his side.

SEVEN

Michelle could almost say she missed these brand trips and the countdown to when the shiny veneer of luxury began tarnishing by having to spend it with the worst people.

Almost.

The thick curtain raked closed behind Ian, and immediately Olivia stage-whispered, "What the hell was that about?"

Before anyone else could answer, Sarah Pruski's drawl rang out, loud and clear. "Dear Lord Jesus, please let this man fly us to safety, and please let his alcohol recovery be going well, in your name, amen."

Sanjeev repeated, quietly, "Amen."

The two squeezed hands.

Rowena sneered. Or maybe that's what her face always looked like. "*That* is what happened."

"He drinks?"

"He drinks, and he flies," Rowena said. Her head popped up over her seat, looking back at Sarah and Sanjeev. "Did either of you smell alcohol on his breath?"

"I wasn't close enough," Sanjeev muttered, at the same time Sarah shook her head, pointed to the ceiling, and said, "God will take care of it."

Michelle rolled her eyes. "And god knows that it's gonna be a long flight." The refreshment table caught her attention, gaze zeroing in on the champagne in the buckets of ice. "Anyone else want a quick drink?"

"Don't you think that's insensitive?" Rowena sneered again.

"He's literally in another room," Michelle said, kicking her feet off the opposite chair, her braids swishing around her waist as she walked over to inspect her options. Snagging the champagne from the ice bucket, she worked the cork from the bottle, the telltale, satisfying *pop* coming seconds later.

From her periphery, she spotted the heads turning around her, the shrugging of shoulders, and only as the plane began slowly rolling out of the hangar did Cody and Sarah stand, joining her. As Michelle grabbed a glass, Sarah reached over her, snatching some snacks and tossing them to Sanjeev, his laugh filling the air as he caught them.

Pale yellow bubbles filled the top of the champagne flute, and Michelle turned back, stepping over and handing Ivy the drink even though she hadn't asked for one. "You'll need this," she said, side-eyeing Rowena, who'd already buried her nose in a book. Ivy let out a mixture of a snort and a burp.

"How's the Excelsior, anyways?" Michelle asked as she returned to the table.

Next to her, Cody performed some kind of magic trick involving ice, orange peels, and whiskey, all their various glasses clanking as the plane shifted again, pulling forward now.

Forgoing another glass, Michelle brought the entire champagne bottle with her, settling into her seat as she clinked it against Ivy's Excelsior can.

With both of Ivy's hands full, she took a sip of the energy drink, then a sip of the champagne. "Not bad. It sort of reminds me of another drink, but I don't know what. Maybe like a piña colada?"

"Hmm," Michelle murmured, bringing the entire bottle to her lips and chugging. She needed to get through at least half before the people on this plane became tolerable. The bottle *popped* as she brought it from her lips, just as Cody walked by with two beautiful, caramel-colored cocktails. "Oooh, what'd you make?"

"Old Fashioned, with a little twist." He winked.

"What's the twist?" Michelle asked, glancing away from Ivy and back to Cody, as he sat and extended the second drink to Olivia. Michelle had never watched any of the TV shows or movies the actress had been in–granted, there had only been a handful–but she had once subscribed to her OnlyFans for inspiration, back when that was a consideration. She was one of the few as beautiful in person as on screen, and between her and Cody, they looked more like they were modeling some adult beverages than merely consuming them. "I took a bartending class a while ago and loved it. They had us make our own signature cocktails. Mine was a Monroe Mojito."

"Is that what you are now?" Rowena muttered, though loud enough for everyone to hear. "A bartender? Or was it a co-pilot?" The book she held in front of her face couldn't hide how far stuck up her nose was in other people's business.

But Michelle ignored her and blinked prettily in Cody's direction, waiting for an answer.

He answered, "It's just a few dabs of–"

The intercom dinged on, interrupting. "Alright, folks. If you'd please buckle up for the next five or so minutes, we've been given the go-ahead."

Michelle sat back, snuggling into the oversized chair as she fastened the seatbelt around her waist. She was facing opposite the cabin door and had a great view of the beautiful, Miami sunshine as they sped across the tarmac, slowly lifting into the air.

The ride was bumpier, the plane smaller, but she felt confident as the bubbles slid down her throat. An all-expenses paid vacation with enough clout-having and clout-chasing influencers around her to make the trip interesting. She didn't know for sure why the rest of them–save Ivy, maybe–said "yes," but she'd gladly take advantage of it.

Once they reached sufficient altitude, a chorus of metal scraping against metal and shuffling feet and rearranged bags echoed throughout the cabin. Michelle took a vertical video of the sky as they floated past clouds, then turned her phone and took the exact same footage horizontally, but this time she panned around the cabin, taking in Ivy as she switched between beverages, Cody as he sniffed his cocktail, Olivia as she ran her hands through her hair, Rowena as she stared off into the distance–her eye-line above her book–and Sarah and Sanjeev, pulling notebooks and iPads from out of their bags.

She turned the camera back to her and said, "This is boring, let's go see what the pilot's up to!"

She walked toward the cockpit, knowing that as soon as she left the others, the mood would shift.

People didn't like reminders of what they soon could be. Once upon a time, these people would have relished her downfall. One fewer person to take a piece of the prize. But now, she was just a warning that any day, any week, any month, they could be next.

"Hey there," Ian said.

Michelle panned her camera up to him, and his enthusiastic grin. Seconds after she closed the curtain behind her, muffled chatter picked up again in the main cabin.

EIGHT

"I really don't mean to be rude," Ro began, trying to keep her tone light and easy, clear from the fact that she was, in fact, about to be very rude. "But how did Michelle Monroe score an invite to this?"

"The same way I did?" Ivy asked, sipping the top of her drink. How many was she at now?

Ro narrowed her eyes, and Cody stuffed his fist in his mouth to keep from laughing. Ivy kicked him with her boot. Clearly, everything was water under the bridge with those two.

"I mean," Ivy said, barely meeting Ro's gaze. "I get what you're saying, but maybe they just want an even spread of people, you know? Plus, like," Ivy dropped her voice, leaning in, "she is the only Black girl here."

"Ivy!"

"I'm just saying!" She crushed the energy drink in her hand, finished. "Maybe they have a soft spot for her *and* knew they weren't diverse enough. I like her."

Ro pinched her lips together, but couldn't stop herself from hissing, "You only like her because she has fewer subscribers than you and she poured you booze."

"*Ro!*" Cody hissed.

Ivy's jaw dropped.

Olivia squirmed.

"What?" Ro said, unable to tear her eyes away from her once-friend. "I thought you were all about the truth now?"

Under her breath, Ivy muttered, "The truth will set you free, the truth will set you free," as if she were repeating something she'd heard from a twelve-step program–maybe she was. She rose from her chair, brushing past Ro as she downed the rest of her champagne.

Cody sent her a glare and mouthed, "What the fuck, Ro?" But if he had any idea–if he knew what Ivy really did–he'd be on her side.

"Can you hand me one of those, Ivy?" Olivia's singsong voice called, as if she hadn't just witnessed old friends acting like jilted lovers amid a decades-old fight. "And speaking of the truth..." she began, with a soft "thank you," to Ivy as they both popped open the tabs of their Excelsior drinks. They clinked the metal together, and the actress continued, "What do any of you know about this campaign? I mean, I got the letter, talking about the opportunity, but no one was appointed to me as Brand Director or Influencer Outreach or anything. My manager said it was weird, but not like, *that* weird. Did anyone reach out to you guys?"

"Nope," Cody said. "Just the invite with the little gifts and the plane ticket. Then, like a week later, I got my 'assignment' and itinerary in the mail."

Ro stopped her glaring at Ivy to turn Cody's way. He had Ivy and Olivia's attention too.

"Same here," Sanjeev's voice came, a row back.

"Wait, you got a second letter, too?" Ro asked, turning around in her seat and sitting upright, so she could see over the headrest. "Both of you?"

Sanjeev looked at Sarah, following her lead and nodding.

Sarah asked, "Did y'all not?"

Ro's eyes narrowed even more. She wrote books for a living–well, now she did–and used to read them professionally before. If there was one thing she knew, it was mystery. Suspense. Intrigue.

And why the fuck didn't *she* receive a second letter? Especially when her first one had been so…so…infuriating.

"What was in the second letter?" she asked, trying to keep her voice light, tone a pleasant interview breezy.

Sarah's mouth scrunched together before she licked at her front teeth, her red-painted lips, the wrong tone for her skin, moving up slightly as she did so. After a moment, she just shrugged, the smile breaking through despite her best effort.

Ro's gaze flitted to Sanjeev for a single moment, before rolling her eyes, hopeless. She fell back into her seat.

"I'm sure we'll all get itineraries when we arrive, and then we'll have a point of contact, too," Olivia offered up, a reassuring smile on the wannabe-starlet's face. Ro knew she was trying to keep in her good graces, just in the off chance she really could affect casting.

Everyone always wanted something from her now.

The plane dropped, and her stomach lurched.

Someone shrieked from beyond the cockpit door.

Another laughed.

It couldn't have been more than a few meters–or lasted more than a second–but it sent a collective shock through the group, more giggles breaking through their own hysteria.

"Sorry folks," Ian's voice came over the intercom moments later. "Let my co-pilot touch something. *Thaaat* was a mistake. No turbulence up ahead, so feel free to continue moving around the cabin."

Michelle's unmistakable honk of a laugh came through, being cut off halfway as the intercom died.

"That man is going to kill us," Ro said, picking up the book she'd tucked to the side as she stood, apologizing as she jostled Olivia and Cody's legs. Ivy moved hers into the aisle, avoiding a collision.

Keeping a hand on the storage bins, she traced her way to the front, gaze picking through the remaining drinks and snacks with a scowl. Only a few gluten-free items remained.

She kept a single hand on each chair as she made her way back, nuts and dried fruits in hand, before opening the compartment she'd stored her backpack in.

The first item she retrieved was her gold-embossed, hand-woven, leather-bound notebook. She'd been sent a stack of them for free, on a sponsorship deal, though she would've paid her own money for them. But she was glad she didn't have to.

"Oooh, are you going to write your next hit?" Olivia asked as Ro grabbed her blanket out next, tossing it onto the extra-wide bench seat that Michelle had abandoned.

"Hopefully. My editor is expecting a new proposal after the trip. I told him this was my vacation, though."

"I'm sure it'll be great," Olivia said, and Ro managed a smile in her direction. But just beyond her, Ivy sat, quietly looking through the lens of her phone.

Ro's smile dropped.

No doubt she'd be the next to appear on Whisper. Only her "blind item" wouldn't be so kind.

NINE

"If there's one person fame changed..."

Ivy looked to where Cody nodded, over in Ro's direction. As if there could be any doubt whom he was talking about.

Though Ivy, try as she might to remain relatable, knew fame had changed her irreparably. The anxiety, the lip filler, the capital gains, the penthouse, the fear of losing it all.

Maybe Ro, too, was always dealing with a crushing weight on her chest. Worse, because Ro was still on top. She hadn't experienced the fall, not yet.

Ivy sighed. She felt like she was existing as two people. The Her Before Therapy, and The One That Knew Better Now. But sometimes she wasn't sure which would come out to play. And sometimes she still wasn't sure if she had done the right things for the wrong motivations. Did that count as The One That Knew Better Now? Or was it some mysterious, third part of her, some amalgam in between?

"Excuse me," Cody said, stepping into the aisle and walking over to an empty space to do some squats.

The partially comfortable silence settled again. In the rows ahead, Sanjeev whispered into a microphone, maybe recording part of his hit podcast. Occasionally, he stopped to take pictures of Sarah, who'd turned the snack corridor into her private photoshoot.

Ivy could already imagine the post when they got back to the Internet. "By the grace of God, I've been treated to blah blah blah blah blah."

Cody squeezed past her, his forearms flexing as he poured another drink.

Ivy tilted her head to the side.

Maybe she could have a flirtationship with him. Olivia could become her new best friend. She and Ro could bury the proverbial hatchet, even though, today, on this plane, it felt more like an axe was still lodged in her back. Ivy had no idea what she'd done to deserve Ro's ire. Before now, she assumed they'd just...drifted apart.

Ivy glanced over at Ro, who was staring straight at her. Their gaze locked for *1, 2, 3* seconds before Ro looked back at her book, conveniently turning the page.

Ivy sighed and turned to Olivia. Her future best friend, at least for this trip. "Did you like the drink?" She motioned to the one Cody had made her, still mostly full.

Olivia shifted, looking around, making sure that Cody's back was still to them before blanching. "Sweet, I like sweet," she whispered.

Ivy laughed and extended her hand.

Silently, Olivia passed her the glass, and Ivy downed it.

She preferred sweet too, but this was a bonding moment. The whiskey burned her throat as it went down.

She stood, empty glass in hand, and staggered. " *Whoa.*"

"You okay?" Olivia asked, her dark brows, contrasted against her golden hair, pinching considerably. For a moment, Ivy concentrated on the elevens present between her brows and wondered if Olivia's Botox was wearing off.

Or maybe she preferred to be natural.

"Fine," Ivy laughed. "Yeah, I'm fine, just, y'know, stood up too fast." She staggered slightly down the aisle, hesitating as they seemed to hit an actual patch of turbulence, before staggering forward some more.

The curtain to the cockpit flew open and startled her, and Michelle closed the gap between them, reaching out, catching her wrists. "Sorry, sorry," she said, dropping her grip and Ivy stabilized. "I was just gonna use the bathroom."

"Oh," Ivy hiccuped. "Me too."

It took only one lingering up-and-down for Michelle to gesture her forward. "You first."

Ivy smiled, her eyes lazy as they fluttered to stay open. "I knew I was right to like you. *Thanksss.*"

She struggled to shut the door all the way, and Michelle helped pull from the other side. Ivy slipped the lock sign, waiting for the overhead light to flash on, indicating the bathroom was occupied, before she slumped onto the toilet.

TEN

Cody watched as Michelle kept her hand on the door, even as the Occupied sign turned on. "Is she okay?" came the whisper, waiting until Cody nodded before dropping her arm and walking off. Michelle plopped onto the long bench seat, immediately kicking her feet up, and Ro continued her impression of a bitch as she yanked her blanket away, so that no part of Michelle could touch it.

"She's fine," Cody answered, a few seconds too late, surprised at how much the alcohol had already filtered into his bloodstream. He only ever let himself drink on planes, the altitude getting him drunk for fewer calories. After this brand event, he had a bodybuilding competition he'd be judging. Cody was the "celebrity draw" and this was their first widely televised showing, so he knew he needed to look as bulky, but as lean, as possible. All his shirtsleeves had been tailored to cut off just above the largest part of his biceps. A good tailor was half the illusion. But he was glad he'd been in peak physique when he received the second invitation from Excelsior.

He hadn't responded to the first one, but the second promised even more money, had leaked some of the guest list, and asked him to film guided fitness routines three of their seven days on the trip, with the understanding Excelsior could use the content and repackage it for the next year. He needed an energy drink sponsorship, and he had hopes this could be the next Red Bull or Monster and he'd be getting in early. Trend-setting had been his secret weapon his entire career.

He'd been one of the first amongst a natty pushback, tired of juicing taking over, especially as increased science revealed the dangers of taking steroids before twenty-five.

His heights truly soared when he admitted that he'd been one of those young kids to take steroids. And when he opened up about the negative side effects he experienced, complete with pictures of his body in full frontal, barely blurred, along with a chronicle of health issues, it was *mostly* not exaggerated, though it was all sensationalized.

Plus, Excelsior sounded strong. *Kingly*. A great addition to his portfolio.

As he sat down, Michelle pulled out her phone. "And this here is Cody, of Cody Planks fame. Cody," Michelle prompted, and he turned around, camera ready. "You gonna help me slim down my arms?"

"Your arms are perfect as they are," he said, staring directly into Michelle's phone camera. "But if you want to be stronger? Yeah, we can work on that."

"Harder, better, faster, stronger."

"You bet."

She turned the camera back to herself, swinging her arm around, nearly hitting Ro in the face as she extended it out. "Alright, before that, are we going to get this party started? I thought that was the point of a private charter jet. Like, where's my sex, drugs, and rock 'n' roll?"

He wasn't sure if he was still on camera in the background or not, but either way he felt the pull of the lens. He stood again, downing his drink. "Yeah, where can we get some music going?" His tone convinced Olivia to help him look for an aux to connect their phones to the speakers. Snaking under the snacks, they found it.

"Ooh, me first," Sarah said, launching out of her chair, pulling out her phone, and snatching the cord from his hand. Immediately an angelic chorus erupted.

"You've got to be joking," Sanjeev said, and Sarah threw her head back and cackled. She passed her phone over to Sanjeev, who took only three seconds to move away from Gospel and onto something Top 40s.

Clearly, those two were getting along again.

Cody searched for Ivy, but instead found Ro. Her left brow pulled up, the most acknowledgment he could expect that she, too, was surprised.

He'd tried to put that night in Cancun far, far behind him, but she'd been there. Ro had seen it all. And maybe more than him, if the blow-up of her friendship with Ivy meant anything.

And even more, they'd all seen Sanjeev and Sarah's fight.

If those two could come back together, maybe the three of them could, too...

With the music thumping so loud, he could no longer hear the rush of the wind. He could almost forget he was flying.

When Olivia asked for another drink, he obliged. Something sweeter, fruitier, with a splash of Excelsior. They posed for pictures, and soon Sanjeev, Sarah, and Michelle wanted the same. They laughed and shouted over the music, clinked glasses and drank and laughed some more.

Even Ro set down her book and offered up her edibles, a five-leaf olive branch from her snippy attitude. Cody accepted, and the booze let him give a smile in return.

Ian cleared his throat as he came over the air, the music automatically turning down. "Ladies and gentlemen, girls and gays." Sanjeev whooped. "We are rapidly approaching our destination and will be touching down in about thirty minutes. Please begin the process of securing your valuables. You've got fifteen minutes, and I'll need you in your seats."

The music turned back up, but Olivia and Ro began their return to their seats. Sarah twerked on Sanjeev.

Michelle snaked around them. "Okay, I can't hold it anymore!" She shouted over the music.

Her drink sloshed as she avoided a wayward white girl arm in the air, and Cody stepped aside, offering more room through the narrow walkway.

"Ivy!" Michelle yelled, banging on the bathroom door. "What are you doing in there? This is the longest shit anyone's ever taken in their life, I gotta go!" She banged on the door again, but her face morphed from annoyed to concerned.

Something was wrong.

Cody set his drink down, not caring that he missed the table as he rushed over.

"What the hell," Michelle muttered.

The music thumped in time with his fist against the door. "Ivy! Do you need help?"

"If you need me to grab you some different clothes, girl, no shame in that, okay?" Michelle tried again.

Still no response.

"Shit," Michelle said, pushing her way past the cockpit curtain. Someone behind them must've realized something was wrong and cut the music, the plane now eerily silent.

"I'm sure she's fine," Cody said, but there was no audience aboard who believed him. "Ivy?" His voice strained.

"Was she that messed up?" Sanjeev whispered.

"No, not that bad," Olivia answered. "I mean, just…normal drunk? Happy drunk?"

Sarah hadn't gotten up, but looked over in concern, and even Ro managed an anxious scowl.

"Got it, got it," Michelle said, coming out of the pilot's nook, leaving the curtain open and Ian visible to the crowd, glancing back every couple seconds.

A green rubber keychain dangled from Michelle's wrist as she tried the first two keys without success, before finally unlocking and shoving the door open. It stopped after a few inches, blocked by something.

Ivy's black boot was visible on the ground, her body clearly slumped over.

"Shit, shit, shit," Michelle said, panicked brain clearly taking over, futilely pushing the door back and forth, trying to get more room.

"I got it," Cody said, shoving his way in front.

It took two seconds of evaluating, but there was no gentle way to do this, and Ivy, clearly, was already unconscious, her body limp and crumpled on the floor. He stuck his foot in, nudging her slightly as he inched his way inside the bathroom. His chest and back scraped against the doorframe.

Blood. Blood splotches. Stained toilet seat. A foul, sour smell came from where Ivy had clearly thrown up the contents of her stomach, bits of pretzel and other snacks he recognized from the plane. His own stomach lurched, but he pulled his eyes away and refocused on his old friend, lying helpless on the ground.

"C'mon, Ivy," he said, grabbing her waist to set her upright.

Muffled orders and shuffling, hustling, came from outside the bathroom stall, but none of it could pierce through the ringing in his ears as he held Ivy up to her knees and tried to force his fingers down her mouth. He had too few hands, and she kept slipping before he could get his fist down far enough. Shit, shit, shit.

"Dump the water on her." Michelle thrust a large, open bottle into the bathroom.

Cody glanced back, meeting her dark brown eyes, wide with horror. He took the bottle and poured it over Ivy's dyed black hair, the bottle glugging. Nothing happened. Nothing, nothing, nothing, as the water dripped down her hair, his pants soaked, the floor slippery.

"I'm gonna hold her." With Ivy's limp body tucked against his torso, he pulled open the door with his other hand so Michelle could shove her way through. "You make her throw up."

Before he could finish his command, all five of Michelle's fingers were down Ivy's throat. A moment's pause.

"What the fuck!" Michelle yanked her hand back, eyes like saucers. "Cody…" she stammered, taking in the pale, fragile, lifeless body held in his arms. "Cody," she shook her head, backing away, accidentally closing the door on the three of them in the tiny, cramped quarters. Her voice broke finally with one more repetition of his name. "Cody."

He dropped Ivy. He hadn't meant to. The shock. It froze him. She was…

Ivy was…

Dead.

THE DINNER

ELEVEN

Dylan Goddard stood at the edge of the tarmac, the ocean breeze ruffling her black *Mercer Staff* t-shirt.

The plane had landed over twenty minutes ago, and still no one had exited. Crackling came through the walkie-talkie attached at her hip, then a bark of, "What's taking them so long?"

Dylan sighed, setting two of the cocktails back down on the bamboo stand she'd brought with her. Condensation had begun dripping down the glassware, rolling down her wrists. She wiped her hands on her black-wash jeans before grabbing the walkie-talkie and turning around. An exorbitant number of fairy lights hung around the bungalow. Exorbitant because her bosses kept insisting on more, more, *more.* It had taken her the better part of this morning to finish the outside of the bungalow oasis, and the early afternoon had been filled with panicked screeches from all three of them.

Monday, they'd crafted and curated the arrival goodie bags. Tuesday, they decorated the common spaces. And yesterday, they'd received their shipments of food and beverages from the other island and begun prepping the kitchen.

Finally...they were ready.

They just needed their guests to get off the fucking plane.

Dylan held down the push-to-talk button and said, "I can't tell what the holdup is. Want me to go over and check?"

"No, no," Lauren Mercer's voice crackled over the radio. "Wait another five minutes, then I'll see if I can find a way to call Ian. Don't leave your spot."

But as soon as Dylan turned back around, running a hand through her pixie cut hair, the plane door swung open.

Ian stepped out first, waving his arm from right to left in a giant sweeping motion.

"Stay where you are," Nick's voice commanded at her hip. "We need this shot."

Dylan froze, increasingly aware of the five cameras pointed at her back. Even though she'd been the one to set them up–close-ups, slo-mo's, an overhead shot hidden in the trees, as well as a tiny action camera affixed to the bamboo serving platter–she'd almost forgotten about the cameras. Ten million thoughts raced through her head, as Ian rushed down the stairs, now waving both arms.

She didn't move.

A few figures emerged next, carrying their own bags: a tall, muscular man, a woman dwarfed by a large fur coat, another woman with voluminous blonde hair. They were too far away for her to make out their faces, though she could guess at who each was.

Dylan grabbed the two drinks she'd just set down, and extended them out, ready for the first person as Ian barreled toward her. "Hey Ian," she called, putting on her best customer service voice. "Did you all go Fast as Fujii? Welcome back to–"

"Sure did," Ian yelled. "Got a dead body on board, gotta take care of that."

"I–you–what?"

He brushed past her, gruffly taking a drink out of her hands without stopping. The second one spilled a little as Dylan stepped back, messing up the shot of Camera 3. She glanced down, wiping the soon-to-stain mess off her pants, looking over her shoulder as Ian sped away, downing his drink in a single gulp. He knew about the cameras. That had to be it. This was a joke, a prank he was pulling.

Dylan took a deep breath and straightened, grabbing another drink and standing at the ready, waiting as the rest of the group seemed to take ages to catch up.

"Hi everyone," Dylan called, her customer service voice now sounding like she'd worked an eighteen-hour shift already. "Welcome to Isle de Cairn. Are you all ready to energize your vacation experience with Excelsior?"

But her forced smile dropped as the setting sun shone on haggard faces.

Ian hadn't been joking.

Someone had died.

Still, it was like her body hadn't caught up to her mind as she stretched out her arms, ready for the next person to take a drink. A happy drink. Filled with rum and grenadine and pineapple and–

Holy shit, there was a dead body on the plane behind them. Glittering waters danced in the distance, and she was sure that Camera 2 was capturing the other influencers as they slowly descended the steps. There, on board, would be one of the eight who wouldn't be getting off.

"Who?" Dylan asked as Sanjeev passed by without a word.

Sarah simply shrugged, a sort of deranged smile on her face. Like she felt she had to smile as a greeting but realized only halfway through that it was wrong.

It wasn't until Michelle whispered, "Ivy," as she passed, her arms wrapped around herself despite the warmth of the island, that Dylan's jaw dropped.

Tears streaked down Olivia's pretty face.

Rowena and Cody were in hushed, intense conversation as they passed.

Not a single person, save Ian, had taken a drink.

“Umm, what the fuck?” Lauren’s voice crackled at her hip.

“Why didn’t you give–” Nick’s voice came in, and soon neither did as they both undoubtedly tried to talk over each other.

Dylan stared at the plane, at the place where Ivy Strohl’s body lay. Then she brought the extra drink to her mouth, pulled the umbrella out with her teeth, spit it out, and chugged.

TWELVE

Cody stomped across the wooden boardwalk, past the outdoor recreation area and bungalows, the sun and his anger blinding the path before him until he dropped his bags, *thunked* to the floor, and crossed his legs. The heat of the wood seared into his exposed calves, but he didn't care. Couldn't care. Hands resting on his knees, he began to meditate.

THIRTEEN

Michelle had to break the news to Nick and Lauren too, since no one else would answer the questions they barked, and she desperately needed them to answer hers. Where was her room?

Slack-jawed and wide-eyed, Nick raised his arm and pointed down the hall.

She wound her way through the large, airy mansion, their home for the next week, a stark contrast to the Highlife. Passing room after room, eventually she found an oil painting of herself hanging on a white oak door. Michelle wanted to smile as she pushed the door open to find more gifts splayed across the bed, but her cheeks wouldn't work.

She wheeled her suitcases toward the large window, practically the width and length of the back wall, and simply stood, staring at the tide as it receded and roared, receded and roared.

FOURTEEN

Olivia took a shower, wiping away the makeup she'd meticulously applied that morning, what seemed like weeks ago, wishing she knew how old Ivy was.

Had been.

FIFTEEN

Ro searched for a spot in her room with reception, needing to ask her agent about the new idea she just got for her upcoming novel. Upon confirming what the crimson letter said was true–there was no internet on this island–she zipped open her backpack, brought out her second spiral-bound notebook. She dotted the tip of her pen to her tongue–something she'd seen in her favorite movie as a kid and now, unfortunately, ironically, had become a habit–and began writing.

SIXTEEN

Sanjeev slumped onto his bed, complete with five pillows–as he'd requested–and a thread count that rivaled his sheets back home. Soon he was falling, falling, falling, so exhausted, so drained, and so very quickly asleep.

SEVENTEEN

Ian downed the last bits of his paradise drink as Nick slumped into the seat next to him.

The table before them was filled with flowers, Lauren's crudités, Dylan's award-winning cocktails, and all sorts of fruit nectars and sparkling wines. The two men had both spent days, at this point, working for Excelsior, readying the trip for what had promised to kickoff their comeback.

With a sigh, Nick sat up and clapped Ian on the back. "It's not over yet," he whispered. "I won't let it be."

EIGHTEEN

Sarah knelt at the edge of her bed, palms together, fingers intertwined, as she thanked God for answering her prayers.

NINETEEN

"Lauren? Nick?" Dylan's voice crackled through the speaker. The radio sat upright at the edge of the marble island. "I have an idea." Her voice sounded haggard–as haggard as Lauren felt–and a little winded, as if she was hoisting something with one hand while speaking into the radio with the other. "Let's change the decorations in the dining room. Anything black. I'll let everyone know to wear whatever outfit they have that fits a mourning and we can host a wake–or a celebration of life–or whatever, and then..." her voice trailed off for a moment, as if not wanting to say it out loud.

But as the silence hung in the air, something like hope swelled in Lauren. She set her chef's knife down and wiped her hands on her apron, closing the gap to the radio with buzzing, quick steps. Her hands shook as she reached out and said, "And then everything can proceed how it should?"

Yes.

Yes.

This could all still happen for the rest of them.

Not Ivy, no, but Lauren still had a shot at reclamation...

TWENTY

Fuck, he hated himself like this. His mom would've called this look "raccoon eyes," but he'd made it glam and dark, perfect for a dinner meant to be a performance of grief. As specific a look as any other.

Sanjeev stared in the mirror, not seeing his own reflection, as much as seeing the thumbnail he'd eventually put up. Some take on "funeral-core" and maybe an RIP to Ivy in the title.

It would get him millions of views. Maybe even a few million more than usual.

The battery pack flashed red, and he tried to ignore how long his memory card had been counting. The seconds had led to minutes, which had led to nearly an hour of rolling, rolling, rolling.

Whatever.

His editor could work around this.

Clearing his throat, he held up his brow pencil and said in falsetto, "Okay, so what you want to do next..."

He could now perform half-asleep, had filmed before countless redeye flights, recorded from the hospital after his mom died, streamed his acceptance at the GLAM Awards while embroiled in a very public lawsuit.

This, he convinced himself, putting the final touches on a dark, juicy, burgundy lip, was a drop in the bucket. Just another Friday.

When the Mercer assistant walked in–Daniella? Danielle? Dani?–stumbling over her words, pretending to act all innocent about how "the show must go on" or whatever, Sanjeev could barely bring himself to feign shock. He'd already filmed the intro to his vlog for the day, meant for his second channel. There was nothing people loved more than death. Nothing more dramatic, more tantalizing. Everyone with the same questions, even people who didn't know him, those who hadn't watched him in years, would be too curious not to click.

Ivy's pain was their gain, to the tune of thousands of dollars in ad revenue. He'd just have to bleep out certain words...

But then again–Ivy didn't feel pain anymore. She couldn't see this betrayal. She couldn't care.

He signed off his funeral makeup tutorial–he'd have to workshop that title a little bit more–with his standard phrase, "Stay gorgeous, besties," and stood. The Mercers had requested all black, or dark blue, if possible, but Daniella or Whatever was right–he'd packed for a beach vacation, not a bummer.

And it *was* a bummer, he thought, smoothing out the pajamas he'd packed on a whim. Dark gray, flow-y, thin, and soft.

He'd known Ivy–or known of Ivy–for as long as he'd been in the business. He'd never chatted with her, even though he'd wanted to, at first. He'd looked up to her for so long, her effervescence, her lightness, something he couldn't quite capture.

The emotion had never been envy, so much as he knew her vibe wasn't his. And he had to find his own. In another life, maybe his next, he could be more like her.

Well, the her *before*.

Then Sarah warned him to stay away from her, and he did as he was told. Because Sarah was his friend–his first friend, his only industry friend, and, for a long time, his only friend period–and now, here he walked the wide halls to discover the open dining room transformed, and realized he never would know Ivy Strohl.

He knew her about as well as her painting, the one they must have all received, placed on their respective doors. Now it sat at an angle on the table, surrounded by flowers, as bright as the Ivy he once looked up to. He'd memorized the Portrayed Her, the Camera-Ready Her.

But he knew as well as the rest of the people on this brand trip that their personas weren't reality.

"Rest well," he said, bowing his head for a moment, keeping his eyes trained on his black loafers as he turned, walked a few steps, pulled out a chair, and waited.

TWENTY-ONE

Dylan stood in silence, watching as Sanjeev followed her lead, quiet as he took his seat. She stepped forward, overturned his glass, poured water from the pitcher, then settled back to the side, blending into the walls, doing the part of her job she was always best at. Disappearing. Sometimes she wondered if it was her superpower. Or maybe just that the villains she was up against were always so self-absorbed.

Michelle joined next, sitting across from Sanjeev, staring adamantly at the portrait of Ivy, her brows pinched and mouth tugged to one side.

Sarah floated in next, hair teased higher than ever before. Ro wore a slinky midnight blue dress that she continuously pulled down with every other step, and Olivia had opted for a black bikini and black fur coat cover-up.

With each new guest, Dylan overturned goblets and filled them with ice water. Every few minutes or so, Nick would drop off one of Lauren's creations, and a mixture of stage voice and real bickering could be heard mingling from the far-off kitchen moments later.

In the distance, through the sliding glass walls, Dylan spotted Cody slowly untangle himself from where he'd sat for the last two hours. As he approached, there was no frown on his face, no smile, hardly any acknowledgement that he knew where he was or what they were doing.

She'd tried to tell him before, but her words seemed as lost to him as the last few hours. Meditated away as if they'd never even existed.

He floated into the room, heads turning to look at him, and he took one of the remaining empty seats. For a while, that's all there was. The soft, delicate sound of heads turning and clothes rustling, glasses brought to mouths and water sipped, until someone brave enough disturbed the silence.

"Where's Ian?"

Of course it would be Ro.

"Like, can we start without him, or...?"

"I think, um," Dylan cleared her throat. "I think he's handling the...well, he's trying to talk with air traffic control about the...well, the issue." Her gaze jumped across the group before landing on the portrait. Keeping her eyes on it, she slowly backed away, trying to disappear once more.

"I'm not usually one for prayer," Cody said, sitting upright, as if his spirit had returned to his body. "But maybe you could lead us in something before we eat, Sarah? Or Sanjeev, with your God?"

"I'm agnostic," the beauty guru said.

"Right, yeah, can we do, like, a moment of silence then?"

Despite the microaggression, Sanjeev bowed his head first, followed quickly by Sarah, Michelle, Olivia, and Cody. Ro was the last person to bow her head, after Dylan caught what she thought was a roll of her eyes.

"Are they ready for drinks?" The question came from her walkie-talkie.

When she didn't answer–trying desperately not to disturb the moment of silence, the question repeated shrilly.

"DYLAN," Nick squawked. "More drinks, yes or no?"

"I'm just gonna," Dylan began, stepping back and covering her mouth with a finger. Into the walkie, she hissed, "They're taking a moment of silence, one sec."

But instead of giving one second, Nick squawked again. "Why the fuck didn't you tell us before–" His complaints faded quickly as Dylan wheeled her volume down to mute.

When she turned back around, armed with more apologies, all heads were up and looking at her.

All except Cody.

"I'll take a drink," Michelle said.

"I'll take two," Sarah agreed.

Sanjeev raised his hand.

Olivia requested, "Me too."

Dylan glanced sideways at Cody, who'd gone back to astral projecting himself somewhere, anywhere, else. If only she could do the same.

She stepped forward and scooped up the two bamboo service plates, nodding once to the cameras she'd set up in the distance, before walking down the hallway, taking a right bend before the stairs. Soft-spoken conversation rose in the main dining hall only as she disappeared completely from their view.

Meanwhile, she was treated to the growing resentment between Nick and Lauren as she swung open the kitchen door.

"They all want drinks now," she said.

"Of course, of fucking course," Lauren said. The anger, the outburst, was very real, but as she turned back to look directly into the camera, she laughed. "Well, what the client wants, the client gets."

Nick echoed the phrase from the walk-in wine cabinet out of frame.

Dylan muttered it under her breath.

Any other time, Lauren might have chided her, told her to say it again, made her put her hand in a huddle with theirs, like they were some underdog team in a children's sports movie.

"Thanks for making your famous Aperol Sours," Lauren said, in that same fake voice she'd used for the camera.

Dylan nodded.

Lauren had used a much different voice when she'd called a month ago, begging Dylan to join her. "Please, please, *please* come help us," she'd said. "We can't do this without you."

And they couldn't. They couldn't because Lauren and Nick didn't talk.

The crimson letter had arrived at one of their three shared homes, this one in the L.A. area. Lauren was the first to find it, read it, and tell Dylan before she even called Nick.

What she'd failed to mention–until the day Ian Fujii picked them up from L.A. to shuttle them down to the island–was that this was their chance, a shot at a daytime television show.

Their being Lauren and Nick's.

Not Dylan. Never Dylan.

A decade she'd worked for these people, and still they tried keeping secrets from her.

Lauren turned back to her chopping board, slicing and dicing, one camera trained on her hands, the other that she stared into as she said, "Nick, have you selected the wine?"

"White, like you requested." Nick emerged from the wine cabinet, two bottles in hand.

"See, getting separated was the best thing to ever happen to us." That voice was back. The one she'd been putting on for the last two days. Dylan didn't have the heart to tell her that she'd been on the internet for over a decade and everyone already knew what she sounded like. Grief could do a lot of things, but this? "We're better friends, better work partners, than we are lovers."

It didn't help that the statement took on a shrill tone at the end. As if the harsher she said it, the more she could convince herself it was true.

"Right," Nick said, not even half trying.

Dylan grabbed her cocktail shaker, her mini strainer, and piled out the ingredients. She tensed as Nick passed her, tearing off a paper towel and barely wiping at where a drop of egg white had dared touch the counter. He crumpled it in his hand, tossing it onto the growing pile. She'd have to deal with that tomorrow–their tiny trash mountain on an already tiny island. She'd be lucky if she slept at all tonight.

As she shook the concoction, arms pumping back and forth, back and forth, Dylan glanced at the large calendar display where Lauren had attempted a bit of meal prepping and listing out all the known allergies and preferences of their guests. This was Day 0, technically, by how Lauren had organized things. Dylan tuned out the clattering of silverware, the tinkering of metal against glass, Lauren's droning on and on to the camera about how long it took to familiarize herself with new ovens, how these were so much closer to the ones in their home out in Martha's Vineyard. This was Day 0.

Only Day 0. There were still seven more days to go. Seven more days of this, over and over and over and over, as the room slowly began squeezing in on her, choking her, never-ending, suffocating, she felt too big–too, too, *too* big, and–

"Try to pitch this show with me, Nick, damn it!" a cry came.

Dylan exhaled out, the calendar returning to its rightful place on the wall, and the walls returning to their rightful space away from her. She breathed shallowly, turning to look at Lauren, who'd taken over the huffing and mania she'd felt only seconds ago.

"This whole fucking thing is proof of concept. If we don't have this–" Lauren's voice rose, hysteria creeping in. "If we don't have this, we have nothing! Then we're just *divorced!*" She spat the word out as if it were dirty.

As if she hadn't been trying to "reclaim" it two minutes ago.

"I need to calm down." The knife was still in her hand, the blade shaking. Lauren closed her eyes, taking a deep breath, then let the knife drop limply to the side, clattering against the island. "Give me ten minutes. I'll be back."

Dylan stared after her, not daring to say another word until she was sure Lauren was out of earshot. "Stop fucking with the chef," she snarled.

"Oh, c'mon," Nick said, and she hated the way his eyes twinkled with some kind of deranged glee. "Think about it. A Meal with the Mercers," he held out his hand, as if weighing one option, then lifted out the second, "or Dinner with Your Divorced Dad. C'mon, tell me which sounds better?"

Dylan narrowed her eyes. "Oh, you're a father now? Have you been keeping that a secret from her, too?"

"I mean, like, 'Internet Dad.' *Daddy.* It sounds good, right?"

Dylan didn't answer his question, just like he hadn't answered hers. He always managed to weasel his way out of things. Or into things. Into pants, into lives, into hearts he'd undoubtedly break.

"Get back to work," she snapped, not caring about the cameras. She'd barely be on them anyway.

"Hey now, who's the boss here?"

"Your wife."

"*Ex*," he hissed.

"Fine," Dylan said, wiping her hands on her pants. "Your *ex*-wife is the boss. She always has been. And she always will be. Because despite your fucking cowboy boots and your–"

"Hey," he pulled at her wrist.

She hadn't realized she'd gotten so close. Hadn't realized she'd stabbed him in the chest with her finger. Didn't like the way he'd grabbed her, like back when she allowed him to do that. She pushed him away and snatched up the tray of cocktails and bar snacks, storming out of the kitchen, through the hall, a battery of emotions firing in her own mind so loud it shocked her when the thoughts were swallowed whole by a completely different fight.

"Her body isn't even cold yet!"

"This is low," the next grumble came. "Even for you."

"Even for *me*!" another voice objected.

Dylan didn't know whether to retreat or freeze, but she couldn't imagine that alcohol would help...whatever this situation was.

"Oh, thank god. Drinks," Olivia said, her chair scraping against the concrete floor as she rushed over.

No turning back now.

"Hi, sorry it took so long."

Olivia grabbed an entire fistful of homemade Chex Mix, stuffing it into her mouth, not caring as several pieces tumbled to the floor and cracked, breaking into food dust.

Dylan made a haggard mental note to clean it later. "There's an Aperol Sour and–"

But Olivia didn't need an explanation, and neither did Sanjeev, nor Michelle, as they grabbed two drinks each and started chugging.

Sarah, Ro, and Cody glared daggers across the table.

"Is everything okay?" Dylan asked, though she wanted to stuff the words back into her mouth as soon as they'd left. If she, too, could crumble into dust onto the floor, that'd be nice.

"All I asked," Ro said with a definite edge to her voice and a clench to her jaw, "was if we were allowed to talk about what was on that bi–on *Ivy's* phone."

TWENTY-TWO

"What was on her phone?" the assistant asked, breaking the tension.

Ro could see it in her eyes, could see the mix of shock and horror. If Ro were writing this, she might have called the expression "aghast," or "staggered," or "wholly appalled," which her publisher would cut in favor of something else.

Something better.

A woman was dead, and here she was caring more about what was on that dead woman's phone.

But Ivy had been dead to Ro for much longer.

Ro glanced back at Cody, who tried to hold her gaze, imperceptibly shaking his head, as if begging her not to say it. But she was tired, so very tired, of staying silent. Tired of letting Ivy get away with it. In her lifetime, she'd succeeded.

But now...

Ro licked her lips.

Besides, if she didn't want to be found out, she would have tried harder to hide it. Ivy wanted people to know. Wanted *Ro* to know. It was all in the way her phone slipped from her grasp, so casually that night in Aspen, the screen aglow against the dark of night.

Ivy had wanted to get back in the hot tub, but Ro insisted on staying out, on bundling up with her spiked hot chocolate, and Ivy had left her there, with the phone sitting face up, the Whisper account open, a blind item ready to post.

This famed BookTokker's been harboring a secret, and it's not just how she landed on the NYT *Bestseller list...*

Now Ro sat back in her chair, crossed her arms over her chest, and clenched her jaw. Cody couldn't save Ivy now. He couldn't even save her life.

"Her submission to Whisper–sorry," Ro said, giving a little shake of her head and a forced, exasperated laugh. "I meant, her Whisper account that she was posting to. Had been posting to for years."

She expected a different reaction. Not sideways glances, chugs of drinks, and more silence.

The assistant broke the quiet again. "What's Whisper?"

At the end of the table, Michelle clucked her tongue. "You need to get better at lying."

Next to her, Olivia pulled her black fur coat across her shoulders, as if the frigid glares had chilled her to the bone. Sanjeev kept his gaze on his plate.

"Not to speak ill of the damned," Sarah said, Southern drawl stronger than ever before, wide-brimmed hat with the word *Relax* stitched in the center, mocking Ro now. "But didn't we all already know this?"

"I didn't believe you," Sanjeev whispered to his plate.

"Is now really the right time to do this?" the Mercers' assistant asked, setting the empty platter onto the table between Michelle and Sarah.

Cody gestured wildly at the woman, as if in agreement.

"Plus," she continued, her voice lowered, "there are cameras." She pointed to them, as if every single person in the room hadn't already picked their seats based on their best angle.

Hell, Olivia had been pruning ever since she sat down.

Ro rolled her eyes. "You're not going to use this footage. None of us are. You think Excelsior wants to be associated with any of this?"

Hands hesitated. Food dangled off forks, halfway between plate and mouth. No one dared drink. No one dared even breathe. For the first time, Ro heard the gentle sea breeze against the half-closed glass wall, a slight whistle in the air.

Here they were, with seven days remaining, on a trip they wouldn't be able to monetize.

Well, they wouldn't. Ro could. *Would.* This was shaping up to be an excellent story. Ivy had given her one of her first–who could have predicted she'd give her another?

Ro bit her bottom lip, now itching for her notebook.

Cody's stern gaze kept her from straying.

"Did any of y'all download your contracts before?" Sarah said. "I realized I forgot when I…" she paused, looked around, then shrugged. "Oh, hell, when I filmed in my room. I did this whole special blessing for poor little Ivy and then realized I might not even be able to use the damn thing."

If she heard her own words back, she didn't flinch. Or she didn't care.

"It was a good one, too," she continued. "One I wanna post. One I wanna find out if I can post, when we get back."

"I did a makeup tutorial," Sanjeev confessed. "Funeral-core."

Sarah squawked with laughter, tipping over and smacking him on the arm.

A tiny smile spread across his face.

A snort came from the other end–from Michelle–and Ro almost found herself smirking, too.

This was deranged. Her ex-friend-turned-nemesis was dead, and people were vlogging as if nothing had happened.

Or vlogging as if *everything* had happened.

Ro hadn't posted a video in ages. For the first year or so of her whirlwind success, she took her old following around on book launches, on tour, to the premiere of her first movie adaptation. She kept them in the loop, promising she'd never leave them behind.

But then work got busier, more traditional. She entered the echelon most aspired to, a realm that rapt her attention so completely, a space where mystery and intrigue mattered more than openness.

Or maybe Ro could no longer stomach the comments.

She was a sellout. She was a star. She was a prodigy. She was a plagiarist.

Ro choked back the critiques still burned into her brain, found herself returning to the dinner table, staring straight into one of the cameras.

If only she'd brought hers…

The radio crackled, and Ro tensed, preparing herself for the shout.

"Dylan!"

Without another word, the assistant slipped away. "Isn't she famous now? Dylan, Dylan Grove, Dylan Goode? Dylan G …" Ro asked, repeating the name, trying to find the last part of it.

"Definitely," Sanjeev said at the same time Sarah added, "I thought I knew her from somewhere."

"How old was Ivy?" Olivia asked, barely loud enough for Ro to hear her, even though she was sitting right next to her. The others–save Cody, who refused to participate and held his silence–continued their shared brainstorming, trying to remember where they knew Dylan from.

But Olivia's question niggled when Ro knew the answer so completely. She and Ivy had bonded over their shared love of astrology, their signs so compatible. The hours they spent dissecting their Ascendants and predicting what their Saturn Return held would have been crazy to anyone else.

That had been a different Ivy. It'd been a different Ro, too.

"Thirty-three," she answered, also hating that it made her thirty-two. She'd pushed through accomplishment after accomplishment, but she was nearing the time when it wouldn't matter. Who cared if you were a *New York Times* bestselling author at twenty-five if you are now forty? She was aging out of the lists. Out of the time when she'd be considered "remarkable" or "impressive." Society valued novelty, but after it was cashed, found it worthless.

"So young," Olivia whispered. Her mouth moved a little bit more, but Ro couldn't make out the other words. Then the scraping of a chair, and the fur coat swished past her, pulling at one of the window-doors. The other conversation stopped, their attention following Olivia until she disappeared, a speck on the island, adrift in the gentle island breeze.

As if that pressed a reset button to let them start over, Sarah's unhinged laughter filled the air. "You know, when Whisper first started, I thought it was you. God bless."

The wave of heads turned to Michelle.

Ro tilted forward, resting her elbow on the table, her head in her hand. Whatever concoction Dylan had served was finally hitting, and she hadn't eaten nearly enough of Lauren's gluten-free spanakopita or scallop tostadas.

"Me?" Michelle pointed to herself. "Why?"

"Because of Aspen."

"Aspen?" Michelle repeated, her big brown eyes glancing away, as if searching for what the hell Sarah meant somewhere else in the room. She clucked her tongue against the roof of her mouth and said, "You thought I, what, ratted you out for stealing my oat milk? My non-dairy ice cream?"

"People have held grudges over pettier things," Sarah said, ignoring the fact they all knew *she* was one of those people.

Ro's eyes shifted to Sanjeev, waiting for him to call her out on it. He didn't.

He never did.

Sarah shrugged. "Realized pretty quickly after Whisper leaked my church construction and Ivy had been one of the few on the Cancun trip with me. They were the only ones I told. And besides, there was all that stuff about Rowena's first book and her stealing–"

"Lies," Ro interjected, the anger creeping up again. She focused on Cody, as he began shaking his head. At first just a little, then a lot. "And she accused me of more than just stealing, you know."

"No," he whispered. "No, Ivy wouldn't do that."

"Didn't the account accuse Ivy of having a drug problem, though?" Michelle asked.

"She clearly OD'd," Sarah said. "Right? I mean...right? Like, it's not that her stupid account spread lies. Necessarily. I mean, sometimes. In my case, they were. All lies." They weren't.

"And mine," Ro insisted, putting a hand up to stop the speculation. "And she talked about you, too, you know! Not just today. Several times!"

Cody's chair scraped against the floor, and he began pacing back and forth.

"The Whisper account talked about how you had some kind of affair with that girl you hired last year. Your assistant or whatever?" Ro snapped, acting like the specific blind item hadn't been burned into her brain word for word. That Ivy would sink so low as to try canceling Cody, too. If she was going down, she'd try dragging everyone else with her, friendship be damned. "She also said that you fired the girl after she declined your advances."

Some turned more slowly than others–Michelle's head whipped around so fast, she hissed, bringing a hand up to her neck, trying to massage away the crick–but eventually everyone's attention was on Cody.

On the man who paced against the backdrop of their oasis.

Head still shaking, as if he couldn't believe it–refused to believe it.

"I don't want to talk anymore," he finally said, changing the direction of his pacing, passing their table, striding across the large atrium, heading toward his room. "Not tonight."

Ro stared after him, grinding her teeth.

"Don't know why he's acting all shocked," Sarah said, tilting toward Sanjeev, their familiar angles. "Pretty sure he sent in a tip about another fitfluencer."

Ro rolled her eyes, focusing her attention on the beach in the distance.

The evil twins continued their whispered accusations, as the setting sun cast pinks and purples and oranges across the sky. The sea breeze drifted lightly from where Olivia had left the door-window open.

Ro could almost hear the ocean's prettiest song beyond the chattering. The tide rolling, rumbling, rushing in, and slowly pulling away. Rolling, rushing, rumbling in, crashing, crashing, *crashing*.

"She has the right idea."

Ro's vision refocused on the actress. Even from afar, the pose was too telltale to be anything else. Arm outstretched, phone in hand, changes so minute most would think it ridiculous that she'd fill her camera roll to the hundreds with the same shot.

"Can you take some pictures of me?" Michelle asked. The question wasn't directed at Ro. "Too good to waste, right?"

Sanjeev stood immediately, Sarah joining with a squeal.

"Photoshoot time!"

And off the three bustled, craning the glass door ajar, and setting off toward the ocean, leaving Ro to stew in her own righteousness. She could have used a new headshot. What better than one on the very island that was about to make her a *New York Times* bestselling author thrice over?

But with pinched lips and a shrug to the nearest camera, Ro stood and exited in the opposite direction.

TWENTY-THREE

"Don't forget. You are the star. The draw. The Hollywood actress. They all want to know you, be seen next to you, make content with *you*."

Olivia stared into the front-facing camera, her reflection back hyping her up more than the words could.

She'd learned long ago never to meet her heroes, and yet, when the invitation arrived, she thought she was the luckiest girl in the world to see the included guest list. It was a brand deal to die for, not because of the gifts or perks or promises of attention, of followers, or a lifetime supply of Excelsior. But because, for the first time, she'd get to meet some of the greats, people she'd spent years following, watching, being influenced by, long before she influenced others. Long before she understood the extent of what that meant.

But to them, she–*Olivia Blakely*–was the prize.

She needed to remember that. Remember that she was the celebrity draw, an echelon that none of them yet touched. Remember that despite their accolades, she was the one with the IMDb page.

They'd heard of her, but she *knew* them. She was the one with the advantage.

"You're gorgeous, you're talented, you're an icon. You're Olivia Blakely." In the bottom corner of her phone, so small she hadn't noticed until now, she spotted the plane in the background. She whipped around, dropping her hands to her side. The idyllic landscape looked like it was out of a movie. The hint of a wrap-around infinity pool blocked by the impossibly large mansion, a grass so green that gave way to the whitest sands she'd ever seen. An ocean so vast, a setting sun painting the sky in gorgeous pastels, and a breeze so gentle it barely lifted her waves from her shoulder.

This was a lavish, opulent, monetized escape, wish fulfillment now at the expense of her psyche. How had she said all of that with the plane in the background?

Dylan Goddard had said, "The show must go on," but the show would only last until their plans changed. Until Excelsior found out what happened. Until they canceled the trip, brought them back home, and all the headlines and buzz Olivia anticipated, hoped for, would morph into bare mentions.

The biggest blip would be from the single Whisper post, and there would be no more Whisper without Ivy Strohl.

She clutched her stomach, sick at the thought. There was no more Ivy Strohl. And no one, least of all the approaching influencers, seemed to care.

The way they chatted as they ambled over sand, walking toward her, she might have thought they were friends. But content creators manipulated moments, and no single moment could tell the whole truth. Certainly not the one she'd seen on the plane ride, even before Ivy's freak accident. There was no love lost between the lot of them. The snark subreddit dissertations and hour-long drama channel summaries were right.

Reality crashed down on her like a wave, submerging her in the truth all their vlogs and socials had hidden.

These people hated each other.

TWENTY-FOUR

Through her phone, Michelle stared at Olivia as the actress arched her back, cocked her hip, and accentuated already impressive curves. The rising star dropped her arms to her sides, slumping as Michelle reset the angle.

"I just keep thinking how poor Ivy will never take another picture again," Olivia said. "Never see another sunset." She whirled around, staring at the water as it glittered in the distance. The coat slid off a single shoulder, and she glanced over it, blinking her blue eyes in the direction of the camera, as sparkly as the ocean waters.

"Her acting seems more fitting for a tampon commercial than an Oscar," Michelle muttered, "but I appreciate that she's really going for it."

Sanjeev, standing next to her, snorted as he squatted down and took another photo of Sarah.

"When's it going to be your turn?"

Sanjeev didn't answer. Michelle didn't press. She rolled her eyes and stepped forward, closer to where Olivia twirled, slowly, in a circle, as if being coached by some unseen director.

"Switch with me," Michelle instructed, offering her phone. Once upon a time, she'd taken a photography course and gotten pretty good at portraits. Back when she owned a DSLR and was Tumblr famous. That was before the iPhone made photos so easy and long before she had to pawn her good camera off to make half her rent for the month.

Olivia's twirling ended, but she seemed lost. Dazed. Michelle followed the direction of Olivia's feet, her attention on the plane on the far-off runway. A small figure–Ian, probably–was walking away from it, but when Michelle turned back, Olivia's eyes were still rooted on the plane.

"She had more than beauty to give, right?" Olivia whispered. "Did she give beauty?"

Sanjeev snorted again, but when the actress whipped her head over, the smirk dropped off his face.

"I just mean...what did she give?" Michelle asked, shaking her hand with the phone, still waiting for Olivia to take it. "What do any of us give?"

"I serve looks," Sarah said, "And God."

Michelle rolled her eyes, catching what she thought was the tail end of Sanjeev doing the same, but he shifted, turning slightly, the wind ruffling his hair.

Olivia shook her head. "So young..."

Michelle dropped her arm. This girl was never going to take her photos. "She feels sort of ancient in some ways."

"That's what happens when you get famous at sixteen or whatever," Sanjeev said. "Wait, how old are you?"

"Twenty-seven," Olivia answered.

"Aww, baby!" Sarah added. "Wait, so I'm thirty-one, you're twenty-nine," she pointed to Sanjeev. "Michelle, that makes you the old woman."

"And yet I still look younger than you."

Sarah lifted a hand to the corner of her eye, as if she could wipe away an imaginary tear. No doubt she'd gotten a couple of ccs of Botox before arriving.

"Don't worry, we can cover that up." If Sanjeev meant it as a whisper, he failed. It came out far too loud.

And, by Michelle's own taste, was rather cruel. But she bit back her smile. Maybe he could talk back to Sarah after all.

"Here." Michelle passed Sanjeev her phone, Olivia clearly too cocooned in her own thoughts to help. "It's my turn."

He stepped back a few paces and squatted again, angling the camera to get the last drops of twilight.

"Give me a sexy smolder," he said. "Give me a pout, give me a fellow influencer just died. Perfect."

THE FALL

TWENTY-FIVE

In the dim light of dawn, the villa took on a hollow, scary presence. Shadows cast from angled architecture made it more mausoleum than museum. Every morning, Dylan had awoken early, feet padding gently against the harsh floors, trying not to disturb someone else's slumber.

She crept out now, needing to set the table. For the first time, she wasn't the only one awake at such an hour.

Hand to her chest, she stepped back. "Cody," she breathed out, the dark presence slowly standing. "I didn't think anyone would be up."

"Sorry," he whispered. "Thought I might see if anyone wanted to do some morning yoga on the dock. Maybe I could lead the session. I was going to film it, but…"

He trailed off, and her tired morning brain pieced together what he'd left out.

"But you're worried it would be insensitive?"

The silence answered what words could not.

"I can make you some pressed juice," she offered. "Lauren will be up in a bit to start breakfast."

"Pressed juice sounds good," Cody nodded. "Thanks. And hey, if you have time, you should join."

Dylan grinned. "I'd love that."

"Yeah, of course. If you see anyone, let them know, alright?"

"You might be alone for a while."

"Nah," Cody said as he walked over to the window-doors and pulled them open without so much as an *oomph* of effort. The first day, Dylan had flagged Lauren down to help her. "They'll probably be up for a photoshoot soon."

A statement that would sound absurd anywhere else. But here, amongst other content creators, they could be honest: They weren't lazy. They worked with natural light, slept during the day, and stayed up late into the night editing.

Well, until they could pay for those things. Then they forgot what hard work was like.

Dylan wasn't there yet. But she could feel it. So close.

She set the hand-squeezed juice on the table, alongside today's freshly picked flowers and festive decorations. Nick wanted to go for an "island vibes" theme as their base, their introduction to the splendor. They'd meant to use these yesterday, but…

Dylan smoothed the place setting like she smoothed away her thoughts of the day before, erasing the woman she hardly knew.

Out on the beach, someone had joined Cody, and there was movement in the opposite hall as others stirred. The first trickle of light had changed their space completely, making it feel more welcoming, homier. She wouldn't have to creep around so much.

Dylan retraced her steps for a fourth time, now changed into tight leggings and a yoga mat tucked under her arm.

"Morning," the voice said through a yawn as she entered the lobby. Sanjeev stretched his arms above his head, then let them fall free with a sigh. "I'm so sorry, Dylan, but could I beg you for a coffee?"

The pitcher of juice now sat empty, and only one of the pitchers of water remained. She glanced into the distance, and Cody had been right. Those not on their mats were at the sandy hill, taking photos.

Dylan screwed on her smile. "Of course. What kind?"

"Latte."

"Milk?"

"Non-dairy."

"Sweetener?"

Sanjeev shook his head. "And two espresso shots, if you could. Three if you still think it would taste alright."

"I'll see what I can do."

From her periphery, she spotted the pretty actress flouncing across the greenery. "Hi, good morning," she said as she floated inside, looking ethereal in an all-white outfit and not a trace of yesterday's nerves. "Cody's hosting a sunrise yoga, if you want to join, Sanjeev."

"Hasn't the sun already risen?"

"Yeah, but he's been out there for a while. I'm sure he'll do some tricky camera magic to make it look like the rest of us have been, too." She flipped her hair over her shoulder, the streaks of blonde glistening. "Oh, and Dylan, if we could have some more pressed juice, that'd be great."

She turned before she could see Dylan's smile fade into a thin line, before she bit her tongue and slipped her sliders back on. They slapped against her bare feet, the sound echoing, as she crossed down the hall, letting her purple mat slip out of her grip next to the kitchen entryway. She pushed through the door to find Lauren chopping onions, cilantro, and all sorts of vegetables, readying an omelet bar and fresh, Mediterranean-inspired "breakfast salads."

"You're back quick," Lauren said.

Dylan didn't answer. She simply pulled open the double doors of the fridge and began grabbing ingredients.

Lauren sighed, "I'm worried this won't be the right food."

None of the dishes from last night had been washed, except for the small collection Dylan put into the dishwasher. The piles, with crumbs and scraps of melted food, towered in all corners. Remnants of wine stained the glasses as much as lipstick lined the rims. Chills rose up her arms, goosebumps forcing her hair to stand upright. A mess. A mess everywhere.

"Do you think I should wake the stragglers in an hour or so? I'm worried they'll sleep through the meal, and since this will be the first real one with everyone–well, almost everyone–together, this really needs to make an impression, and..."

Lauren prattled on and on and on.

Dylan eventually found the juicer hiding amongst the colander and cheese grater, and she rinsed it off before returning to the large island.

Lauren still prattled.

Dylan had learned long ago to just let her talk.

That was Lauren's system. To get out all her worries, foist them upon others, and then when the lights were on and the cameras recording, she appeared collected and in control.

Meanwhile, her staff walked on eggshells, tiptoed around her emotions, stiffened at any dropped spoon or clatter of plates, lest they finally and irreparably break Lauren's barely-held-together sanity.

Harnessing her stress, her frustrations, Dylan squeezed the grapefruits, the lemons, the pears and plums and pomegranates. Freshly pressed juice–that's what they'd all get. And thinly sliced cucumbers to place over their eyes for their spa later, which Dylan had also helped organize even though she wasn't the fucking party planner, Nick was, and–

"Dylan!" Paring knife in hand, pointing upward, Lauren kept her eyes pinched shut. "Dylan, can you *please* go see what Nick wants?"

The squawking came from the radio. Dylan had tuned that out too.

Lauren's eyes remained closed as she sighed. "I'll go see what Ian, Sarah, Sanjeev, and Cody want for breakfast. Or if they want it in their room, we'll just forget the whole breakfast altogether."

"Sanjeev is down at the docks with Cody and Olivia." Dylan squeezed her anger into the last small quart of juice, the lemon searing into small cuts at her cuticles. "A couple others were out taking pictures, so it's fine. It'll all be fine. I'll go find Nick. Hey, hey," Dylan whispered, hating herself even as she did, "we'll be fine. It'll be fine, okay?"

"Yeah," Lauren breathed in deeply through her nose and slowly out through her mouth. Her hands still clutched the knife, but she repeated the words. "It'll be fine. I'll be fine. Go, go," she shooed.

Dylan's arm flexed with the weight of several juices atop the platter. A lifetime of working in kitchens or behind bars had toned her body in a way that Cody Planks never could–but she watched the group she so desperately wished to join before calling out, a touch louder than necessary, "Fresh juices! All kinds. And one latte!" She kicked the bamboo tray table out, setting the platter on top, enjoying the way her muscles gently burned.

Only Sanjeev opened his eyes and looked back, his regret clear. He glanced at Cody, his latte, and back again.

Dylan could practically hear him groan as he felt compelled to stay. Her pinch of kinship disappeared as Nick's radio message interrupted her thoughts.

She reached for the radio secured to her black jeans–having changed back into her uniform after giving up all hope of joining the group–and asked, "On my way. Where are you? Over."

"Setting up for the Excelsior Game Night," he said, voice rising. "I need someone to get the ladder. Over."

"Be right there." She clipped the walkie-talkie to her belt loop, sighing as she turned away from the idyllic ocean and the small group stabilizing their emotions–or, at least, trying. Pretending.

Dylan kicked her shoes off as she traversed over wooden steps that gave way to sand. She sank into it, the grains giving her the only massage she'd get on the island.

The large gazebo sat quietly in the distance, a lone solace, all glass walls, nestled within the tree line. Once upon a time, someone probably rented this spot alone, a honeymoon oasis.

"You rang?" She knocked on the doorframe as she entered, already clocking Nick standing precariously at the top of the ladder, straddling either end. The ceiling reached a height of twenty feet in its domed arches. Dangling lights wrapped around Nick's shoulder and flowed to the floor, snaking around in a coil amongst the ladder legs. "You idiot," she muttered under her breath, then, more loudly, "Stay still."

She scampered forward, unwinding the lights, removing the danger, and feeding them up to Nick as he secured them along an invisible string. They worked in silence for nearly twenty minutes.

It was a simple trick, one they discovered together, one she'd utilized on the first episode of her online show *Drinks with Dylan*. The credit she gave them had been a courtesy, because she was still working under the Mercer brand then.

That was before the whispers of divorce turned to mangled shouts. Before the late-night calls, the sneaking visits, the begging and pleading.

Nick cleared his throat as they finished. “Have I told you how nice it is to have you back?”

“Not nearly enough.”

He climbed down the steps, hopping off with three remaining, the ladder rattling a bit. He always did like to show off.

“Your hair looks good too, I never mentioned.”

“Maybe you shouldn’t.”

“Oh, come on,” he said. Instead of staring up at his masterpiece, like Dylan did, he stared at her. “It’s a compliment, Dylan. Take it.”

Dylan tilted her head down, glanced in his direction. “Thank you. Is that all?” Her gaze shifted away from those familiar blue eyes and out toward the door, but she couldn’t bring herself to walk away. Not yet.

She hated the power this shitty man still had over her. He didn’t even need to touch her, hold her, for her to feel ensnared in his shallows. “You stopped answering my calls,” he said. “I don’t know if you ever got my messages.”

“I got them,” she said, still eyeing the group in the distance.

“And you never called back?” He asked, that low rumble of a whisper turning into a familiar purr. “C’mon, why don’t we go somewhere to talk?” He lifted his hand to rest against the small of her back.

“Don’t touch me,” Dylan smacked his arm away. She glanced over her shoulder, taking half a second to find the nearest camera pointing in their direction. It didn’t take much, anymore, to realize that there was a wide lens attached, and that they most definitely were in view. She sidestepped out of the way, only to find herself in view of another. “Not here. Not now.” She shook her head. “Actually, not anymore. No.”

“Look, can’t we talk about this?”

“You’re not even divorced yet.”

“That didn’t stop us before.”

“Because you lied to me.” She shoved him out of her way with an elbow into his stomach.

Nick opened his mouth to argue, to defend himself, to lie some more, but he was cut off.

A scream pierced the air.

TWENTY-SIX

From the docks, it took a moment to figure out what the sound was.

Ro thought it was her internal monologue. Just the high-pitched screeching she'd been hearing at any mention of Ivy, after every time Sarah spoke, or she remembered she had only a week to turn in her book proposal.

But this time the scream kept going.

Ro fluttered open her eyes, the morning light harsh despite her sunglasses. She glanced to the right as Sanjeev opened his eyes too. Squinting into the distance, she tried to make out where the sound was coming from.

Only as the scream grew louder, closer, did she rise to her feet, did Cody rush past her, did the others fold out of their Virasana pose, did she run toward the villa, as the scream turned into a wail.

A tear-stricken Lauren sucked in a mighty gasp, blubbering into Dylan's arms. Her eyes wide and terrified, jaw quivering, as if she couldn't find the words she needed. All she could do was shake her head, shake her head, shake her head, as the people behind peppered her with questions.

Dylan pulled out a chair.

Nick grabbed a napkin to fan her.

Sanjeev stayed to the side, wrapping his arms protectively around himself.

Olivia and Michelle huddled together, at times bent down, at times standing, still trying to get Lauren to talk.

It was only as a rowdy clomp echoed through the hall that attention pulled away from Lauren, still speechless. A pair of cowboy boots, just barely visible below a fluffy pink robe, stomped across the floor. “What on God’s green earth is all this screaming about?”

Ro had to blink a couple of times to recognize the woman in front of her as Sarah Pruski.

A sleep mask scrunched her bangs up, but the rest of her hair was pin straight, flat, and lifeless. “Oh my god, not another panic attack. Lauren, I told you last night, you just gotta breathe through it, babe, alright? What? *What?*”

Everyone stared at her in silence.

“Fine, don’t tell me!” Sarah threw her hands up in the air, mumbling under her breath something about going to get coffee, her boot clomps masking most of her words.

“Shh, shh,” Cody whispered to the chef. “In through the nose, out through the mouth, right? Count of five. Hold it at the top and–”

But Lauren’s next breath came out a haggard, deep, shaky wail of terror. “Ee–ee–” she tried to get out.

“What? *E* what?”

Nick glanced over Lauren’s head, and Ro followed his gaze, settling on Dylan. She shook her head.

Ro repeated the mystery, trying to guess the ending. Were they out of eel? Eggplant? What would terrorize her so badly? If she could get over Nick’s blatant cheating and continue working with him, what else could there be?

Did she manage to get on the internet?

Get news from outside?

Ro crept forward, a sick hope twisting in her stomach.

"Ee–," Lauren heaved. "Ee–*Ian*!" She choked out finally. "Ian. He was…he's…he's *dead*."

Her heaves of breath echoed through the hall as everyone took a second, waiting to hear more. Surely there was more.

"What?" Nick demanded, the first to recover.

Olivia backed away, crossing herself.

Sanjeev's jaw dropped.

Cody started pacing again.

Michelle squatted down on the ground, holding her legs.

And all Ro could do was stare, the word not computing.

Dead.

Dead.

Another one of them, dead.

TWENTY-SEVEN

Ian Fujii's body lay limp on the first floor of his two-story suite, bits of broken wood paneling chipped and lying in the wreckage. It hadn't been a long fall, but sometimes it didn't take much.

Cody reached for Ian's phone, face down several yards away, and turned it over in his palm. The screen was somehow better protected than his head had been. He swiped up and was met with an error–his face not recognized.

Internally, he swore.

"Anyone know Ian's passcode?"

"80085," Michelle answered.

He looked up from the phone in his palm. The others glanced at her sideways. "How do you know that?"

"Took some videos for him when we were in the sky." She tutted. "Hard to forget that one. The man was *not* creative."

Cody input the numbers, the phone opening automatically to the Photos app. The first, open picture was of the ornate stained-glass window, depicting a beach oasis, and an island with a lighthouse on the second level. "I guess we know how…"

What was there to say? He'd once seen a fellow gym rat–big, burly man, always there, a staple of early CrossFit–land wrong off a toes-to-bar dismount. He had to be wheeled out in an ambulance. The man never came back to the gym.

Cody didn't look him up–didn't want confirmation. But he'd seen more than a fair number of accidents happen from a miscalculation only a few feet high.

He swiped through to the next photo. And the next. All repeating images of the same stained-glass window from different, blurry angles.

"Did you get the number for the local police department?" Dylan asked, her voice hushed.

Cody glanced up, too late to see who she was asking.

"I thought Ian was checking on that?" Lauren whispered. She'd explained earlier, through choked sobs, that she'd gone into his room to ask when he wanted breakfast–"if he wanted it brought up to him, or if he wanted to be served with everyone else"–and that's when she saw him…lying there…helpless.

Dylan squatted down, inspecting the bits of blood pooled around his neck, discoloring his otherwise white button-up pilot's uniform. To her right, Michelle asked, "Does his phone show if he was able to contact anyone?"

Cody flicked through to the next photo, looking up at Michelle, realizing belatedly the question was for–and all eyes were on–him.

"Oh my God, *ew*," Sarah gagged, taking a step back from where she'd been looking over his shoulder.

He glanced back down to see a photo of Ivy.

A photo of a very *dead* Ivy.

Splayed on the back of the plane where he'd carried her and Ian swore he'd "take care of things." Vomit down the front of her shirt, her dark jeans stained darker, limp hair pressed to her cheeks.

Cody swiped and swiped and swiped.

More photos.

All of Ivy and her sallow skin and pried-open eyes. Up close, from farther away, from one seat over, from the back of the plane.

His hand shook, and he dropped the phone. "Fuck!" It bounced off the ground with a clatter and tumbled until it sat face-down in the pool of blood. "Shit, shit, shit," he said, as if trying to curse away a demon. He pressed his thumbs into his eyes, trying to remove the image. "That's seriously...so fucked up. He's so fucked up. Why would he do that?"

"What?"

"What was it?"

"It was Ivy!"

The voices clamored, clawing over each other, begging to be the loudest, to be noticed, to be heard.

Cody pressed his palms into his eyes until all around him turned deep purple and splotchy. He dropped his hands, blinking it away. "Just…check the call log."

Only Ro braved grabbing the phone, using a pair of gloves she pulled out from somewhere, and turning the phone over, wiping away the screen, the image gone.

A few clicks later. "Nothing," Ro said. "His last call was two days ago. To someone he saved as 'Booty Call 305.'"

A chorus of groans, then a hiss, a breath sucked in, and Cody knew what Ro had done. Michelle's eyes bugged out as she looked over Ro's shoulder, the two, no doubt seeing Ivy again. But their surprise was silent. Until the women turned to look at each other. "You don't think…"

"I do."

"What?" Cody demanded, cutting through the bubbling confusion from the others.

"Texts, maybe? Or an email?"

"What?" He demanded, striding around the perimeter they'd formed, Ian's body in the center. "What about his texts?"

He stood behind Ro and Michelle, watching as Ro navigated through Ian's email app, toward the Outbox, where several sat, clearly awaiting reception.

Ro glanced back, met his gaze, and he saw the young woman he had met all those years ago. When they were both starting out. When they thought they'd just gotten lucky to be invited to their first brand trip at all. Her large, dark-rimmed eyes turned back, and she opened the email, scrolling through the text too fast for his reading comprehension.

It wasn't my fault.

Let's get ahead of this.

Here are some photos. How much do you think they'll sell for?

Make sure we get the best deal.

"Damn," Michelle said under her breath. "Baby girl wasn't even cold yet." Then, as if a single second was long enough for her to process things, she added, "How much you think he'd get for those photos?"

"Well, he won't get any of it." Ro held out the phone, pinched between her fingertips, and passed it to Cody.

No one questioned why he might take it back.

The rest fell into silence as everyone's gaze slowly drifted back to the second dead body of their trip to paradise.

A paradise that was starting to look more like hell.

"What should we do?" Michelle asked. "Like...with the body. Won't it decompose or whatever?"

"Yeah," Ro said, "yeah, in a few hours." She spoke with such authority no one questioned how many hours Ian's body must have already spent lifeless and decomposing.

Dylan dared to reach out, everyone's eyes widening, as she touched Ian's forearm with the back of her finger. "Cold," she said. "I think he's been dead for a while." She stood up, pinching her nose with her other hand. "And I think he shit himself."

"Bodies usually do," Ro said. "Once they've...you know, served their purpose."

"And what purpose is that?" Sarah asked.

"Can you not be antagonistic, for *once*?" Sanjeev asked, his voice shrill. Everyone turned to look at him, and he paled under their gaze. "I just...not right now, Sarah, okay?"

Cody shifted back to Sarah, her jaw agape and her eyes morphing through shock, distaste, and settling somewhere near acceptance, her jaw clenching. She took another moment before lifting her hands up in defense. "Sorry, the body has me shook is all." Except, in her faux Southern drawl, that somehow sounded like a threat.

"Chocolate," Dylan whispered. Then, louder, "Hot chocolate, anyone? We can discuss next steps over some hot chocolate and, um, grab some blankets?"

Nick and Lauren started nodding in tandem. "Great idea."

"Yes, of course. Everyone, let's lead you out of here."

Slowly, one by one, the group trickled out of Ian's room.

Cody held the heavy door open, waiting for the last of them–Dylan–to stride out. Each person glanced at the oil portrait of Ian, then back into the room, as if trying to memorize both versions of him. Chatter increased the farther they got away from the suite, as they walked down the hall, their voices echoing. As if the distance allowed them to forget.

When they'd all turned the corner, Cody stepped forward, letting the door close with a whoosh. He entered *80085* one last time and navigated to Ian's text messages. Scrolling only once, he found the text burned into his brain, under the nickname *Chodey*. He didn't bother opening it. He swiped to the side, and deleted the entire chain, forever.

"Good fucking riddance."

TWENTY-EIGHT

Nick had never been good in emergencies.

He'd never been good at much of anything. That, he'd been told. Repeatedly. He was a menace at school, barely better at home. He exhausted his teachers, his parents, even his childhood friends fell away when they learned how to better control their energy. There seemed to be an unwritten rule of when "adding to a conversation" became "interrupting," and he'd missed that lesson.

So, it was no wonder to him that, in the aftermath–the second aftermath of an already short trip–he found himself leaning against the marble countertop, watching Dylan run in and out of the kitchen, manically taking care of things, and Lauren, eerily focused on conjuring together a comforting soup.

Conjure. Like she was a witch. Now *that* was funny. He'd called her something close to that plenty of times.

He opened his mouth, vaguely aware that Lauren wouldn't appreciate it, but more aware that it would get a laugh.

Even if the only laugh was his own.

"Have you ever–"

"Nope. Nope, not now. I don't want to hear any more of your amateur comedy hour." She gestured wildly with her mixing spoon, flicking bits of deep liquid across the stark white cabinetry. "Hand me my notes."

He rolled his eyes at the camera and mouthed, "Get a load of this."

Even though she called it amateur, Nick's only true skill all his life had been his humor. His humor and his charm. That's how he managed to woo the audience, entice all the women that came before–and, okay, *during*–his marriage to Lauren, and how he convinced their hired editors to make him look better. He could imagine it now. They'd zoom in on his face, on his amenable gesture of grabbing the notes after her harsh demand. The commenters wouldn't be the least bit surprised the Mercers were getting a divorce.

His eyes scanned the scribbled handwriting, a wave of familiarity registering as he handed over the page with Baked Feta Soup crossed through in favor of Lauren's Luscious and Light, Literally Divine Sumptuous Soup.

"Isn't this Dylan's recipe?" he asked. "From that *Food Magazine* spread or whatever?"

"Oh, now you've decided to learn how to read?"

A scoff erupted from him. "That was almost funny, Lauren. See, you can make jokes, too."

Her only answer was a glare.

He leaned against the counter again, closer to her this time, watching as she diced shallots. "You used to be fun. Didn't we used to have fun?"

He almost couldn't remember now. He remembered the sex. The wild, crazy sex they used to have and *that* had been fun. But it was hard. Hard to remember the early years. The reason they ever got together in the first place seemed tucked away, in a place neither of them could access.

The kitchen door swung open, smacking against the wall as Dylan strode through, both hands occupied with a cascading tower of used dishes. She sniffed and said, "That smells great. I'll get started on the hot chocolate soon."

Lauren surreptitiously turned over the recipe without looking up, saying only, "It will need to simmer for a while."

"That's fine." The dishes clattered into the deep, farmhouse sink. "I'm not sure anyone has much of an appetite right now."

"Right."

Lauren's clipped tone would have been dangerous if sent in Nick's direction, but Dylan breezed through the door without a second thought.

Only then did his soon-to-be ex-wife's gaze flick up in his direction, an almost imperceptible request in those large brown eyes.

Nick pinched his fingers together and brought them from one side of his mouth to the other, zipping his lips closed. It was a promise they both knew was only good for so long without payment.

TWENTY-NINE

It took longer than expected for everyone to gather in the living room. Some needed their emotional support blankets, others their plushies.

Lauren had made the marshmallows two days ago, in preparation for Nick's "Cozy Night in with Excelsior" event but didn't bother stopping Dylan as she sliced through the confections and placed them gently in a serving bowl. She didn't bother helping as Dylan whisked hot chocolate in two saucepans–one dairy-free and as "skinny" as possible, the other a full-fat, delicious version. The only thing Lauren did was hold open the door, as her once-assistant passed through. She wrung her hands together as she followed, taking the final seat–no emotional support to be found. For her.

As everyone settled into the large, square room, on the impossibly plush couch cushions, all facing each other with warm mugs in hand…they had nothing to say.

They all sat in complete silence.

Lauren waited for the rest of Dylan's grand idea, but it seemed corralling everyone had been the entirety. Now the poor woman stared at her hands, as if she was remembering how cold Ian had felt.

A gag crept up Lauren's throat. She'd touched so much meat in her life–had worked in so many kitchens before rising to fame, that squeamish wasn't typically in her vocabulary.

But the blood…the way it had seeped out…his skin, so weathered, looked so thin, the way the veins…

A shiver crept up her spine, remembering when she'd first seen him, alone.

The awful thought that flashed through her mind. That someone had pushed him.

She turned to look at the only man who could've done it, extracting himself from the couch, centering himself in the room. "We need to get help, eventually. That much is obvious," Nick began. "But we can't call. No service. And we don't have the emergency numbers but–as far as we're aware…" he looked right at her, nodded briefly before his gaze slipped to Dylan. It *always* slipped to Dylan. "This isn't really an emergency, right?"

Those who weren't enmeshed in their own thoughts nodded along.

Dylan nodded along.

"We'll be okay until our next batch of supplies comes. That should be in two days. So really, the only thing we need to take care of is the smell. We can maybe put some towels down in the front of the room to block it out?"

Lauren shrugged. So did Dylan.

Good enough. Nick took a deep breath, his chest heaving and his posture straightening. "Right," he clapped. "Well, that just leaves us with what to do in the meantime. Suggestions?"

He walked back to where he'd been sitting, rummaging around with something in his pockets, the gentle chatter encapsulating the group.

Sanjeev leaned over to Dylan, whispering, "Are there any other unoccupied rooms? I was put next to Ian's and, um, I don't..." he trailed off as Dylan assured him there was more space available.

Others around them began whispering, too. Some asked about Ian's email, others asked if they saw Sarah's face when Sanjeev told her off.

And Lauren looked around at them all handling the shock much better than she had.

Handling *all* of this better than she was.

The night before, Sarah had found her huddled in the shared hallway outside their rooms–shaking and barely breathing. It was a panic attack. The kind she hadn't had in a while.

And in that moment, of all people, Sarah Pruski had been a true friend. Selfless and giving as she talked Lauren down off the ledge.

She hadn't been close to Nick in such a long time that the past few days triggered all the old emotions, pent up over years and years. Therapy had done what it could, if only in the two sessions she'd bothered to attend. Rather, it was the illusion that was so painful, so hard to maintain. She never should have taken this stupid invitation, never should have put her ego in front of her own health...

Lauren tried to breathe now, as her eyes fell on the one person she hated and loved the most. He'd found whatever was in his pocket, fiddling with his phone.

There was one bit of good news. He couldn't access any dating apps here. No chance of calling someone in for the night to flaunt it in her face. Not like he wouldn't hook up with someone here.

She rolled her eyes, lolling her head back onto the soft sofa, blinking once.

Twice.

There, in the very top corner, nearly hidden by the sparkling chandelier shaped like a ship, was a tiny red light.

Lauren clenched her teeth. One of the cameras she'd vetoed. They only had so many resources, and this angle, like Nick, was trash for ninety-nine percent of their time.

"Are you recording this?" Lauren hissed.

It was as if someone had taken the air out of the room, the once-bubbling conversation was now a barely-there simmer.

"I..." Nick looked around, as if there could be anyone else she'd talk to in this tone. Maybe he thought that. That she snapped at everyone. And maybe she did.

But he made her that way.

"Well, yeah," Nick said. "Look, it's not a big deal, it's just for–"

"Why are you recording right now?" Lauren screeched.

The other conversations died completely, heads whipped in Nick's direction, or up, around, trying to find the camera. People adjusted, stomachs now hidden with pillows, hair tossed over shoulders.

Even in her mania, Lauren found herself doing the same. Tilting her chin out, jutting it, angling so that the camera got her "best side."

Her best side, according to *Nick*.

She balled her hands into fists, glared daggers, and cursed his name.

Old habits died screaming.

THIRTY

Sarah hid her laugh in her hot chocolate, the liquid bubbling, sloshing, burning the top of her lip. But she didn't feel any pain as she set the mug down and wiped the milk away from her mouth, trying not to laugh again before she could smother it with the couch's throw pillow.

Contrary to what some might say, she wasn't mean. She wasn't evil. She was just…blunt. And found humor in situations others didn't.

Like Lauren, right now. Bless her heart.

At least she'd been able to help her last night. The poor woman wasn't likely to survive another hour spent with her ex-husband.

Nick's hands went up–way up–a common stance for him. Yells and screams rocked him, but Nick never seemed to mind the dramatics.

Probably how he put up with Lauren for so long.

"Hey, hey! Okay. Listen," he said, more quietly. "Listen."

The shouts turned to grumbles and Sarah brought a hand to her hair, fluffing it up. She let her head rest on her hand, angling away from the high above camera.

At least it would be slimming.

"Look, yes, I'm recording, okay?" He gestured with his hands around the room, pointing out several more cameras she'd somehow missed. "We're recording everything. That's the point. But look..."

Sarah barely contained a snort. She'd watched Nick–and Lauren–for years. "But look," was always how he started his worst pitches.

Coincidentally, it was also how he announced that yes, he and Lauren were currently separated. He'd been wearing a cozy knit sweater, linked it in the description, and it went out of stock within three hours.

Sarah had bought two.

In the video, he'd continued his "but look," with "sometimes things like this are inevitable–it doesn't mean it was all bad though."

A stark contrast from Lauren's own announcement, on their original shared channel, that implied they'd been trying couple's counseling and would probably be just fine soon.

This time he continued his, "but look," with "These accidents are terrible, yes, but sometimes great things can come from tragedy."

Sarah held her breath the same way as when she'd first watched that separation video, having clicked the moment it dropped, hearing those words, and waiting for the reactions to pour in.

In person, without a screen or username to hide behind, people weren't so bold to call him out.

Or maybe, like she did, they agreed.

"Okay, before y'all can yell at this man," Sarah began.

Showtime.

"Gross answer, by the way," she said, mainly for the cameras, clocking him up and down with one of her fingers. Plausible deniability. She loved it there.

Standing, taking center stage, she continued, "He's on the right path. Ivy, Ian, they both documented their lives. All of it. Shouldn't we also celebrate them by documenting their deaths? This way they can be heralded. They can be cherished by their fans. And–you better cut this out," she threw a look to Nick over her shoulder before turning back to face most of them again. "It will be good for the rest of us. If we must deal with this obvious trauma, carry this emotional baggage for the rest of our lives, the least we deserve is to make content out of it, right?"

The room sat frozen.

There was a moment during her sermons that Sarah realized she had her audience. Truly *had* them. When they were just captivated enough by some sob story she'd told or anecdote she'd stolen. The time when they walked along the tightrope of wanting so badly to believe to teetering over the edge to fully believing. The place where they fell, allowing themselves to be swallowed whole in her powers.

This was that moment.

She waited a beat…six, seven. "Y'all know as well as I do, what's captured doesn't need to be shown. But if you never capture it in the first place…well…" she trailed off and clasped her hands, letting them rest in front of her, waiting.

Eyes glanced sideways, brows raised slightly and were answered with tiny shrugs.

She no longer had them, she *had* them.

Dylan hopped to her feet first. "Should we reposition the other cameras?" Weaving between couches and through the living room into the dining area, she swiveled one of the wide-lens cameras around. The others scrambled to their rooms to grab their vlogging cameras, their DSLRs, their phones.

Cody had left his on the dock. Ro scrambled to get her phone, mentioning she was filming her first "books I brought on my vacation" video in years, and Sanjeev disappeared, too, promising Sarah he'd bring her an extra ring light.

With a lick of her lips, satisfied, she maneuvered her solo armchair to the side, hoping to get a bit more of the natural light coming in from the large glass windows. Here, she could see their oasis, remember her mission.

She checked her phone.

She'd been checking it incessantly. Religiously. As dedicated as she'd ever been to anyone or anything else. All for it to be the same–no internet.

Somehow, she'd let herself pretend it wasn't a habit–an addiction–before now. It was work. But opening the same app to see the exact same accounts posting the exact same message was starting to break her.

Instead of throwing her phone, she navigated to her camera, turned it to selfie mode, and made sure her hair was adequately fluffed. Sanjeev adjusted the light for her in the background, until she clucked, "Perfect." With a final glance away from her own reflection, she looked back to see the rest of the group had finally settled. "We all here again? Good. Okay, Nick, do you want to take all that from the top? For continuity's sake?" She set her own camera up, pressing record.

"Sure, sure," he said, hopping back up to his feet.

Only Lauren still seemed annoyed with him.

All was right in their world.

"What should I say?"

"You were talking about how we needed to move on," Michelle prompted. "Maybe Lauren can get us all lunch so we can think better, and you can figure out how to contact Excelsior to ask them what we should do in the meantime?"

"Yeah, yeah," he said, nodding slightly, although it slowly came to a halt as he began shaking his head. "Actually, no. I don't have any contact info for Excelsior. I have the grounds people on the next island, the provisions, but no one with the sponsor." He looked at the circle of faces. "Does anyone else?"

"Wait, then how did you set everything up?" Michelle asked, but her eyes were on Dylan, who shared the couch with her. Even Michelle Monroe knew who was really in charge here.

Dylan answered. "I got everything I needed in the mail from those two."

"And we got everything from Excelsior," Lauren said, voice clipped, putting an end to it. "We had no direct person to contact, per se, but they always answered in a timely manner. They honestly gave us more info than we needed. Pages on pages on pages."

"They'd said part of the appeal was all of us together, with no interference from anyone else."

"That's..." Sanjeev started, as if trying to come up with a better word before settling on, "weird."

Michelle sat back on the couch and pulled the matching cashmere blanket up to her chest. "You wanna hear 'weird'? I once was invited on this relaxation retreat. I thought it was like a yoga thing. Free up your mind, all that woo woo shit, which really, I needed. Turns out, it was with a cult, and they were trying to recruit me."

Olivia laughed, spitting out some of her drink, bits of brown bubbles spotting the glass table in front of her.

"I'm serious!" Michelle said, though she started to laugh, too. "I had to pretend I was gonna take them up on it when I got home. I was scared for my damn life."

"I once accidentally caught Andrea Nichols going down on Sophia Remington at a Tarte event," Olivia shared. "I had to moonwalk out of the bathroom, pretending I was too high to figure out what was going on."

"Was that before Sophia was out?" Sanjeev asked.

"Yep," Olivia confirmed, popping the *p*.

Sanjeev let out a low whistle, before biting at his lip and adding, "One time, the organizer for the Shorty Awards left out a seating chart a week ahead, at the Webby awards event, and I took a picture and sent it into Ivy–to Whisper. Under my alt."

Sarah's jaw dropped, glancing with glee over at Sanjeev as she smacked him in the arm. "You never told me that! Well, I'm the one who sent her the tip-off about that yoga studio owner who was gonna get raided by the FBI."

Michelle sucked in a breath. "You did not." She said it like a chiding, but her grin was wide. "God'll get you for that."

"Me and God are good. Don't you mind us."

Not one to ever be left out, Nick hedged, "You all promise to delete this from your videos, okay?"

A collective hush fell over them. Sarah looked over her shoulder and winked at her camera. Sure, she'd probably delete it from her vlogs. But she'd pull it into a separate file before sending it to her editor and store it in a place deep within the folders of her computer. Home to hundreds of files.

"Of course," she swore, folding her hands in like a prayer. A prayer that this would be just as juicy as she'd hoped.

There was a reason they'd all submitted to Ivy–even those who hadn't confessed to the sin. People loved gossip.

All people did, but perhaps influencers more than most.

Their business was done in secret, money made in bargaining, power wielded by the algorithm. When so much of your own fate was left up to Internet Jesus, you'd do anything you could to gain favor. If a brand was choosing between you and another person–and that other person had posted something harmful, something foot-in-mouth, in the past, well…

Someone should make that known.

Everyone else solemnly swore and Nick took a deep breath. "After Kitchen Contraptions said how much they were getting paid for the *Big Game Cook-Off* event, I sent in how much they were paying us. It was such a lowball offer, almost insulting, and because our fans rallied around us at the news, *Big Game Cook-Off* ended up paying us triple."

Before Sarah could ask the question, Dylan piped up. "And how much are you two being paid for this event?" Gazes jumped from her to Nick to Lauren, waiting, waiting, waiting.

"What? Everyone's shy now?" Dylan asked, her pent-up rage finally springing forward after barely hiding underneath the surface.

Sarah couldn't keep the smile off her face now. She loved the mess.

Michelle sat up, the couch shifting with her, the plush fabric moving Dylan, too.

Gazes jumped to her, and Michelle Monroe was never one to let a moment pass her by. "I mean, I wasn't paid exactly. Just the meme coin. Were y'all?" she asked, then shrugged before she got an answer. "Honestly, my situation's dire enough that I'd already planned to hawk the free gifts to make rent." As the rest of the group leered, she *tutted.* "What? Two dead bodies and now I have to hide stuff? I don't think so."

Those were the kind of things to save for confession. Only a priest could get that sort of truth out of Sarah. Not that she was even Catholic…

Across the living room, Olivia shrugged. "My agent thought it would be a good idea. Free vacation, lots of great pictures, good promo for future projects," she shrugged again, deepening the crater of her décolletage, highlighting just how Hollywood skinny she was. "The opportunity was more than enough payment."

Sarah glanced at Sanjeev, his eyes already on her. She spoke for both of them. "We weren't paid either."

Cody agreed. "Same story as Olivia. Good promo, can't pass that up. I've been wanting a drink sponsorship for a while to really take me to the next level. Sometimes exposure really is payment enough. I'd never tell sponsors that though."

"No, never."

"Hell no."

Their heads shifted toward the Mercers and Rowena, who so far had barely spoken a peep since she'd explained how long it took for bodies to begin decomposing. She kept a notebook at her side though, one she must've grabbed when she'd picked her phone up from her room. Her phone acting as a camera, unlike everyone else's, was positioned behind her, almost looking over her shoulder at the rest of the group.

"This served as the perfect excuse to get away," Rowena said, removing her tortoiseshell glasses and pushing them up into her hair. "No internet? No way to get in touch?" She forced out a laugh. "I thought I'd finally get some writing done."

A couple of the others laughed with her.

Not Sarah.

And not Dylan. The poor girl was glaring at the still-married Mercers, whose attention was on each other for the first time in a while.

Nick opened his mouth, but Lauren beat him to the punch. "Just enough to reinvigorate the business." It was clipped and curt. A perfectly mysterious answer, but Nick could never let anyone else have the last word.

"Both together," he said, his gaze meaningfully resting on Dylan, "and apart."

That could have been the end of it. Except Sarah had the same infliction as Michelle. Maybe they all did. She just couldn't let a good opportunity pass her by.

"Oooh, so Ivy was right, huh? Y'all are finalizing the divorce after all?" Sarah leaned forward, resting her elbows on her knees and her hands in her lap. She didn't bother trying to hide the twisted smile that worked its way up her face. "Guess now's a good time to tell you, Lauren, that Nick cheated with me. You know, before I found God."

She'd glanced upward, pointing to the sky, and missed the throw. But when she looked back, she saw the rag Nick pulled away from his face.

"Hey now, you already knew about that."

"About us, too?" Dylan asked.

Sarah gasped, feeling very much like a Housewife during a reunion. Andy Cohen would have *died*.

Like an out-of-body experience, she saw it all. Dylan's set jaw, Nick's bulging eyes, the mix of shock and painful amusement on everyone else, awkward biting of lips and ducking behind hands.

Ro scribbled away with some kind of manic glee, fake prescription glasses still tucked away in her hair.

Lauren escaped from her corner of the couch, rushed stomps quickly encapsulated by crashing furniture, shattering glass.

"That poor woman," Sarah said, shaking her head, having already repented for her sins so thoroughly, she genuinely believed she had nothing to do with it. "Don't worry, she'll calm down." She looked straight at Nick. "Though she might kill you first."

THE SEARCH

THIRTY-ONE

The rest of the group scattered after Dylan's confession and Lauren's meltdown, some recording in corners, others laying out in the sun.

Olivia had tried to calm Lauren down, but the sobs, the painful aching questions of how she could spend so much of her life devoted to someone so shitty wore Olivia down.

And being worn down was something Olivia could never, ever be.

The dining room table remained the centerpiece of the influencers coming and going, ebbing and flowing, but whatever grand plan the Mercers had for their own videos had clearly evaporated hours ago.

It had been another life since Olivia stacked plates on her arms, wiped down glasses, cleared tables. She recognized Dylan's tight smile, the eyes dancing around the room, looking for something–*anything*–to do.

Olivia straightened in her chair at the dining room table. That was all behind her now.

"Thanks," she said, as Dylan refilled her tumbler with another Excelsior. She washed her sip down with a gulp of white wine. She mostly pushed the roasted Brussels sprouts and kale salad Dylan had served earlier across her plate, trying to make it look like she'd eaten more than she had.

On the other side of the table, Nick, Cody, and Sanjeev made a pact not to let "all of this" ruin the trip.

Well, Nick and Cody made the pact. Sanjeev politely nodded, his head rotating as he looked around the room for his other half.

It wasn't the first time Olivia had joined a group that already knew each other, shared a history so deeply intertwined.

Stranger that she knew the deep intricacies from her years of watching them. From library computers, when her mom would have to drop her off for hours, to her very first smartphone. She followed them all, watched every video, liked every post.

That was the real reason she'd said yes to this trip. Her twisted parasocial need to find out if they were just like she'd always imagined.

But she was beginning to regret it.

"Oh?" Nick laughed, and it took her a moment to realize she must have sighed.

"I just..." she shook her head. "I'm getting old."

The men laughed back. They always did.

"You're only twenty-seven," Sanjeev accused. His chuckles were polite in a different way, a trained way, not the kind of laugh that was hoping to get into her pants.

"Only for another two-hundred twenty-five days." She shrugged one sleeveless shoulder. "I did the math last night. Deaths always make me think..." She trailed off. They didn't push. Deaths had that effect on everyone. Forcing you to think about your own demise. When it would happen.

How it would happen.

"Did you know Jennifer Lawrence already had an Oscar by my age? Ayo Edebiri won an Emmy for work she did when she was my age. I'm just…I'm behind. For so many actresses, all we have is our youth. The roles start changing. And they don't care about you unless they knew you from before. Unless you were accomplished 'back then.'

"And it's not just traditional media! Social media is so ageist. Michelle Monroe won two Webby's before she was twenty-seven. Ivy had already hit two million followers by then. And I'm pretty sure that's when Ro signed her first book deal."

Cody shook his head. "You're not going to get much sympathy from the girls here."

Nick rushed to reassure her. "You're already way more accomplished at your age. Social media just isn't the same. You know how many of us would kill to make the jump to where you are? That's where the real power is."

Olivia gave the two of them the smile she knew men loved.

But her words, at least, were genuine. "I have a lot to learn from them. These women made something of themselves on their own. Or, as on their own as any of us can be. I don't have that yet. And I'm running out of time to make people care."

"That's not true. You've got your, umm–" Nick snapped his fingers, as if he couldn't place the word. As if it wasn't ingrained in his brain. As if he didn't go to that site to jerk off the moment he heard she was coming.

She wondered if he downloaded a video whenever Excelsior told him there wouldn't be Wi-Fi. He seemed the type.

"It's changing, though," Sanjeev said, ignoring Nick entirely. "Not fast enough, maybe. But it is changing. I know lots of girlies who are getting into the game in their forties, fifties, even sixties. Makeup wearers who want to know what it will look like on *them*."

Sanjeev leaned back in his seat, slumping, crossing his arms over his chest. "Although the comments are awful. I've debated putting a filter on my videos so people will stop talking about how I've 'changed.' And that's just from five years ago!"

"Oh, I live for the Sunset filter," Olivia said, leaning across the table, trying to get just a little closer to him. "Smooths everything, brightens it up. A nice tan."

"Your tan is already so nice."

Olivia gave Nick her practiced, pitch-perfect fake laugh and stood. "I'm gonna go freshen up. See you three later?" She walked off, leaving her plate for Dylan to clear. A few steps later, she paused, flipped her hair over her shoulder, turned around and basked in their captive attention. "And thanks for making me feel better."

"Of course," Nick said. The other two smiled. "Can't afford for any more of us to bite it."

Ever the gentleman.

She grabbed her white triangle bikini and a few different shawls. Primping quickly in the mirror on her way to the bathroom, Olivia checked her waves. No touch-up needed. She tossed her outfit change over the side of her jacuzzi tub and opened the door to the toilet.

Dark green, jungle-themed wallpaper with pops of black leopards wrapped around the entirety, accented by deep golden appliances. Someone knew this was her exact aesthetic when they chose this room for her–or maybe they all looked like this.

Regardless, she pulled her linen pants down and sat on the gold toilet, waiting, her eyes darting around, one hungry set of eyes to another. Not so different from when she'd been at the lunch table.

With a wipe, she pulled her hand away. Splotches of blood.

Olivia sagged in relief, resting against the cool wall. No wonder she felt so crazy, so obsessive, so stressed, so panicked. Her period had come early. Travel always fucked it up.

She wiped and flushed and stood, looking at herself in the reflection. Leaning forward, she touched the sides of her eyes, pulling with her ring fingers at the burgeoning crow's feet. Or laugh lines. Whatever they were, she wanted them gone.

She stepped back, looking at herself all the while. "How do I turn that into a positive?" She pruned, checking her angles, pretending her mirrored eyes were the lens of the camera she'd need to stare down. Tilting slightly, chin angled up, an inquisitive but serene look. Unbothered, but intrigued. "Well, yes, I really resonated with my character as someone who also deals with a debilitating–no. As someone who also has a chronic–no."

She licked her lips. She needed to be relatable, but not so relatable she lost her air of mystery. Mysterious, but not so mysterious that she was deemed a bitch. And only a bitch when it was necessary, or if she could make it funny. But not too funny. People didn't like women who tried to be too funny. Especially pretty women.

And if a joke were to go awry, they'd find a reason to try to cancel her. That's all anyone needed. A hint of a reason to dig into her past.

Olivia shook her head.

She had to be perfect now.

"Hey," Olivia tapped her fingers on the half-open door. "Would you want to trade off taking some photos? I need to shoot a short video for this upcoming release."

Michelle sat in front of the tripod, camera pointing at her, as she glanced over her shoulder with a withering look. "Are you actually going to take pictures of me this time, too?"

She deserved that. "Yes." Olivia grinned as she watched Michelle unfold her long legs with an exaggerated sigh, as if this were really putting her out.

With an expert hand, the woman zoomed her camera out, and Olivia could just see a tiny speck of herself in the viewfinder. In Michelle's other hand was an Excelsior, which she chugged the last bit of before crinkling it and bringing it close to the camera lens, tapping it, the camera going dark.

Olivia had watched so many lifestyle vlogs from when that trend had taken over. The screen going dark in one location, brightening back up in another. A clever transition, if dated, though Michelle kept with it. And Olivia loved her even more for it.

Michelle waited until she stopped her recording and packed away her things before asking, "What'd you think about all that with Lauren and Nick?"

As if she'd just been waiting to gossip.

To be fair, Olivia had been, too. "So strange," she agreed. "Plus, I'm pretty sure he was just openly flirting with me in the dining room."

Michelle rolled her big brown eyes, exhaling out, "Men," as they passed by the next room–Sanjeev's new one. He'd even brought over his oil painting, though the door was closed.

Olivia had been watching for so long, she knew exactly where the photo was from–the thumbnail announcing his first ever skincare line, so many years ago. The bright, dewy look was as impressive in oil as she imagined it had been in person.

"I hate to say this," Michelle said, dropping her voice as they exited the hall, spilling out into the large combination living and dining room.

They gave the boys a wide berth, but waved as they passed by, Sanjeev clearly taking his leave not long after Olivia had.

"But I think Nick might just be dumb. I know, I know," she put her hands up. "Everyone always says that about us. But you gotta actually be smart to get this far, I think."

Olivia believed it.

“Not that man, though. That man is dumb as dish soap. And far less useful. Ain’t no way he’d be where he is now without Lauren.” She held her arm up, shielding her face from the sun, and Olivia closed the sliding glass door behind them. “Ain’t no way those two would be where they are without Dylan.”

“I bet they realized that on the Vail trip,” Olivia replied. She remembered the vlogs. The strange shift in atmosphere that no one mentioned. Some had been doing dailies, others a summary of the whole trip. And still, something on the second day must have broken the group.

Dylan had been a prominent fixture in the Mercers own vlogs, so much that people had called for her to have her own spin-off channel. She’d been on that trip and suddenly, *poof.* No evidence of her anywhere after the second day.

But she could be seen in the background of Sarah’s. In Sanjeev’s. Even Ro’s. Picking up a plate here, serving a dish there.

Of course, Ivy had suddenly been scrubbed from Ro’s vlog as well. She’d been doing dailies and then *whoosh.* No more Ivy. Not even in the background. As if Ro explicitly stated she didn’t want a single trace of her in the edit. Cody had remained in both Ro’s and Ivy’s videos, as if he were being pulled side to side, even seconds later.

People matched up the backgrounds and angles of the sun to figure out how close the three must have been standing, but neither Ro nor Ivy mentioned the other.

Sanjeev and Sarah, too, were noticeably absent from each other’s long vlogs, encompassing the whole week. They’d been posting each other like crazy in daily snaps, but that suddenly stopped. Sarah even quoted the iconic Mariah Carey “I don’t know her,” when asked about Sanjeev.

“How’d you know about that?”

“Huh?” Olivia asked, tilting her head to the side. Her companion had stopped walking. Olivia slowed, turning around, blinking away the memories of old Internet forums and obsessive spirals.

She was supposed to be Hollywood. A *starlet*, not a fan. If she were higher up, if she were even C-level, it would be cute that she loved them. She could admit to her hours spent watching. But that wasn't her trajectory. Not yet.

"Oh." Olivia shrugged. "Umm, I think Cody was talking about it with…well, with…"

She let Michelle fill in the gaps, the content creator's voice hollow. "Ivy."

Olivia nodded. It worked as she'd hoped, memories tainting the topic, forcing Michelle to drop the question.

Playing dumb worked on women as easily as it did men. People wanted her to be stupid. It made them feel safer.

Michelle shook, as if a chill ran through her. Then, shedding the thoughts as easily as she shed her previous internet personas, asked, "What are you thinking? Close-ups? Far away? Focus on the jewelry or the fit? Your face? Your ass?"

Olivia laughed. She'd always liked Michelle. The same way she'd liked Ivy. They both had some inexplicable magnetism. One she'd worked hard to identify, copy, channel, and make into her own.

Only theirs were genuine personalities people ran away from, too.

"I need to say a few words about the show and my character, so maybe if you could start far away, and then come close."

"Horizontal or vertical?"

"All vertical for me."

"Short form," Michelle nodded. "Let me get my timelapse set up and then I'll record you. But you better shout me out, okay? Like 'filmed by Michelle Monroe' or something. You can say it or tag me, I don't care."

"You got it." Olivia laughed her promise.

She turned, letting the salty breeze carry her beachy waves over her shoulder. Closing her eyes, she felt the heat through her lids, the sun radiating into her skin.

If this had been a normal vacation–the trip she was promised–she would have been out here nearly every second of every day. She would have laid in the sand, would have swam in the ocean, would have posed on the rocking swing at the gazebo. She might have even read one of Rowena's books she brought with her or taken up Dylan's offer to learn how to make a Mai Tai.

Instead, she opened her eyes, shivering as she looked straight at the two-story annex Ian had been staying in.

That his body was still in.

"C'mon, blondie, let's get the shot!"

When Olivia whipped around, she was no longer herself, nor any version of herself she'd been before. She was her character. A femme fatale. A part she'd been born to play. The only part she'd ever been offered.

Twenty minutes later, a video had been shot, re-shot, and shot again. They finished their work, and Michelle went to pick up her own camera. "Damn, I just recorded the whole thing. Ahh well, I'll speed it up."

"Is that hard? Wouldn't your editor do it?"

"Nah," Michelle shook her head. "Besides, I can't afford one right now. And I like the control, anyways. Okay, can you get in here with me?"

"Of course," Olivia said, trying not to sound too giddy. She ran a hand through her hair, staring at herself, not in the camera lens, but in the viewfinder.

"Alright, we're done with the photoshoot! What'd you think, should I be your next director?"

"'Director MM' does have a nice ring to it," Olivia agreed.

"Doesn't it? Right. Okay, now let's pose for a thumbnail really quick."

Doing as she was told, Olivia grinned, twisting her fingers to make half a heart. Michelle made the other side. The time on the recording ticked up, measuring the interim between events, all this time that would be snapshotted, cut, then forever forgotten.

In the background, Cody and Dylan exited the villa. With a wave in the girls' direction, they turned left, heading toward the white sands of the beach.

"You know," Michelle said, still eye-fucking the camera, so Olivia continued, too. "Lauren and Nick aside, I think this is the best everyone's gotten along in ages." Her braids flipped over her shoulder as she turned back and said, "Only took two people dying." Then, side-eyeing her camera, "I'll cut that out. Anyways! It's time for food. Definitely some alcohol. And some more Excelsior! Let's go!"

Michelle's other hand closed over the camera lens, smothering it in darkness. She dropped her arm, turned off the recording. Ian's annex loomed ahead.

The same chill from before ran through Olivia, as an awful thought raced through her head.

If Michelle died now, the last vestiges of her presence, the last clip immortalizing her forever, would be her hand covering the camera.

Darkness.

The end.

THIRTY-TWO

With Lauren's blubbering, Nick's ineptitude, and Dylan's specialty with drinks, Sanjeev was tipsy and starving as the hours ticked closer to dinner.

Instead of feasting, he sat in the kitchen, being taunted by half-prepared entrées and simmering soup, made extra salty by Lauren's tears.

"I don't mean to be insensitive," Sarah began, crossing herself, her prayer silent but her performance loud. "Lord knows it's tough to develop a good picker. But surely you knew the kind of man he was before you married him?"

Sanjeev sometimes wondered if Sarah was right. Because if there was a Hell, then they were certainly in it now. The kitchen was its core, and they were doomed to repeat this same conversation every half hour.

"No!" Lauren gasped from her sob. She hiccupped too, as if her body didn't know how to handle the lack of oxygen mixed with too many tears, too many fears, all in one day. "He was... he was..." she choked out. "He was so *good*! He was kind and sweet and funny and charming and yes, I knew he was a flirt, but not like that! Not the kind of man who'd run the second I was too busy for him, too busy building our life up."

"Oh, sweetheart," Sarah came up close and rubbed Lauren's back. "If it makes you feel better, I don't know that he was ever that man."

"Me neither," Sanjeev said, quietly throwing in his support. "Rumors ran rampant for ages. They gotta start somewhere."

Lauren rolled her shoulder, Sarah's arm falling back to her side. "He was. He *was* good," she repeated, sounding more like she was trying to convince herself. With a shaky breath out, she picked up the large paring knife. Her steady ease in the kitchen couldn't overwrite her nerves, her pain, and it shook with her, the blade glinting and gleaming off the dazzling fluorescents.

"What are you going to make?" Sanjeev asked, his voice small, his stomach rumbling louder.

He cringed, as if that might set her off again.

But she was too busy pressing her eyes closed. He could almost imagine the ringing in her ears, the internal screaming.

She took a deep breath, then opened her eyes, blinking the two of them into focus. She screwed on a congenial smile, and it scared him even more. "Do you have any requests?"

"Um," he shrugged, his gaze hopping from her to Sarah. "Whatever you make sounds good to me." Anything sounded good right now.

"I'd like another one of those delicious kale salads from before," Sarah said, risking bringing her arm back up and patting Lauren on the back again.

The chef didn't cringe away, and it was all Sanjeev could do to not imagine where Sarah's hand had touched Nick before.

If Lauren wasn't picturing the same thing, it was only a matter of time.

It didn't take long.

Lauren slammed her knife down onto the cutting board, making Sarah jump. "Salad," the chef repeated. "Fine. Great.

I can do salad." She whipped around, facing the fridge. "Why don't you two go get Dylan for me? I'll need help."

Sanjeev held the door as Sarah muttered, "With a salad?"

He dared not answer within earshot, letting the door slam closed before said, "Odds we get dinner?"

Sarah shook her head, then linked her arm into his, the two entering the large foyer as Michelle and Olivia entered from the opposite side. Both wore bikinis and cover-ups, but between them they carried a clear shower curtain.

"What on earth are y'all doing?"

"We got a plan," Michelle said as they breezed past the two of them.

Olivia deigned to explain, "Michelle's in the room next to me, so we're going to share showers and use the curtain from her bathroom to see if we can wrap…if we can wrap Ian up in it. To help with the smell."

Sarah extracted her hand from Sanjeev's arm and began to slow clap as the other two women disappeared. "Well, put enough of us in a house together and a good idea or two is bound to happen."

Sanjeev lifted a brow. He remembered a host of collaborations and shared views, but not a truly good idea that had ever come from one of these trips.

"I'll get some more towels and we can stuff them at the door," Dylan said, appearing from out of the corner of the room, as the sound of gagging came from the end of the hall.

"I'll help," Nick's voice came. Sanjeev took a couple more steps inside the living area, their once-meeting place. The man was still sitting at his seat at the head of the table, only a spread of Excelsior and beer cans to account for his time in the hours since.

"I'll do it alone," Dylan said.

"*Alone*," Sanjeev whispered and Sarah snort-laughed.

No one payed them any mind over Dylan's stomps.

She reappeared moments later, a handful of soft, plush towels folded and stacked in her hands.

"I'll take those," Sanjeev volunteered, though he could already feel his stomach turning at the imagined scent.

Before Dylan could insist, Sarah cut in. "Lauren was looking for you."

No response.

"Don't worry," Sarah said, in that voice that she could turn on at any moment but chose not to. Her real voice. That's what Sanjeev always thought of it. Sarah played a part ninety percent of the time, but there, hidden, tucked away, was the real her. "I was with her for a while, and she wasn't trying to kill me. And we stand guilty of the same crime."

Still nothing.

Sarah gently prodded again. "Good luck."

Dylan lolled her head back, a tiny groan exhaled out before she straightened up. Without another word, she walked down the hall, like a soldier marching to her death.

THIRTY-THREE

Once the tiny matter of the dead body stench was handled, Michelle suggested a dip in the swimming pool, and to her surprise, Sanjeev and Sarah agreed to join. Olivia's response didn't surprise her, especially since she already wore her swimsuit, and Nick surprised her even less, since this was an easier chance to ogle the actress.

Michelle fought the need to keep one eye open around the group and rested her head on the tile deck, her body floating freely in the saltwater pool. Heat from the sun radiated against her skin, every part of her warm, gentle, and at shocking ease.

"This reminds me of Santorini," the actress's voice was wistful, though the mood quickly shifted when Nick asked, "Wasn't that where you were papped with that guy? He had a weird name?"

"It wasn't weird. It was French," she said, and Michelle had to open one eye just so she could slip her gaze to the side and confirm that Sarah and Sanjeev were as amused as she was.

"It was a pool like this, too," Nick said, not even pretending to be the least bit cool. "The infinity kind, with the clear glass people could see through the other side."

"You think people can see us swimming?" Sanjeev asked.

Michelle took a deep breath and sighed it out, letting it be carried away by the wind. "If anyone else were here, maybe."

"Didn't that happen to Bieber, too?"

"It's happened to a lot of people."

"Kinda hot, right?"

Michelle wished she could turn her ears off like she could close her eyes.

"It wasn't," Olivia argued. "It was an invasion of privacy."

"The headlines were hot, though," came Sanjeev's voice, interrupting them. "I mean, you dominated the news cycle for a good three days or so."

"It wasn't worth it. The whole thing was arranged with my agent and his publicist anyway and it just...ugh. The paps weren't even the worst part. The worst part was that my stalker showed up, too."

"You only have one?" Sarah's laugh was as fake as her accent. She clucked her tongue, "Aww, precious."

"Sounds so Hollywood."

"Not even," Sanjeev said.

Michelle hated that she agreed. At least one of her stalkers found out when she'd moved from an apartment to a new condo through Ivy's Whisper.

One bonus of falling off the proverbial cliff–even her most ardent followers had stopped caring. But that obsession scratched an itch for her, too, and she sunk deeper into the water, trying to cleanse herself of the thought.

Sanjeev continued, "I've had several. One even broke into my house when I was gone on that...oh em gee, on that trip to Hawaii, with all the beauty girls and Veronika Janika. You remember her?"

"Was she the one that tried to be a relationship coach and then transitioned to mommy vlogging? And then got arrested for abusing her kids?"

Michelle opened her eyes to find everyone's head turned toward Olivia.

The actress pulled her sunglasses from the top of her head and covered her eyes. "I saw it on the news."

"That was *definitely* her," Sanjeev nodded as he fanned himself with his hand. His skin sparkled in the sun, as if he'd applied a glittering body spray. No doubt coming out next summer. "That was right after she lost all her money in that lawsuit for online gambling, too."

"You know all about that, right, Michelle?" Sarah began, her over-inflated lips contorting as they twisted up into a smile.

Michelle had seen enough of that sinister grin from Sarah's sermons to know that she wouldn't like what came next. A threat, or a pep talk about how she walked the line to eternal damnation? Either option sucked.

"I mean, how did you lose *all* your money?" the faith grifter continued prodding.

Somehow less annoying than her expectations, Michelle matched the deranged glee on Sarah's face and mock-grinned in her direction. "It's not lost…it's just…currently tied up in some investments."

"Mmm, guess those aren't working out well."

"We'll see."

"We sure will," Sarah laughed, and when she looked at him, Sanjeev did, too.

Olivia's mouth pulled down in a slight pout, and Nick continued his ogling.

Michelle closed her eyes again. "At least I don't have to create a fake church and scam people out of their hard-earned money to pull myself out of debt."

The lounge chair squeaked behind her, as if something other than Olivia's breasts had finally grabbed Nick's attention.

"I'm not in debt," Sarah objected.

"*Anymore*," Nick said before Michelle could, and she could tell this trip would be full of unlikely alliances.

"I didn't say anything," Sanjeev whispered his promise. Again, too loud.

"He didn't need to," Michelle said. "Ivy was hinting at some big takedown on Whisper. How many other 'reality trash turned sanctimonious twits' do you know?"

"Yeah," Nick snapped in her direction and Michelle immediately removed him from even her temporary list of allies. "Awfully convenient for you that she–"

Before he could finish his sentence, a splash of water came rocketing in their direction.

Nick barked out a laugh.

Michelle gasped, her head sliding off the pool deck, forcing her eyes open to blinding sunlight. "Not the hair!" Arm chopping through the water, she splashed Sarah back, whose shriek dwarfed the shouts from the others about getting them wet in a *pool*.

"Can you all shut up!" The shout came from the second floor and everyone's heads whipped upward in unison. *Ro.* "Some of us are trying to read."

Michelle pantomimed gagging, and Sarah nodded in agreement as she rolled her eyes.

Nothing brought people together like a common enemy, and none was so obvious as the woman who looked down her nose at them.

THIRTY-FOUR

Sweat trickled down Cody's forehead that he wiped away as he gasped for oxygen. "Alright, now for our longer break. That was a great tabata. Hard. Very hard. To make yours harder on vacation, I recommend trying it out on the sand. The resistance is–" he couldn't think of the word and instead gave a thumbs up as he wandered off screen, ready to choke down some more water.

Today was infinitely harder than his usual routines. Not just because of the sand–though he'd pretend that was why. He hadn't slept well since getting to the island. Had barely eaten. Normally food wasn't something he cared about–a necessity rather than a pleasure. But his protein powder could only do so much. He needed chicken. He needed steak. At this point, he'd settle for fucking ham slices out of a fucking Lunchable.

He shook his protein shake, the blender ball rocking around the container, as he came back into frame for a plug. "Don't forget to have some of your Planks Protein Powder. And some Excelsior to keep your caffeine up! It will work wonders, I promise." Following suit, he downed the last bits of his drink. It was cookies and creme, a new flavor about to hit the market. Gritty, he chugged some of his Excelsior to wash it down.

Chest still heaving, he walked off camera again, set the drinks down, and tried to mentally prepare himself to go again. Another four minutes of peak intensity and–

Fuck it. He'd just change angles. They wouldn't need to know he had to catch his breath. What did it matter? He could do all of this and more any other day of the fucking week.

He turned the camera off, rotating the tripod so he could review his footage so far. Six minutes captured for that round. He sped through the setup, the initial chatting, and moved into the first tabata. He looked a little sluggish.

Whatever, they'd put some music pumping, some fun cuts, descriptions on screen. No one would notice.

His six-week cut had worked though. The evening sun glinted against the sweat on his abs. His pecks were popping and his shoulders looked huge. The gains he'd made over winter looked staggering on film.

All the reward he needed.

He finished chugging the last of his Excelsior and crinkled the can in his hand just as a blur raced across the screen behind him.

As if forgetting this was minutes ago, he whipped his head up, staring at the villa in the background. He furrowed his brows. Nothing amiss. He went back to the footage, rewound, but there it was.

Not a blur.

A person.

Unmistakably a person.

Wearing all black, a hood pulled over their head. They stood on the second level of Ian's room, looking at something, before dashing across the stained-glass window.

What the fuck?

Cody raced across the sand, barely noticing his calves burning, muscles straining, as he sprinted the quarter mile back to the main house. Sand flew up behind him, and he gulped down air in heaving breaths. If only he'd seen them before he'd done his workout. If only he'd seen them when he was–

The doors were already open as he slid through.

Only Dylan stood in the hallway, eyes wide at his mania.

"Have you been into Ian's room?" he demanded. "Has anyone gone in there? Hell, has anyone seen–"

"Slow down," Dylan said, mirroring his concern back to him. She set a platter of appetizers onto the dining table. "A couple of them went in to wrap up the body and we stuffed some rags under the door, but no one–"

"Who? Where are 'they'?"

"They're all in the pool. Why?"

Foregoing an explanation, Cody sprinted through to the living room, his bare feet slapping against the tiled floor as he searched for the door to take him to the other side of the villa. They'd barely had time to tour the place between fights and deaths and he'd staked out the upstairs gym, not the pool.

"Where is it!" he screamed.

"To your right," the meek voice came, but he followed her instructions and tore through floor-to-ceiling curtains on the right, on the right, on the right, until he found the door and threw it open. It ricocheted, the glass warbling before beginning its slide back to close.

"I don't know what's going on, but you need to calm down. C'mon, hun, have a drink." Sarah pointed with her half-full glass toward the swim-up pool bar, currently stocked with what looked like pre-made mojitos.

"I caught someone."

When no one responded, Cody clarified. "On camera. In the background. They were up in Ian's room."

Concern pinched Michelle's face and Olivia stared at him wide-eyed.

Sarah looked to Sanjeev, and Sanjeev to Sarah.
Nick downed the rest of his drink.
“We aren’t alone here.”

THIRTY-FIVE

Never let it be said that Lauren Mercer–no, Lauren *Alvarez*–didn't take requests. The kale salad sat, covered, next to the parmesan crisps, the butternut squash ravioli, and extra sides. For the non-vegetarians, she also seared ahi tuna steaks, the crackle of fish in oil silencing the whispers outside her kitchen.

She appreciated how everyone had placated Cody. When he barged into her kitchen, Dylan begged–nearly on hands and knees–that he not disrupt her work. That he wait to share whatever "big news" he had until dinner.

She appreciated it even though she could feel it tinged with the reality that it wasn't for *her* sake, but everyone else's.

She'd been ridiculous. Dramatic. Monstrous.

Hurt.

So *publicly* hurt.

Still, Cody only managed to wait until they were all seated, as Dylan tonged the first bit of salad onto his gold-rimmed plate, before he pulled out his phone. "I took a picture."

"A picture of your video?"

He cast a withering gaze in Sanjeev's direction, who immediately shrunk down despite Sarah's honking snort.

"Do you want to see it or not?" He pulled out his phone, turning it around to show him without waiting for an answer.

The broad, lithe man hesitated only a moment before leaning forward.

"Do you see?" Cody asked, swiping from left to right, setting down the fork he'd held in his other hand without taking so much as a single bite of her salad.

Sanjeev studied the photos. The rest of the group studied his face. His perfectly painted crimson lips parted slightly, and his lined lids narrowed as Cody scrubbed back and forth.

He blinked and looked up, seeing everyone waiting on him. His long lashes barely moved as he glanced around, some part of him clearly reveling in the attention.

Then, a single nod.

Chairs scraped against the floor, everyone clambering to stand behind Cody–to get a look over his shoulder, needing to see the photo of the video for themselves.

Lauren stayed seated, giving Dylan a curt "thank you" as she served the salad onto her plate. When she was out of the way, Lauren reached forward, gently tapping her unused soup spoon against her glass of white wine. "Please, everyone, enjoy this meal. Our first of many together. Served family style and inspired by this beautiful island." She repeated the words she'd rehearsed before.

Before she learned Dylan and Nick slept together.

Before Ian and Ivy died.

Before the others had even stepped foot on the island.

The words meant nothing anymore as they flowed from her mouth. When she finished, she looked over to the camera shooting across the room, and gave it a thumbs up and a smile, as if it wouldn't be edited away by Nick later.

Then, just as she stabbed the first bite of her kale salad, Cody spoke. "I saw a large compound in the distance, a little way up the mountaintop. Maybe we should ask them if they've seen anyone walking around?"

"Or if they have cell coverage!" Michelle said.

"It'll be about a three-hour hike, I think."

Michelle groaned. "Not sure internet is worth all that."

Ro asked, "And what would it be worth?"

"I could do an hour," Michelle answered, clearly ignoring the other woman's tone. "Get all cute, wear my two-piece matching set, take some pictures–"

"I'm always down for more pictures," Olivia agreed. Then, added a defensive, "*What?*"

Cody's jaw tweaked, but as more attention drew to him, he said through gritted teeth, "I just thought there would be more important things than pictures right now."

Lauren knew the tone of the words unspoken. The way Cody stared Olivia down. She'd thought them so many times before. *You were supposed to be on my side.*

He continued, "Like what if this person had something to do with Ian's death?"

Forks froze. Eyes glanced to either side, all of them trying to make sense of the words.

"And then what," Ro said, "they came back to look at their handiwork? I don't mean to shut you down, I'm just saying. What would be the point? You think there's someone else here, hiding out?"

"I don't know!" he nearly shouted. "But you saw the video! What else could it be?"

To that, Ro didn't have an answer. Only a mumbled, "picture of a video."

Lauren bit at the chunks of her lips that threatened to flake off. She tore at the skin, pulling too much. It began to bleed, the familiar rust-like taste filling her mouth. She sunk down in her chair, trying to hide her shame, nibbling more.

"Okay, so we get a search party going?" Nick asked from the opposite side. He was too far away to see her lips. Otherwise, she knew he would have commented. "After dinner, we can all go check Ian's room. Then we can leave tomorrow–"

"Morning," Michelle said. "Tomorrow *morning*. For the best lighting." Then, her mouth half full of food, she gasped. "Do you think…I mean…could it be a reporter?"

"A reporter," Ro repeated, but she was nodding her head this time. "Maybe they found out we were here–"

"How?" Cody asked.

"I posted about it," Michelle said. "Pretty sure Ivy did, too. I mean, I posted the invitation. The car ride to the airport. I was streaming from the plane before take-off."

"It wouldn't be too hard to figure out," Ro agreed. "They know we're all on some beautiful island in the Caribbean. And maybe Ian was able to contact someone after all–maybe the person heard about Ivy and wanted to be the first to break the news, or…"

Lauren couldn't tell if Ro was legitimately speculating about their issue or brainstorming her next bestseller. But either way, it made more sense than someone trying to kill Ian. He was a dipshit. She'd learned that quickly. But her husband–her *ex*-husband–was a much bigger one. If that was the justification, *Ian* wouldn't have been the first to die.

"Just…please," Cody said, "Try to think about it another way. It's crazy that two people died on this trip already."

"Okay," Olivia jumped in, her voice that easy, placating tone used on toddlers or grown men. "Let's just think. What did the two of them have in common?"

"Umm, they're both Asian?" Nick said.

"Oh, so you think they're killing the Asians?" Sanjeev asked.

"I mean…" The answer came only with a shrug.

"So what? You're saying I'm next?"

In that moment, it was clear Nick had forgotten that East Asians weren't the only Asians even though he'd traveled all over the world with her.

"No?" her ex answered.

"They're both addicts?" Ro again. Someone–Michelle, probably–must have kicked her under the table because she hissed, "What?" Then, "Fine, fine. Both their names start with I? And are three letters?"

Cody gestured in Ro's direction, as if they were finally getting somewhere, though no one else seemed convinced. Ro probably only knew that because she'd written their names down in her little notebook she took everywhere.

She was probably writing about all of them.

Lauren glanced down at her plate. What would Ro write about the food? All her hard work, and it would be cold by the time Cody let them finish. Only Dylan, to her right, continually stabbed into her salad, plucked off bits of her dinner roll, and sliced through her ahi tuna.

It was the reason Lauren couldn't even be mad at her. That, and because she knew the truth. She couldn't function–*survive*–without Dylan by her side. There were battles to be chosen, but to win the upcoming war against Nick, she needed to keep in mind who her true enemy was.

"They were both shitty people?" Nick tried.

Think of the devil…

"Ian ruined a couple of lives. Ivy…what," someone scoffed, "a couple reputations?"

"For some of us, that's all we have."

Lauren processed the words, looking up to see who'd said them, but all eyes were on her. *She'd* said them.

And she'd meant them dearly.

The last vestiges of her reputation were all she clung to. It's why she couldn't let go of this moment, why she tried so hard to make it work, why she bothered with this last-ditch effort of a brand trip at all.

Ro cleared her throat. "If that's all the reason we have, shouldn't we circle back around to it being an accident? He drank too much, he fell–that's it. It's almost...poetic. In a twisted sort of way. The pilot falling."

Michelle pointed to Cody with her drink. "Why are you so convinced he was pushed?"

"Besides the random person I saw?"

Ro rolled her eyes.

The silence made it clear it didn't seem like enough proof for anyone else either.

Cody's fork scraped against his plate, and a chill raced through Lauren.

She stared as he set it down, hardly taking another bite even though he'd been so insistent on her making all this fucking protein for him.

"Because..." he hedged, "he was into some bad shit. Blackmailed some people."

The reason Cody knew this lingered in the air, none quite willing to ask more questions.

For a single moment, they'd all seemed to have forgotten the cameras.

It wasn't until Lauren really pondered his words, as her eyes naturally grazed over, that she found herself staring directly into a lens.

She straightened in her chair.

The others moved around too, adjusting. "Cut that out, please," Cody said, picking up his fork again.

"Were you one of them?" Nick asked.

Cody set his fork down, brought his napkin to his mouth and patted at the imaginary food he'd eaten in that time. "Pardon?" It was a question, but also a warning.

"Was Ian blackmailing you?"

And though Lauren didn't dare look at him, she could imagine the smirk on her ex's face. That awful, taunting sneer he made.

If she were Cody–and she had been on the receiving end of Nick's fixation plenty–she wouldn't answer.

But Cody did. "Yes," he confessed.

That only begged more questions. It's all it ever did.

"What for?"

"Does it matter?"

Nick shrugged. "I'll tell you if you tell me."

Cody leaned back in his seat and crossed his arms. "So, you were also being blackmailed?"

"Oh, yeah," Nick said. "And mine was for something bad. I bet yours was, too. What was it, hookers? Drug addiction? He flew you out to some other island where you…"

Cody's entire torso rotated to face Nick, his muscles clenching as he wound his hands together.

For a moment, she wished that Cody would kick the shit out of him. And then the next image, of Nick hurt, wounded her so badly that she chastised herself for ever wishing for it at all. Lauren's heart lurched, and she hated it.

"Is that what yours was for?" Cody said, voice even.

"Nick!" Her warning fell on selective hearing ears.

"I mean…" Nick shrugged. "Yeah. All of that. And more."

Jaw clenched, eyes shut, Lauren whispered, "Shut *up*."

"Our therapist said I'm not supposed to lie, Lauren."

"*Shut up!*" she all but yelled.

"Dude, shut up," Cody added.

A chorus of others joined in.

"Fine, fine." He relented, hands up in a faux defensive pose he'd so perfected. "I'm gonna get another beer. Anyone want to join?"

Chairs screeched, plates were pushed, people grabbed their wine to join. Even though they'd all collectively yelled at him, even though they surely agreed he was the biggest asshole to walk this villa, people still wanted to be in his presence.

"SIT DOWN."

Everyone froze.

Everyone but Nick, who was already halfway down the hall. He wouldn't have come back even if she'd begged. He would've love that, would've laughed.

Lauren gripped the steak knife in her hand so hard her knuckles turned white. She could see the panic in their eyes. The worry she'd turn it on them, or herself. Slowly she rotated her fist back to her plate, the knife's serrated edge coming closer and closer. "If you people do not eat this meal, so help me..."

She couldn't finish her sentence.

Chair legs squealed across the marbled granite, and elbows smacked against the table as everyone hurried to sit to begin stuffing their faces.

"Mmm, so good."

"This is the best meal I've ever eaten."

"Wow, thank you so much, Lauren."

Placated, at least momentarily, Lauren cut her already thin slice of ahi tuna in half. She brought it to her mouth slowly, and it melted as she chewed. *This* was good. *She* was good.

Good, good, good.

"I don't know why you bother with that man," came the drawl at the other end of the table. The one that haunted her nightmares for so many months when Nick finally confessed. "People love divorces. They would *love* watching you build your life back up."

Lauren stopped eating. She felt like she stopped breathing. Slowly she glanced up from her plate, across the immaculately set table, tracing her way up the bedazzled cross hanging between Sarah's cleavage, and straight into those blue eyes.

She was still talking. "You know how many second chances I've had? And that was me doing it to myself. People will give you the time of day, Lauren. Especially since he's such a dipshit. Just kick him to the curb, make a tell-all, and watch those views flow in."

"I don't want your help."

"Sarah," Sanjeev whispered, reaching over to take the influencer's hand, but she didn't listen.

Instead, Sarah snapped. "Fine! You don't want my help? You don't get to cry to me." Turning to face Sanjeev but speaking loudly enough for the whole table to hear, she added, "I hate when people won't help themselves. Why should I care if you don't?"

"Sarah–" Dylan tried to chastise, but Lauren was done.

She stood back so quickly, the chair buckled behind her, clattering to the ground.

Someone gasped, others winced.

And Lauren stormed off, plate of food still in hand, no doubt giving more fuel for Nick to edit later.

THIRTY-SIX

Nick had just pried the cap off a bottle when the kitchen door swung open to reveal the last person he expected.

"I swear, there's going to be so much leftover food," Lauren harrumphed. She scraped a fork across her plate, the metal screeching against the porcelain, bits of lobster mac and cheese tumbling in clumps down the trash chute.

While it was still open, Nick arched his hand back, "Swish," he said, sending the bottle cap flying through the air, missing the bag entirely.

Lauren hissed. "Nice."

She didn't bother grabbing the cap as it rolled right next to her foot, wavering back and forth until it came to a stop. He didn't bother either.

"What?" Lauren demanded.

He looked up from the cap. "Nothing," he said, unable to help the chuckle under his breath as she practically threw the plate into the sink. It clattered among the other dishes. The ones she or Dylan hadn't gotten to yet.

"What?" She demanded again, this time picking up a dirty dish towel and hurling it at him. "What's so fucking funny?"

He caught it on his chest and tossed it back to her.

She hurled it at him again, and he nearly howled with laughter at the absurdity.

"I just can't believe," he said, bending down to pick up the towel and tossing it into the corner, "that after all this time, you really don't know."

Lauren gripped the edge of the island and bent over, lunging slightly. "I'm so tired of all the cryptic bullshit. That's all you ever do and it's exhausting."

"Oh, *I* exhaust *you*?" he asked, no trace of laugh left. "That's fucking rich. Fine. *Fine!* You want to know what I'm laughing at? Dylan always gathered up your food and gave it to the hired help. All the waitstaff ate your leftovers. And there were fucking piles of it, pounds of it! Never touched by all those fancy people that hired you."

Lauren lifted her head, but the rest of her remained half on the island. "You..." her voice came out gravely and low. "You're serious?"

"Oh yeah. All those people raving about how great you are?" Nick asked. "Wait, wait, I remember a good one. Remember The Met afterparty? When your 'biggest fan' called your food–what was it?"

"An inspiration," Lauren answered softly.

"'An inspiration!' Yeah, she ate one bite," he laughed. "*One* bite, then just moved the food around her plate, and went to the bathroom to snort some coke. Oh! And that time the head of *Cosmo* said you were an icon, a titan of the industry? She never even–"

"I'm going to kill you!" Lauren threw herself off the island, looking like a woman possessed, moving across the kitchen so fast he barely had time to flinch as a half-full pot came hurling toward his head.

He ducked out of the way just in time, old pasta water splashing everywhere, metal clanking against tile, echoing.

"You're gonna *what*? You're gonna try and do what? I fucking have you now, bitch. I got that on fucking record–" he threw his hand out, pointing toward the constantly running camera affixed in the upper corner of the room.

Lauren acted like she didn't hear him.

A pan came next, another pot, then a crash as she ripped open one of the drawers and started throwing forks and spoons and knives.

He dodged out of the way, his laughter echoing along with the clanking, clattering, smashing, banging.

Until she reached behind her, toward the magnetic knife board, and grabbed one that gleamed.

"*Whoa*, okay, hey," Nick said, both hands in front of his face. "Easy now, I know you don't mean it."

Lauren cocked her arm back.

"Okay, hey, I'm sorry, I'm sorry–help. SOMEONE *HELP*!"

Three bodies barged through the door and Lauren turned, now pointing the knife in their direction.

"We were listening on the other side," Olivia explained, her hands up, too. "It's okay, no one blames you," she said. And from the edge of her voice and the glare she cast at him, it was clear his chances with the actress were *donezo*.

Dylan stepped forward, her voice calm and slow. "I promise, everyone always loves your food. So much that I never wanted it to go to waste. The staff was always so appreciative, always spoke so highly of the leftovers."

She took another step forward, and Lauren's arm seemed to grow heavy and weary.

"It's okay, it's okay. There you go," Dylan said, as the knife passed from Lauren's fingers into her own grasp. "Olivia, Ro, could you take Lauren to her room?"

"Of course," the actress said, interweaving her hand into Lauren's and pulling her out of the kitchen.

Ro looked between Nick and Dylan.

"I'll be fine," Dylan said.

The writer nodded and left.

Nick finally dropped his arms down as the door swung closed. "Why's she so worried for you?" He asked. "I'm the one who was just held at knifepoint!"

Dylan just stared.

"Oh, c'mon. You know she's as crazy as I do."

More staring. And slowly, ever so slightly, she began shaking her head.

"Whatever," he said. "I've got it all on camera. You think she's getting half of everything now? She's lucky if she'll even be able to set foot near me." The words continued to flow out of his mouth as he waited–kept waiting–for Dylan to interject. For her to do anything other than shake her head. "We could take it over together, you know. You built it up as much as she did. More, even. C'mon, we–"

"You *disgust* me," she said, the venom dripping from her mouth, the knife the least of his concern as her words finally cut him. Setting the blade back on the magnetic cutting board, she turned and looked at him as if it were the final time. "And one day, you're going to get what's coming to you."

Then she, too, stormed out of the kitchen, leaving him alone with the mess.

THIRTY-SEVEN

It had been so easy to hold the knife in her hands, to point it at him–it must have been how Lauren felt. Dylan knew she should check on her, but in the few short seconds it took to extract herself from that kitchen, all matters of "should" left her.

She stared at Lauren's portrait as voices trickled from down the hall. The woman had chosen that room as much for its proximity to the kitchen as its distance from Nick.

Now it seemed an entire floor wasn't enough to separate them. Nowhere would be far enough.

Dylan breathed in through her nose, exhaled exhaustion through her mouth. How long had she been up today? Yesterday? All week, she'd been running around, prepping, setting up. It came crashing down on her now.

Feet shuffled against the granite floor as a large figure stood, arms crossed over his chest, at the end of the hall. Cody kept his voice low. "I'm going out. *Tonight.* I'm not waiting until tomorrow, and I think someone should come with me."

She should go with him.

She knew as well as he did. The only chance at reaching the outside world was the hike. And only the two of them stood a chance at making it in the next few hours.

Nick said supplies were due to come in a few days, but she doubted any of them could wait that long. Antsy nerves pinched at her skin. "Yeah," she said, letting the brief comfort wash over her. She could get out of here–away from Nick, away from Lauren–at least for a few hours. Maybe permanently. "Yeah, I'll go with you."

"Where?" Olivia asked.

Dylan turned, looking to the side.

The actress exited Lauren's room. Ro followed behind.

Cody hesitated. Then, "Out. To see if we can find help. Or cell service."

"Cell service?" Came the loud drawl. Sarah and Sanjeev's conversation had died out at the worst moment, the two stepping forward, joining Cody. "Where'd you find that?"

Cody sighed. "We haven't yet. We're going out. Dylan and me. To try to find some."

She appreciated his short, clipped response. She could barely rally herself to spend time with him, let alone with Sarah Pruski.

"I wanna go, too," Michelle said, her voice carrying. Great. Dylan rolled her eyes. Now they were all here. "No way someone else is breaking this before me." Her eyes shifted to the side, sizing Sarah up. "Or at least…we'll all be breaking it at the same time."

"Agreed," Sarah said. Then, turning back to face the rest of them, barked, "What? As if y'all weren't thinking about it! Tell me, Cody, if you found this cell service, you weren't going to post? Weren't going to snag all the attention? I don't think so."

"I wouldn't–"

Michelle tutted. "You so would."

Sanjeev nodded.

Dylan didn't rush to defend him. She knew, if given the chance, every single one of them would have posted. First, for the attention. The eyes. Thousands–maybe hundreds of thousands, maybe millions, with all their followers combined–of people, curious where they'd all disappeared to.

It would be huge.

Besides, sometimes things happened faster over social media. People cared more. Or, at least, pretended to care more. Why complain about mistreatment to a poor call center worker when you could just @ the company and rally thousands of others to badger them with their own complaints until they rectified the situation?

And, also, sent a PR box or two.

No doubt rescue missions would be the same. Someone, somewhere, would rush to find them. To gain their own clout by being the heroes. And they'd deserve it.

"I should probably stay behind," Olivia said. "I think I'd just hold you all back."

"We don't have to go fast," Cody insisted.

"No, no." She brought a hand down to her stomach. "My cramps have been brutal."

Half the group groaned in sympathy.

"Anyway, good luck. Be safe, okay?"

As she weaved her way past the group, Ro piped up. "I should stay back, too. Get some real work done."

Cody seemed noticeably less upset about her absence, barely looking at her as she walked past. No doubt he was holding a grudge, replaying in his mind how Ro shot down every theory about the person in the hoodie.

Dylan would have bet all the others were thinking the same.

Especially as he said, "Poor Olivia. She doesn't deserve this." Sarah cocked her hip to the side, and he rolled his eyes. "Not that any of us do, but it's gotta be hard. New people, totally new place, doing a new job, influencing for the first time, and then this happens?"

"I'm gonna start a bet that you to sleep with her before Nick does." Sarah turned to Sanjeev. "You want to take me up on it?"

"Sarah," Sanjeev scolded, but his grin was wide. He asked Cody, "You're going to try, aren't you?"

Michelle snorted. And Dylan had to chew at the inside of her cheek to keep from snickering.

Cody turned on his heel. "Be back here in fifteen. If you're not back by then, Dylan and I are leaving without you."

She continued chewing on her cheek as she walked to her room, leaving the others behind as they argued back and forth about what the betting line should be.

It took thirty minutes, but eventually Sanjeev, Sarah, Michelle, and Cody rejoined her at the dining table, still messy with remnants of half-eaten dinner. They all wore athleisure, some likely sponsored or gifted. Cody was the only one sporting his own designs.

A year ago, Dylan had started showing off her yoga routine, posting a snippet here and there. Not enough to mess with her carefully curated algorithm, but enough to garner some interest.

Now she was drowning in clothes, so many PR boxes she had trouble remembering what she got from where and when.

"Twins!" Michelle checked her with her hip, wearing a similar leopard print two-piece, though she'd clearly forgotten to take the tag off.

Or maybe she remembered and simply stuck it up the back, intending to return it. She could always Photoshop it out of her pictures.

And pictures were clearly the primary goal, if the fumes from Sarah's hairspray that wafted with the evening breeze were any indication.

Dylan hesitated as they neared the bungalow–the only place she'd been alone with Nick. All willful intention of ignoring his existence flew away with the breeze and the hairspray. She glanced over her shoulder, heart thumping as she stared at the mansion.

"What's up?" Michelle asked, slowing, sticking with her.

Dylan cleared her throat, projecting, "Should we really let Nick and Lauren stay there together?"

The rest of the group turned around, pausing, waiting.

"Lauren's resting," Michelle answered. "Plus, Ro and Olivia are there. Besides, do you really want Nick with us right now?"

"No," Dylan shook her head. *Hell* no.

"That's what I thought. Now take this," Michelle said, slipping her phone into Dylan's hand without a moment's hesitation, "and take a slow-mo of me walking once we get to the front, okay?"

The two sped walked their way past Sanjeev and Sarah, and Dylan called out to Cody, "Wait up!"

He hung back, watching with what looked like distaste mixed with intrigue as Michelle now led the group.

Dylan did as instructed, ducking a little to get the angle.

Michelle whipped her hair over her shoulder, turned, and smized at the camera. "Okay, once more," she said.

Dylan obliged.

Sarah, having seen this, insisted Sanjeev do the same for her, only she repositioned herself to be walking back toward the mansion.

Cody sighed, running a hand through his perfect blond hair. "We're not making it up to that penthouse, are we?"

"Doubt it," Dylan said, returning the phone back to Michelle, her eyes already glued to the final product.

"Alright, then can I bother you? Can you take a few photos of me, too? I'll return the favor."

"Deal."

After at least twenty minutes, they eventually made it off the boardwalk and began traversing across the sand.

The process repeated with each new background: the place where the sand gathered into small dunes, the angle where the fairy lights created a bokeh effect in portrait mode, the moment more palm trees dotted the sand. What should have been a ten-minute walk took them at least an hour, and only then were they completely out of earshot.

"Okay, seriously, what the fuck was all that?"

"Have they been like that for a while?" Sanjeev asked, his question less directed outward, at the universe, and more to Dylan herself.

She huffed as she took a step up, over a large rock. "Honestly? I haven't seen the two of them together in months. Since before the news of the divorce broke."

"You mean the one you leaked to Whisper?" Sarah asked slyly. Cody offered his hand and helped her up the same step the rest had just climbed.

"Yes," Dylan rolled her eyes, turning around and staring wearily ahead. "I'd hoped it would help Lauren leave him."

"It was their business," Sanjeev said. His scolding was light, but there all the same. Dylan eyed him as he walked past her, beginning to understand how he and Sarah maintained their friendship for so many years. So holier than thou...

"I know it was their business," she hissed. "But I think it helped. She'd started to move on. *Actually* move on. What with the...evidence pointing to how quickly Nick had."

"You mean how he'd never been fully in?"

"I think they were...once upon a time." Dylan remembered the early days, when they'd first hired her. Back when they still openly flirted with one another, in a way that made her feel both giddy at seeing such strong love and hopelessly jealous for not having that for herself.

Maybe that's why, as soon as Nick made a move, she'd been willing to betray Lauren's trust. To experience some of that giddiness for herself. She was young, not even twenty-one, and so the older, wiser Dylan knew better now than to blame herself. At least, not fully.

She looked at Sarah, only a couple years or so older than her, and wondered if that's how she'd felt too. Almost taken advantage of by a man fifteen years their senior, who'd seen the way of the world and decided to prey on those who didn't yet know it.

Dylan remembered the news breaking that Sarah and Nick hooked up. The blame she copped. The references to how she'd always been the "easy" one, even back on her first reality show. In a house filled with hot, young people, and producers who prompted drinking to deal with problems, big or small, or celebrations, big or small–who cared if someone liked hooking up?

The public, apparently.

Maybe that's why the woman became a born-again Christian. Why she preached so strongly about letting Christ "save" you. Harder for her biggest haters to blame her if she'd "redeemed" herself through the eyes of their shared Lord.

At least some of it was an act. It had to be. No influencer rose that high without blending fact and fiction. Dylan just wondered where that line blurred between Sarah the Preacher and Sarah Pruski.

"Look, it's all fine and good that they don't get along. They don't need to. Who cares?" Sarah huffed, taking Cody's hand again to lift her over a small incline. "But the knife? Unwarranted. Regardless of what a shithead Nick might be."

"Is," Dylan corrected.

Sarah just rolled her eyes. “Can we take a break?” She breathed out heavily, leaning against a large boulder. It overlooked the vista slightly, and they could just barely make out… how truly little they'd traveled.

“Oh my god, we're barely higher than the bungalow,” Michelle realized, leaning against the stone next to Sarah.

“But what a view,” Cody said, his admiration clear. “Wait, watch this.” He took a running leap and then scrambled up the boulder, in an almost gravity-defying dare.

“Holy shit,” Dylan said, “can you do that again?” She whipped out her phone, ready to catch him descending and ascending. Then–“Oh my god. I have a bar. I have a bar!”

Michelle pushed off the boulder and rushed to look over Dylan's shoulder. “Quick, call 911!”

“No!” Sarah cried. “Call your agent! Or your publicist!”

“Or your assistant,” Sanjeev said.

“911 won't work,” Cody agreed, hopping off the boulder and gathering around, as Dylan held her phone up to her ear.

“It's ringing,” she whispered as she began to hop in place. “Oh my god, it's actually–fuck, it's dead.” She pulled her phone back to see the bars had vanished.

“Maybe if we keep going,” Cody said, “they'll reappear.”

The bars did not reappear. Not for any of them. Not as they scaled uneven, damp terrain. Not as they slipped and fell. Not as they cursed their agents, publicists, and even themselves for deciding to come on this stupid trip. They also laughed so hard they cried and then laughed at their mascara-stained cheeks.

For the first time in over a decade, Dylan finally felt like she was part of the trip. Not in Rome, Vail, in a cabin on the Michigan lake, Paris, Miami, or Las Vegas. She never felt like she belonged, felt like the rest of the influencers saw her as a person.

And she also knew, that as soon as they left the hillside, as soon as they scaled across the dunes, as soon as they trudged through sand to reach the mansion, that would be it. They'd expect her to go back to serving them, to her role as the help, to a person meant for catering to their every whim.

She didn't know how much longer she could do it.

"Is my hair flat?" Sarah asked, her face nearly as pink as the lipstick she was currently reapplying.

Sanjeev wisely said nothing, and Michelle placated with a "Girl, you're always stunning. Now take the damn picture."

"Fine, fine," Sarah said with a laugh, stepping up to the old swing dangling from a large mango tree, one that overlooked the ocean far below. Vines and roots and overgrowth made it clear no one had used it in at least a season. Still, Sarah took her turn, the last of them, to sit on the swing. Sanjeev directed her to tilt her chin, and the other three commented on how Sanjeev should angle the camera. In the end, they got at least two or three perfect shots.

"I don't mean to be a downer," Sarah said, beginning to swing slightly, her neck craned back so she could see. "But we are still a very, very, *very* long way from the top." The swing squealed under her weight as she moved, rusted metal grinding against leaves and caked dirt.

"Sarah," Sanjeev said, his voice quiet. "Maybe you shouldn't–"

On the back half of her swing, the right chain snapped, and Sarah tumbled out of the seat. Her face planted into the mud, and she groaned, but she'd fared better than the swing. The chain dangled off, the seat falling down, down, *down* until it smacked onto the hill below.

"We should probably head back," Dylan suggested, and everyone frantically agreed.

THIRTY-EIGHT

Olivia always knew she'd die young.

She'd had a dream about it in grade school. Right around the time the Virginia Tech shooting made the news. Recurring nightmares followed, of school shootings, of devastating car accidents, of natural disasters. She once drew a picture of her own funeral and her art teacher called her mother in for a conference–a busy mother, not a lot of time to take meetings other than the most important ones, and Mrs. Moscovitz had insisted it was–and explained that she was concerned about Olivia.

But Olivia's mom had always known the truth too. It was their curse. The Inge women died young.

Her mom survived to forty-two, older than most in their family. Every birthday that passed was a grand celebration, a wish blown on the candle for another year.

Until she got into acting, Olivia thought that meant she'd live to be fifty, at least. She'd survived high school with no problem, survived her twenty-first year with a minimal hangover, made it to twenty-five as unscathed as one could expect.

Now there was one more hurdle. A looming one, approaching with swiftness. The twenty-seventh year.

All the greats, and upcoming greats, died at twenty-seven. Amy Winehouse, Janis Joplin, Chance Perdomo, Anton Yelchin, Kurt Cobain, Kim Jonghyun.

A curse. Her curse.

She stayed away from drugs except the ones that kept her thin. And she stayed away from alcohol, except in times of crisis. But otherwise, she was healthy. She ran, she ate vegan, she only ever walked because of how dangerous car drives were, which had made it nearly impossible to navigate auditions in Los Angeles before the pandemic. Even now, she still wore her face mask whenever she felt a hint of sniffles coming on.

Olivia Blakely–born Gemma Inge–turned twenty-seven nearly one hundred forty-one days ago. She only had to make it seven and a half more months. She was close. So close.

But death surrounded her. Her suitemate in freshman year? Suicide. Her senior year roommate? Cancer. Her first serious boyfriend? Car crash.

Her part-time boss?

Her agent's husband?

Her landlord?

And now, this trip. Two of them.

224 days, 5 hours, and 33 minutes to go.

With a groan, Olivia slowly sat up, clutching her stomach. Period pains were her worst nightmare on set. But she'd learned to cope...or rather, she'd learned to spend copious amounts of money. Massage chairs, heating pads, getting pedicures or manicures or facials to distract herself, and smoke some weed. It gave her voice a nice, husky quality, and helped with the pain.

But she hadn't brought any of that stuff with her. She'd assumed there would be masseuses on site. She had been ready to lap up luxury.

And while she could complain about the amenities, there were no complaints about the space itself. From her king-size bed she could see the sunset, casting dazzling hues of pink above the white-sand beaches. The linen fluttered in the breeze. She lay on a bed of clouds, surrounded by a multitude of plush pillows, tucked in crisp sheets and lush blankets.

The room itself rivaled the size of her first home, and she couldn't tell if the villa was pumping in coconut perfumes or if it was the natural scent of the island, but it wafted by every half hour or so, further lulling her into a state of comfort.

But none of it did anything for her uterus, which was currently trying to break free of her body.

She groaned as she slowly kicked her legs out from under the duvet and cringed as she landed with a small thump on the ground below. Her slippers sat only a few feet away, and she shuffled into them, then shuffled into the bathroom.

Nothing in the medicine cabinet other than a small bag of Tylenol, not even the super strength.

And she hadn't brought anything stronger either. Shit.

Still hunched over, with a hand pressing into her ovaries, she slowly made her way out of her room and down the long hall. The hiking crew still hadn't returned, so the house sat, almost preternaturally still.

Olivia shuffled, forgoing the stairs to the guys' rooms upstairs, and continued down the long hall toward Lauren. She passed by Dylan's headshot, taken when her hair was a cropped, platinum pixie. She passed by Sanjeev's and Michelle's, all three pairs of eyes feeling like they were following her, the hallway closing in.

Finally, when she arrived at Lauren's room, the portrait loomed down at her. Olivia remembered this headshot, the one she'd used to promote herself as a judge for some Netflix cooking show. Lauren's trademark dyed tomato red hair was braided and twisted, pinned to the top of her head, a few pieces dangling, curling down to frame her face. She wore her chef robes, holding a knife painted in gray oils, with a hint of white to make it look like it was gleaming.

Olivia knocked on the door, still staring at the portrait. As she moved closer, she could see the specks and thick chunks where the paint had been piled up, creating texture. "Lauren?" Olivia called, taking a step back as she knocked again.

Still no answer.

Her stomach ached, and she bent down even further. She was about to lay on the cool, granite tile and call it a day, just waiting to be found and carried back to her bed. But she'd already come so far. "Lauren, I'm coming in, okay? I just need some medicine, if you have it–any kind, as long as it's strong." She gripped the cool doorknob, turning and pushing it open.

"Lauren?"

Still no reply.

She glanced away from the bed, where she'd left Lauren to cry herself to sleep earlier. The pillowcases were stained with streaks of black and bits of too-dark foundation. A small breeze blew in more of that delicious coconut smell, and Olivia's eyes moved to the bathroom. "Lauren," she called, her voice a little worn with pain. "If you can hear me, I'm going to look in your bathroom for medicine. My uterus is trying to plummet out my butt, or rip through my stomach like that scene from Alien." She opened the medicine cabinet and found nothing. Lauren had barely unpacked. Her monogrammed toiletry bag was lying partially open, only the skincare neatly laid out on the counter.

For the first time in a while, Olivia let her hand drop from her stomach to use both to rummage through the bag. Pills rattled in various bottles. Anxiety meds, migraine meds, various vitamins, including some that looked like they hadn't yet hit the market yet, with a label that clearly said *All Natural by Lauren Alvarez.*

So, she was returning to her maiden name. Probably smart.

Finally!

Olivia's hands wrapped around extra-strength Motrin with Tylenol, and she poured two out into her hands, downing them dry before turning on the faucet and drinking a few sips directly from the tap.

She wanted to collapse into a ball and cry, in frustration, pain, and relief, no matter how small, but instead she put the bottles back into Lauren's toiletry bag, narrating all the while. "Alright, Lauren, I took two for my period. I promise I will totally pay you back, whatever you want in the future. You are literally saving my life right now, I swear. And I want to know all about this new business you're starting." She finished, with a final, satisfying zip, before placing the bag next to the skincare. She gave herself a once-over in the mirror before walking out. "Will it be like Gwyneth's new line? Or Kourtney's? Like vitamins to relax or…"

She glanced out the open window as the coconut breeze blew in again. Only this time, it twirled the curtains open a bit more, allowing her to see the beach from a new angle.

And to spot the half-bobbing, half-stuck, beached body, wearing the same outfit as Lauren had hours before.

"Lauren? *Lauren!*"

Olivia splashed into the ocean, tripping in the mix of dry and damp sand, sinking as the next wave crashed to the coast. She half-crawled, half-swam her way toward the bobbing body, the red hair practically black.

Another wave crashed, Olivia taking it in the face. She choked out a mouthful of water, gagging, thrashing to grab hold of Lauren's body before she floated away. Her hands tangled in the silk pajamas. Olivia pulled. She yanked. She trudged and sank, submerged underwater again, coughing, choking, spitting out the water, as she trudged and trudged and pulled and pulled until she collapsed onto the damp sand, tugging Lauren's body as far as she could.

"Help!" She called. But she couldn't hear anything other than the sound of the waves crashing. "Anyone," she cried, her tears mixing with the saltwater leaking from her hair. "Help!"

With her last bit of strength, still coughing out bits of water, Olivia turned Lauren over. Blue lips, pale skin, all so at odds with their idyllic getaway. "Lauren?" Olivia's voice cracked.

She had no idea what she was doing. She never did. But she once took a class on this. Well, she took a class on this for a job. For an acting job that she didn't even get, where the hiring director required her to "test it out on him."

Olivia brought her hands to Lauren's chest and braced, pumping down hard. Her body mostly sank, especially as the next wave crested, water swirling around them. But still Olivia pumped. She pumped and pumped and pumped, and then brought her mouth down over Lauren's, and began blowing as much air from her fragile lungs as she could.

She repeated the process.

And again.

And again.

And the only one coughing was her.

Lauren's lips were still just as blue, her skin just as pale, her hair just as dark, even as it mixed with the sand, still warm from the setting sun.

Olivia sat back, staring down at the dead body in front of her. Another one to add to her list.

And then the chill settled on her lips. As if death was creeping its way from Lauren, connected from where Olivia had tried–had failed–to resuscitate her. It traveled down her spine, chilling her deep to the bone. She shivered and stared, and soon, the panic surged.

"*Help!*" She scrambled to her feet, rushing over the small dune, leaving Lauren's body on the banks. "Somebody, please, help me!" She cried. Sand whipped up behind her as she sprinted back through Lauren's open doorframe. "Nick! Nick!" She shouted, sprinting into the hallway. "Nick! Ro! Anyone?! *Someone!*"

Ro appeared first, at the top of the staircase, book in hand. "Olivia?" She rushed down the steps, her footsteps thumping as loud as the beating of Olivia's heart. "What's wrong?"

"It's Lauren. She's...she's on the beach. And she's...well, she's all blue. And white. And she's...I mean, I think she's..."

Ro's eyes widened as she reached Olivia's eye level, the two women staring at one another as the unspoken word passed between them. *Dead.*

Laughter and teasing sounded outside the villa, growing louder as the steps magnified against the wooden paneling.

Olivia didn't turn to look for them, though she could see Ro's head shift in her periphery, and Nick brought his face out of his hands, wiping away at tears. Sanjeev and Sarah squealed as they retold some story the others weren't there for, and all of it sounded...so muted. She still had water in her ears. The ocean swirled inside her brain, and she felt like she was tumbling with the waves that had pushed her down earlier.

The sliding glass door opened, and the laughter–the melody–died. Darkness consumed.

Their garbled questions of what was wrong, and is everything okay, and standoffish panic couldn't penetrate through Olivia's ears. She kept staring ahead at the painting of Ivy. Cast to the side, almost forgotten amongst Ian and now...now it bore witness to another tragedy.

Olivia found her, someone said. She tried to revive her. Then we all did.

Where? They wanted to know.

On the beach. Down on the beach. She...she drowned.

But how? Did she do it herself? Did someone push her? Did they find the hooded figure?

So many questions. No answers.

Olivia stared ahead at Portrait Ivy, realizing, like in all the deaths she'd known before, there would never be answers. None good enough.

224 more days, 3 hours, and 19 minutes to go.

THE LIE

THIRTY-NINE

Ro leaned against the wall, her gaze tracing Dylan's as the other woman closed the door to Olivia's room. Everyone had gone through their own bags to check for medicine, looking for something to help Olivia sleep. Despite the numerous prescriptions for Xanax, Ambien, Valium, Ativan, and more she hadn't heard of, they settled on Benadryl. The last thing they needed was another accident. Another death.

Dylan whispered, "We should check on her in a few hours."

Ro nodded, her eyes finding the portrait of Olivia affixed to the door. Sultry and smirking. Up on the second floor, her own portrait had been taken from her headshot from her very first book. So many to choose from, she'd wondered why they picked that one. Of all the books–all the thumbnails–all the social media–why?

Why *that* book?

It was the only place the photo had ever been used. She took another headshot, a more professional one, when she got her second book deal. She even had an entire photoshoot to show she was serious about her craft.

So why that book? Now she wondered where the inspiration for Olivia's came from.

Dylan hadn't moved either, even as the hushed voices from the main room picked up, people interjecting, now speaking over one another.

"I'm so tired," Dylan said.

Ro nodded her agreement. She wasn't really here. She was still on the beach. In Ian's room. On the plane. As if she was floating in the ether, watching herself discover the bodies. Again. And again. And again.

If she had her notebook now, she'd write that down. It was a good line. Better than most. Her line editor and copy editor might even keep it as is.

"I should interrupt them," Dylan said, and Ro floated back down, returned to the present, the argument coming into greater focus, the voices harsh.

"Come on." Ro kicked off the wall and led the way.

Nick's protests grew louder. "No, no, no," he shook his head, his voice warbling as he rose from his chair and started pacing. "No, no, this isn't on me. This is on her. This is one final 'fuck you' to me. I'm ruined. The business, all of it. *Gone*," he snapped.

"She's *dead*, Nick," Ro hissed.

Leave it to Nick to be selfish enough to make Lauren's death all about *him*.

He glared at her, as if annoyed that she dared join the conversation now. "And now I have nothing!"

Dylan stepped forward, "Oh, so you admit you were mooching off her the whole time? You mean the very thing she accused you of–"

"–our marriage is none of your concern–"

"Hey, hey," Cody said, stepping in front of Dylan, putting himself between her and Nick. Ro fell off to the side, anger vibrating underneath her skin. She never could stand Nick. Never could stand Lauren, for that matter.

Not that it was Lauren's fault, but their dynamic reminded her all too much of her own parents. Seeing their relationship unfold, the snide comments, the panicked confusion, the non-apologies, the blame game, was all too triggering.

She'd grown up with a narcissist, so she'd been able to spot Nick as one from the very first time they met.

It's why she also clung to books. Why she secluded herself in her room for hours upon hours, reading and escaping, disappearing into worlds of fantasy, freeing herself from her mother's constant chiding and her dad's helpless silence. Why she turned to the internet in the first place, searching for connection. Under the guise of sharing her love of books, but really it had been a yearning. A deep sense of missing out, of longing for the friendships from the pages.

It's why, at her first ever brand trip, she'd clung to Ivy so quickly–the only other person who seemed to see past that carefully curated, charming veneer. And Cody was quick enough to join, even if his own dislike stemmed from jealousy. He'd been a much smaller creator then. Smaller, at least, than Nick and Lauren. Overshadowed in ways, even though he'd been doing it for just as long. The overshadowed feeling that bred a sense of resentment, of that deep, ugly envy.

Ro slumped into her chair, trying to drown the memories of her childhood with a glass of wine. Something she couldn't do then.

It barely helped now.

She poured another.

"Start from the beginning," Michelle said to Nick.

He slumped into the chair at the head of the table, where Lauren had sat only a few hours before. All eyes were on him as he took in a deep, shaky breath.

"Y'all left at about five, right? Then I went to the kitchen to clean up. Lauren wasn't–" he cleared his throat. "Lauren wasn't there, so I figured this was the best time to get it sparkling again and ready for tomorrow. I figured we were all understanding that midnight snacks and breakfast would be leftovers or whatever Dylan made when y'all returned."

He took in another shaky breath, his rib cage expanding, straining against the already too tight V-neck he always insisted on wearing. "I don't know how long cleaning took me, but I needed to let off some more steam, so I decided to walk around the house. I checked the huge garage, no cars, but no people either. I checked the library, found Ro. I checked the gym, found equipment. I checked the storage areas where we'd set our extra decorations from the first flight over. Then I started…well," he shrugged, "I started going into some of the other rooms."

"You mean you snooped?" Sarah snipped.

"No! I left everything as it was. I didn't pick anything up. I just…wanted to make sure the person in the hoodie wasn't still here, you know?"

The person in the hoodie.

Ro brought her legs up to her chest and carefully sipped at her second drink, folding in on herself.

Dylan turned to her."And where were you during this?"

"Reading," Ro said.

Dylan kept staring. The others did, too. As if they expected more. A clipped fact or a self-assured theory. She would have shared if her mind weren't too busy racing.

As if her own guilt tricked her into saying more, she added, "Nick came by the library at, I think, six, maybe? It wasn't long after that…I mean, maybe an hour or so, that I heard Olivia calling for help. So, I ran out and raced down the stairs, and that's when…"

The attention turned away from her. Back to Nick. Perhaps the only time he didn't seem to revel in it.

"And were you checking all the rooms?" Dylan asked.

"And did you go to Lauren's?" Sanjeev added.

Nick's attention ping-ponged around the group, finally settling on Sanjeev. "What are you implying?"

"Nothing," Sanjeev shrugged with forced nonchalance.

As if any of them believed his act. Half of the group still glared daggers at Nick. Their questions were accusations in disguise. Their stares demanding.

"I just wondered if you'd seen her," Sanjeev continued. "Before she…well, how long she might have been in the ocean."

"No," Nick shook his head. "No, I knew it was best if I stayed away from Lauren." His breathing had slowly returned to normal, and he looked back at Dylan. "I didn't go through her room or yours. And I thought about checking Ian's, but the smell was…"

"Yeah, our wrap job wasn't great," Michelle admitted. "Sorry to y'all on that side."

"I'll stuff some more towels next to the floorboard, underneath the door," Dylan said. Then she huffed out, almost a wheeze. "I can't believe what I'm fucking saying." She slid into one of the chairs and rested her head against the table.

Sanjeev poured himself some more wine, and five hands, holding empty goblets, shot out at the same time. He finished off the bottle after two, and Nick silently rose from the table, and returned a minute later with a bottle in each hand. He poured to what would have been excess on the first night. Now it seemed they all needed something–anything–to get by.

"Does anyone care if I–"

"No one cares," Sarah answered the question before Sanjeev could finish asking it. "Hell, we all need it."

He pulled a pack of cigarettes out of his pocket and offered one up. Sarah took it and passed the cart along to Michelle, who passed it along without taking one.

Dylan asked, "You finally managed to quit?"

"At least for now."

Ro bit her lip, watching as the lighter was passed around next. "Did the hikers find anything?" She could hear the hope that still tinged her voice.

"We found a good boulder to lay on in our bikinis," Michelle said. "There was a drop-off where you could see the ocean, for miles and miles, until it met the sky. We took some pictures there too."

"She's saying we didn't find shit," Sarah interpreted with a harsh laugh before taking a drag of her cigarette. "Pretty, pretty scenery, and we still had at least five hours more to go to get to that damn house." She exhaled out. "In any other case, I could see why people come out here…complete privacy."

"I heard J. Lo has a place on the next island over." Sanjeev said. "And Diddy."

The group nodded appreciatively, as if they were on the same level simply by proximity.

Cody stood from his chair, having taken neither the offer of wine nor the cigarettes, finally finishing their pass around the table. He stood in the frame of the open glass door, reaching his hands up and leaning against it.

"I hate to be a downer," he began, and Ro's stomach tightened. "But I think it's clear that the hooded figure from before has something to do with this."

"Lauren was sick," Nick broke in, shaking his head. "I'm not saying I think she did it on purpose, but…"

Michelle mumbled under her breath.

"*Huh?*" Nick asked, in the way people did when they weren't actually confused.

Michelle crossed her arms over her chest. "Funny that her soon-to-be ex-husband keeps trying to imply it was suicide. Who *drowns* themselves?"

Ever the peacekeeper, Dylan chimed in. "Maybe Cody is right? I mean, we do have video evidence of someone here. Should we barricade the doors or something?"

"What are y'all saying?" Sarah began, head whipping back and forth between Dylan and Cody. "You think that person isn't a reporter? You think maybe they killed Ian, too?"

More heads shuffled. Knuckles cracked. People downed their wine.

Sarah spelled it out more clearly. "Are y'all suggesting there's a murderer running around?"

"Alright, relax, relax," Cody said, stepping out of the doorframe and returning to the group. He stood behind Sarah, hands kneading at her neck. "We don't need to panic. We don't need any more panic attacks, okay? If we're all here together, nothing bad can happen, right? I'm just suggesting that we do our own search. All together."

"How are we supposed to sleep tonight?"

Sanjeev shook his head. "I won't be able to."

"Me neither," Michelle agreed. "At least..." she yawned, stretching the words out, "not until we've done the check. I think that's a good idea. Co-signed!"

"And if we don't find anything?" Nick asked.

The group shifted its attention to him.

"Look, I'm happy to pretend it's someone else. That's a lot better–a lot more convenient for me. I don't wanna be the dude whose ex-wife was so sad he was divorcing her that she killed herself, okay?"

Even Ro had to roll her eyes. The fear, the anticipation, that had been bubbling up, broke for a single moment. So was the power of Nick's narcissistic gift.

"I hope I'm wrong," Cody started. "I–"

She had to. She had to *now*. "I have something to confess," Ro said, standing. She wanted to put her cigarette out. Taking one last drag, she deposited it in an old coffee mug. At this point, Excelsior couldn't possibly care. What was one mug compared to three dead bodies?

She took a deep breath, regretting that she didn't have another cigarette ready to go. A silence stretched as Ro waited for the go-ahead. Sarah gave it to her. "Spit it out!"

"I..." she breathed in once, closed her eyes, then let it go. Just as Sarah's shrill tone accused her of being melodramatic when there were clearly more important things happening, she confessed, "I was the person in the hoodie."

She opened her eyes and found a camera. One of only a couple remained. Michelle's, and the one that used to belong to Nick and Lauren. Now just Nick. Everyone else seemed to have given up on vlogging the brand trip from hell.

Staring directly into the camera, Ro breathed in deep. "I'm sorry I didn't say anything sooner. I just–"

"You just *what*?" Sarah spat. She shoved Cody off her and kicked at her chair as she stood, all while staring directly at Ro. "You thought it would be funny to send us on a wild fucking goose chase? You thought it would be funny to scare everyone half to death? What if that's what happened to poor Lauren! What if she went out looking for this fucking nonexistent madman and tripped and hit her head or something?"

Ro shook her head, rushing to explain, "It was just for research...for my book–"

"Oh, Lord, help me," Sarah said, storming off. Twenty seconds later, they all heard the slam as her door shut.

Dylan looked up at Ro. "Why confess now? Why not just... why tell us?"

"What if..." Ro said, forcing herself to gulp, the nerves building as she thought of all the stories she'd read, all the movies she'd watched, her greatest, worst fear as a kid materializing not as the monster under the bed, but the killer in the house.

Back then she thought it would be her mother. But she'd escaped her. She couldn't hurt her now. But maybe someone else could... "What if Cody's right? What if someone else really is here too?" She asked. "What if...what if these actually weren't accidents?"

"There's no one fucking running around but you!" Nick shouted. "So, what the *fuck* do we have to be scared of?"

Even Cody seemed deflated. The rest looked on in horror, trying to piece together what all of this–what any of this–meant. Or what it didn't mean.

"I'm going to bed, too," Sanjeev said, getting another eyeful of Ro.

Michelle followed his lead, as did Cody, then Dylan, leaving only Ro and Nick to sit in silence.

The lull the ocean had over Ro before morphed now, inextricably tied to Lauren's body. Now the dark of night fit, a sound without sight, the ocean invisible and unimaginable if not for the waves crashing in the distance.

For the first time ever, Ro wondered what Nick thought. As the two of them stared out the door, at the crisscrossing fairy lights that felt so at odds with their shared discomfort.

Eventually, he asked the only question she hadn't answered. "Why go into Ian's room? Just...why?"

She shook her head, still staring at that place in the distance where their villa succumbed to blackness. "I wanted to see his body up close. And when Cody saw me, I realized how crazy it sounded, how crazy I'd look, and I...I lied." There was no reason to lie anymore. Three people were dead. And maybe Sarah was right. Maybe, somehow, the third was her fault. "And I wanted to see how people would react in this situation. So, I just...said nothing."

Ro finally turned to Nick, only to see him shaking his head. "You really are a psycho."

"Antisocial," she corrected. She cringed, hating herself all the while. Her deep-seated need to be better than the influencers she surrounded herself with was indeed pathological. "Psychopath isn't really a recognized health diagnosis…" By the end, she was talking only to the wind.

FORTY

Olivia lay in her bed, staring at the ceiling, trying to ignore the ticking of the clock, the forward march of time. When she closed her eyes, she saw Lauren's face, so she forced them to stay open.

Tick.

Tick.

Tick.

FORTY-ONE

Nick cried. Real tears. Tears for himself. Tears for his future. And one, single tear, for the Lauren he once knew, for the life he once had, back before fame tainted every moment.

FORTY-TWO

Sarah stopped by Sanjeev's room.

"You know," she began, "even if there is no murderer. Three deaths? With ten total people? Sanji, that's a tragedy."

He waited for the point to be made.

She threw herself onto his bed and gripped his arm. "We're *survivors*," she declared.

He could tell this was just the start. The first time she would say it, the words warbling in his ears. There would be more. On the first video when they got back. On the subsequent ones, breaking down each day. On talk shows. On red carpets. On anniversaries of the trip.

When people asked how they survived, he could imagine her canned response, too. She'd say how blessed they were. He didn't believe her. He doubted she even did.

FORTY-THREE

Dylan and Cody and Michelle ate a late-night snack together in silence, nibbling on their food, not really tasting anything. A boon since the "healthy food" taste itself was nothing worth remembering.

FORTY-FOUR

Ivy was dead.

FORTY-FIVE

Ian was dead.

FORTY-SIX

Lauren was dead.

FORTY-SEVEN

Ro sat in her room, a pen in her left hand, an empty notebook in front of her. She tried to convince herself that she could write about this, too. About being an outcast in a house like this. About the others turning against her. The protagonist in this case would have to be unlikeable. All her main characters usually were. She'd stolen so much from real life, why change the truth now?

FORTY-EIGHT

The tripod sat on three-pronged legs, camera angled down slightly, Michelle framed perfectly in the middle, resting her back against the bed. It was how she often filmed at home, sitting on the floor, feet tucked underneath her. It gave the air of relatability, whether she was in a hotel in Monte Carlo for the Monaco Grand Prix or in a villa on an island where a third influencer had just died.

Night offered no natural light to film, so she'd turned on the clawfoot flamingo lamp, the chandelier, and set her own ring light between purple and blue to offset the yellow glow.

As the recording ticked up ten seconds, she changed her pose, long since learning it was better to take a thumbnail before starting to speak. She dropped the two hearts she formed with her fingers and began, "Okay, right, so it's only day two and Lauren just died. We found her body on the beach. Scratch that, Olivia found her body on the beach, and the poor woman is now comatose. I have to say, I know it's crazy, but I don't think Nick did it."

She held her hands up. "I don't, I don't, okay? I know he's the obvious suspect and all, but the man seemed genuinely distraught. More for himself, right? I acknowledge that, but–"

Something *thunked* against the ceiling, as if someone had dropped something heavy from the floor above. Gentle padding of feet and a slight scrape, that was all Michelle could hear before the sound dissipated completely. The villa succumbed to eerie silence once more.

"I think that's Ro's room. Oh my god." Wide-eyed, she whipped her head down, a gleeful grin stretching on her face, reflected in her camera's viewfinder. As if she were about to tell a very good friend a very juicy secret. In a way, the camera was maybe her best friend of all. "You'll never guess what she did today. Okay, right, we've all been freaking out about the figure in the hoodie, remember? I would've sworn it was a reporter. Like I was so excited, but so nervous. It just kept being this awful thing, lingering in the back of my mind this whole time. What would we do, what would we say, if we saw them? But they never came up again. We only ever saw them on Cody's stupid recording."

She paused for effect.

"Well. Guess who confessed to wearing the hoodie and checking Ian's body?" Michelle leaned forward, gagging. "Look, once was enough for me. The second time–when we went to wrap it up–was god-awful. Smelled like hot shit. *Very* derogatory. Which, everyone else was saying he was a shitty person when alive, to be fair. Didn't take long for them to take his name in vain. Ivy's either, for that matter. I'm sure that by tomorrow people will be cursing Lauren, too."

Her brain skittered and stopped, thoughts flying, emotions bubbling. Was it the island or the people that had this effect on her? All her plans, so many plans, and not enough yet to show for them.

"Where was I? Anyways, now everyone is big mad at Ro. Which, she deserves. I mean, why lie? As if any of us would make fun of her for wanting to check out the body. I mean, not any more than we already do. But that's par for the course with this group, you know? Gossip and backstabbing are the minimum expected. What was it–The Maldives–when that rumor about Sarah and Sanjeev..."

She reached for her phone, remembering before she flipped it over that all it would tell her was the time.

She was addicted. It was painfully and obviously true. The number of times she tapped it on, swiped, then groaned with agitated disgust. This trip was the first time she ever felt how truly pathetic it was.

She wiggled her phone in her hand, attention back to the camera. "You think I'd be used to this by now. Dumb." She tossed the phone onto the bed behind her. As she turned, watching it bounce, tumbling over itself until it rested at her pillow, she caught sight of the outside.

It was hard to see much. Easier, of course, to see inside, with all her lights lit up.

There was no reason to be scared anymore, but still a chill ran through her. She constantly put herself on display, constantly out there for consumption, for people to pick and pick and pick, and yet the idea of someone watching her now made her blood run cold.

Michelle took a deep breath, trying to remember what she'd told the camera. No one else was here.

"The moon is really bright out tonight." She felt its pull, its reflection mesmerizing. It was too high in the sky for her to see from her room, but its glow glinted across the pool and choppy ocean waves. The only other light emanated from the villa itself and distant houses and hotels that dotted the next island over. Not too far by boat, much too far to swim.

And then, because she thought it would be funny, thought it would be dramatic, and maybe, a part of her thought it could be true, she said, "What if this is the last full moon I ever see?" She turned to the camera, and gave her future audience a shrug, before bringing her hand over the lens, smothering the view, and turned off the recording.

THE REJECT

FORTY-NINE

Ro couldn't fall asleep last night. She tossed and turned and threw the notebooks she brought with her off the bed, and then pillows and then the blankets and comforters, until she was left with only sheets. She stared at the ceiling as the dark of night gave way to a patchy blue dawn.

Only then did she rise and open the drapes, staring out at the never-ending ocean.

Some people found the saltwater freeing. Their escape from city life, an oasis.

Ro had been one of them. Every time she saw the ocean, her stress ebbed and flowed away. It had been a reminder–a positive one–of how small she was in the universe.

Until this trip. Until now.

For the first time, the ocean reflected her feelings of isolation. How deep, deep, deeply she felt them. Here they were, on this tiny island, all alone. Or not alone enough.

She gulped down the rising, unexplainable panic. She'd been the one in the hoodie. There was no other piece of evidence that anyone else was here.

And yet, if she were writing this story, that's exactly what she'd do. Make someone a scapegoat. The perfect red herring.

She turned away before she could drown in her thoughts any longer. Picking up her tossed phone, her vegan leather-bound notebooks, and sponsored Montblanc pens, she walked out of her room and down the large, grand staircase. Wearing her thinnest silk pajamas, the breeze off the ocean sent chills down her arms. But she kept her eyes trained on the section of the beach that faced the sunrise, not daring to turn and look where she knew Lauren's body still lay.

The gentle rolling waves didn't wash away her stress, but they did offer company. As she took videos and photos showing off her pens, her notebook, and herself. Pretending to write, to be the author she promised her publisher she would be on this trip.

When the sun rose enough to warm her skin, Ro returned to the villa, more alone than she'd been on the beach. Side-eyes and sneers accompanied the few others awake, returning from their own photography sessions. All gave her a wide berth, as if her lies might be catching.

The worst part of her pathological need to be better than them was she had to be amongst them to prove how much better she was indeed.

She left her things on the large breakfast table and headed toward the squeal of the teakettle.

"Need help? Want a latte?" Nick offered.

Sarah cooed her usual, "Yes, please, sweetheart." She leaned her weight against the kitchen island, staring at Ro with eyes that pierced like knives.

Any other day, Ro would've gone to anyone–literally anyone–else. But today she said, "Me too, please." Then she added, "That is, if you're offering," as she rested on the island next to Sarah.

"I'm not," Nick said, and Sarah didn't bother hiding her squawk of laughter. She needed no words to communicate exactly how she felt about Ro. As soon as Nick handed over her steaming mug, Sarah gave her a single up-and-down and left.

The kitchen fell into awkward silence, interrupted only by the thumping of the espresso machine. A small, wide-angle camera recorded Ro in all her shame.

She cleared her throat as she turned around, hoping it wouldn't capture the flush as it rose from her neck to her cheeks. She needed no mirror to confirm the splotchiness of her face. In a poor recovery, she opened random cabinets, looking for the pantry or a stash of breakfast snacks.

Nick didn't help. He left as soon as his drink was finished.

It took her several more minutes to find the pantry, where she grabbed a thin, gluten-free bagel and then looked helplessly into the hyper-organized refrigerator for any form of cream cheese.

She settled for butter. There wasn't a toaster, and she hadn't worked an oven in years. Part of her brand was working from local cafes, the aesthetics ever-changing, perfect for pictures.

She couldn't find a butter knife, so she settled for merely smashing her bagel into the container of whipped honey butter and then stuffing it into her mouth.

Served them right. They could suffer through her crumbs.

After the disappointing breakfast, Ro rallied herself just enough to stalk out of the kitchen and head toward the gentle chatter. It lowered and lowered in volume the closer she approached, until there was only the sound of her shuffling feet. Eyes burned into her already red cheeks.

As she excused herself around the group, ready to grab her things and stake out a different spot on the couch, she froze, hand extended, to her notebook open to one of the back pages. Not how she left it.

Her pen, too, was haphazardly tossed to the side, and her phone now face-up instead of face-down.

"Who touched my stuff?"

In the silence, the answer became immediately obvious.

It was a group effort.

Sanjeev snatched her notebook before she could, flipping through the pages as he sipped on his steeping tea.

Nick unwound her pen, dismantling it.

Sarah grabbed her phone, groaning as she smashed on the screen, failing to guess the passcode.

"Give it back!" Ro marched through, shouldering Nick, the pieces of her thousand-dollar pen clattering to the ground.

"It's fine," Sarah said, nudging Sanjeev, who tossed her notebook onto the opposite side of the table.

"There's nothing there anyway."

Her pointed accusation was said directly into the only camera still recording–Michelle's.

"What do you mean?" Michelle asked, her voice dramatic, as if she already knew the answer to the question. With a quick spin of her wrist, the camera lens zoomed in.

Ro sprinted, reaching the end of the table and grabbing the notebook before Michelle could rifle through and show off the mostly empty pages.

"Nothing, huh? So, you've just been pretending?" Michelle whipped the camera up and Ro held her hand out in front of her face.

"Turns out she's good at that," Sanjeev chimed in.

"That was another notebook," Ro mumbled, even though, technically, she didn't have much in the other one either.

"Sure, sure," Michelle said, only then setting her camera down next to her bowl of cereal. Unlike the others who stared at her as if she'd grown a second head, Michelle seemed content to capture the drama. An audience, rather than the star. No doubt she'd take all the snippets and cast her own narrative, anyway. That'd always been Michelle Monroe's MO.

The others settled, the silence back, this time intermixed with the scraping of bowls and forks stabbing into plates.

Ro flipped through her wrinkled pages, where greasy hands had gripped. This notebook had meant to be her writing journal. The one where she wrote about the progress she'd made in her story.

Only she'd made relatively little progress, so the updates were pathetic and shallow. Named a character. Found a motivation. Changed a name. Changed a motivation. Half of these weren't even real notes, but ones she'd made to look important to the camera.

Nick set down his own plate, crumbs and remnants stuck to the sides. "You better believe I'm not doing your dishes," he said.

Ro looked up to see Sanjeev and Sarah pushing their plates across the table.

"Where's Dylan?" Nick asked.

"She came out of her room in workout gear and a backpack two hours ago," Michelle said. "She beat me to the sunrise."

"Cody's gone, too. And Olivia's still…in her room."

No one asked if she was functioning. No one expected her to be.

"Maybe they're up in the gym?" Michelle suggested, though there were no grunts or grinding of metal or high-fives emanating from the floor above.

"That, or they're dead," Nick said, callous and cool.

Sanjeev rushed away from the table without another word, everyone's eyes following him up the stairs and across the hall. He returned, moments later, adding, "There was a note on his bed. They're trying to get cell reception again."

"Getting us worked up over nothing," Sarah whispered, but as she side-eyed Nick, she licked her lips into a smile. "Dangerous game you're playing."

Ro grabbed at her pen, jotting in shorthand. A memory of Sarah's bet she overheard. She wondered if Sarah had her own goal of sleeping with Nick or Cody first.

Character unchanged, despite her best efforts at pretending. Wasn't that the case for all of them?

"Whatever," Michelle said, pushing back from the table. "Can anyone take some more pictures of me? I have ten more outfits and if the restock boat is heading over soon, I want to get them all now before we leave."

"I can," Sanjeev volunteered.

"I need more pictures, too. And some video," Ro tried, to no avail. The two musketeers and Michelle left without her.

Only Nick remained behind.

"Don't take this the wrong way," he began, and Ro prepared herself for the onslaught. The myriads of things she could have done differently. She should have been honest at the start. Or she should have just kept it a secret.

Instead, he said, "You'd be prettier as a blonde, I think. Have you thought about dyeing your hair?"

Without another word, Ro gathered her items and strode out of the dining room. She grabbed a beach chair from outside the patio, and dragged it all the way down the beach, a different angle than she'd been before.

She flipped her notebook to the middle, finding a page where she had, in fact, written down a few notes. Nonsensical ones, perhaps to anyone but her.

Midpoint twist? She struck through it, adding a *+1* for the addition of Lauren's body. On a new line, she wrote, *Bad Guys Close In??*

If this brand trip had been a story–and it still could be now–she figured the likelihood was Dylan and Cody wouldn't make it back. Either they'd abandon them, find a rescuer, break the story first, and come back as heroes days later, or they'd die.

There needed to be one final, awful twist. Maybe the resource boats wouldn't make it. Maybe they'd run out of gluten-free food. Maybe she'd lose all her footage, the entire trip for naught.

Sanjeev, Sarah, and Michelle had returned with props, the threesome giving her a wide berth as they trudged across the stretch of sand. Ro kept her eyes glued to them as they posed and preened. Sarah took sexy shots of herself in lewd positions, her large cross pendant dangling in front of her skimpy beach cover-up. Sanjeev requested close-ups, angling his face so his highlighter popped. Michelle brought multiple outfit changes, not bothering or caring that anyone–including Nick, who Ro imagined was leering from some awful perch–could see her.

Then again, Ro almost wished she could be over there. That she could be so free. That she wasn't so obsessed with the accolades and awards and "being respected," whatever bullshit that meant.

Maybe she could've helped Ivy with Whisper. Maybe she could've taken acting classes. Maybe she could've tried painting or cooking or anything else.

Maybe she could've written her own books. Not hired someone to help her fix them up. Not stalked AuthorTube and BookTok videos, stealing the best ideas. Not plugged in countless prompts to whatever AI was popular that month. Maybe then she could've stood behind all her reviews, from the starred Kirkus praise to the cutting Goodreads criticism.

Instead, she took all the unearned credit and felt fleeting joy. What a sham.

Then again…

Maybe this was her second chance. The ocean glittered and gleamed like a siren inviting her to this shiny, new idea. In all good stories, the hero must change and grow. So maybe this was her time. She sells her true story of surviving the worst brand trip in history, a tell-all, and then she's free to write her own fiction. She could write the weird alien porn for all it fucking mattered.

Who would care what she writes then? She'll have changed. Or, at least, the headlines will certainly think so. And they'll have to include her tragedy, her trauma, in their reviews. Who could criticize her for that? Who could criticize her at all?

FIFTY

Sarah used her arms to push her boobs together. Just a hint of cleavage. A God-fearing amount of cleavage. Something to get her clicks, so long as it was in service of a greater good.

"Now pout a little," Sanjeev said.

She did as instructed, pursing her lips, making sure to put the lip filler to good use. Sarah had just lifted her sunglasses up, to give more variety, when she spotted them.

What she'd first written off as specks in the distance, animals or plants moving in the breeze, was now, unmistakably, two people.

"You're losing it, Sarah."

"Shut up."

"Excuse me?"

She lifted her arm, boobs falling with gravity, her necklace disappearing down her shirt, and pointed at Dylan and Cody on the cliffside.

Sanjeev and Michelle both walked over and looked, realizing at the same time.

"Well, at least they didn't die."

"Yeah, but they didn't bring a rescue team back, either."

"Ugh," the three groaned.

"It's not all bad," Sarah said, dropping her voice to a whisper, ever aware of the author not far from their photoshoot. "Maybe one of them can distract Ro."

"Cody?" Sanjeev suggested.

"Nah," she shook her head. "Dylan. She's too much of a pacifist to argue against it."

"She stood up to Nick alright."

"Yeah, eight years too late."

Michelle shrugged. Sanjeev did the same. "Alright, they're coming over."

The three stood back, waving their hands, trying to be a welcoming sight.

As expected, Ro stood, too. Studying, as ever. "Did you find anything?" she called first.

Sarah had never taken Ro for the needy type. In fact, she'd thought Ro had enjoyed being the loner. The bookworm, looking down on the plebeians from a higher perch. It's why Sarah had respected her. At least *that* was a Ro she understood.

This one…this one was just *sad.*

Cody's eyes darted away from Ro and toward the group.

Sarah shook her head.

He didn't answer.

Dylan looked like she might, until Michelle asked, "Any chance we can convince you to make some lunch? My sandwiches are shit."

"I've barely eaten since last night," Sanjeev agreed.

Sarah opened her mouth and smiled wide, using her preacher voice–the one that projected, the one that signified authority. "Plus, you need some of your own content. I'm sure Ro wouldn't mind being a dear and helping out." She left off that it was the least Ro could do. She needed this plan to work.

As expected, Dylan didn't argue. Her RBF–though it was resting *bored* face in her case–had dropped in the past few days to a near constant-frown. She shuffled over without another word, a meager, distant hello exchanged with Ro as they went inside, lone beach chair and umbrella long forgotten.

The group waited until they could no longer see the two women past their own reflections before Sarah turned and hissed to Cody, "We're going to raid Ro's room."

He nodded, clearly needing no further convincing. He pushed his fist into his palm, a couple of knuckles cracking, his muscles flexing. "Now?"

"Once she's in the kitchen."

"What are you hoping to find?"

Sarah led the way, Cody to her right, Sanjeev and Michelle falling in step behind.

"Anything," she said. "Proof she's behind all this. I'm not buying her hoodie story. As if any of us would care if she wanted to inspect Ian's body? Hell, she could've taken pictures of him like he did Ivy. That'd go for a lot of money."

"We still could."

"Sanjeev!" Michelle scolded, but her voice was teasing.

"You know someone's going to get them all, eventually. Us or the press. When the cops get here–"

Michelle slid the glass door closed behind them. "Cops?"

"Oh, c'mon," Sarah said, glancing right, toward the kitchen. She lowered her voice. "You think there's any way this doesn't get investigated? I mean, three deaths are crazy. One, an overdose in the air. Second, a fall–or a trip–off a balcony. And poor Lauren? Nuh-uh. There will be cops crawling all over this place. We'll be questioned."

"All the more reason we'll be survivors," Sanjeev said.

"That's what I'm saying!"

He'd seemed so disillusioned by her last night, but this morning, he was right back to himself. And now he was clearly seeing what she already had. This was *good* for them.

She knew how tough the industry could be. Pivots were needed, unless you became cemented in the cultural zeitgeist…and there was nothing better for that than death. To be so close, but still alive yourself to capitalize on it?

She tried not to grin as she whipped around. "Shh." She led their way up the stairs. They tiptoed around, step by step, passing the library, passing Cody's room–his painting a smoldering recreation burgeoning on caricature–and slowly making their way to Ro's door.

Sarah reached the doorknob first, the metal cool in her hands as she slowly twisted it open. Her jaw dropped as more of the room came into view, an explosion of clothes and toiletries, towels and blankets tossed onto the floor.

"Jesus," Michelle said from behind her.

"Whoa," Cody agreed.

Ro first gained notoriety through her YouTube videos, then TikToks, all with herself in center frame, sleek, stuffed bookshelves behind her. But there had always been an orderly sort of chaos. In the times where screaming had run triumphant, she'd been cool and calm and collected. People turned to her for cozy reprieve, for tea kettles poured just so, and pictures of fuzzy socks adorned on a white bed spread.

This…this was *chaos.*

And not the good, fun kind.

Not the *Michelle* kind.

This was…a mess.

"We'll each take a corner," Sarah instructed, pointing Sanjeev toward the towels, Cody toward the desk, and Michelle toward the nightstand. She took the bed for herself, looking under pillows, under the mattress, ripping the sheets off and checking underneath.

The others started out timid, but as she yanked, stripping the last of the mattress pad off, the others created ruckus, too.

"Nothing," she said.

"Hey, check this out." Michelle tossed her a different leather notebook.

The pages fluttered, Sarah catching and dropping it. She didn't care. She tore it open to the first page. Nothing. She flipped quickly, still nothing. The back was blank, too.

Sanjeev had tossed the towels all around, the adjoining bathroom and closet pilfered through. "Lots of pills," he said. "Nothing too exciting, though."

Sarah could just imagine if Ivy were still alive, what each of them would have submitted to her. How she would've phrased it. "This famous short-form star gets her best ideas from drug-induced psychosis." Or, "This bestselling author, infamously accused of stealing ideas, is a literal mess behind the scenes."

Oh, precious Ivy. She flew too close to the sun. Idolatry wasn't a game, and she was a far too inexperienced player. Whisper needed a face. Anonymity didn't make an icon. Ivy should've seen that sooner. The shock, the attention, the stardom she could've gained if she'd admitted to being behind it all along...

It was a pity she couldn't have revealed more before she died, but at least no more of Sarah's secrets would be shared.

"Take a look at this," Cody said, slamming one of the desk drawers shut. The group reconvened in the center as he flipped the notebook over. On the front of the leather-bound, a tiny drawing of a star. "I remember her writing in this one," he said, unwinding the strap, freeing the binds. There, on the first page. Their names. Descriptions of what they were wearing on that very first plane ride.

"'Hair so high she's trying to get to heaven,'" Sarah harrumphed. "Ivy already used that on Whisper. Birds of a feather." She looked up to see Sanjeev's lips curled as he tried not to laugh. "Oh, nuh-uh. 'Sanjeev thinks piling on the makeup will act like the filters he uses in real life. Too bad his skin is as ugly as his miserable personality.'"

She watched as his smile dropped.

"Go to the next page," he insisted. When she took too long, Sanjeev stepped forward, reaching out and snatching the notebook, doing it himself. He flipped it over, the spine breaking. "What the fuck...?"

Cody looked over his shoulder, eyes squinting. Sarah and Michelle waited for the two to parse through it. "This is...this is gibberish."

Sarah turned back to her search, but still asked, "More mean comments?"

"No. No, it's just, 'I'm pretending to be writing. This is me writing. I hope this shot looks cool. Should I change it? Okay, I think I'm done.'"

"That's...so sad," Sanjeev said.

"Pathetic," Sarah agreed. "Like, I know we all pretend. You really think I'm taking more than a single sip of that Shit Tea every time I forget a line the sponsor wrote? No way." She gagged, remembering the string of awful tummy teas and weight loss shakes. "But I'm not pretending to write shit down when that's my entire fucking *job*. That'd be like me pantomiming on stage and pretending I've given a sermon."

"Maybe you *should* try that," Michelle said.

Sarah threw a pillow at her, successfully walloping her in the face. Michelle threw it back and missed.

Sarah sneered in her direction.

"You've got to be shitting me," Sanjeev's voice came from the small bedside table.

"I already looked over there," Sarah said. "Go check the–"

He pulled open the self-help novel Ro seemed to be studying voraciously–pages earmarked, tabs sticking out in all colors, maybe another concept for her to steal–and turned the book over, letting the pages fan out freely.

Not even a second later, a crimson letter fell from the book, fluttering its way, twirling and spiraling, until it finally landed on the ground.

Michelle gasped. "Her invitation! She refused to tell us what was on it."

Cody strode over and dropped to the ground, reaching under the bed frame and jumping to a stand, invitation in hand. He flipped it over, opened his mouth, and…

"What?" Sarah spat.

"It's a quote. From a book, I think. I don't know why I remember it…"

Sarah crossed the room and pressed up against his shoulder, trying to get a good look.

The first death was her reputation. Enigmas never survived.

"Why would she hide this?"

"Maybe it's blackmail," Sarah said.

Three heads turned toward her.

"That's from the book Ivy accused her of stealing. Well, *one* of them," she shrugged. "I think that's the line everyone went crazy over. It's the role that Olivia wants. *What?*" She rolled her eyes at the surprise on their faces. "I read!"

"Yeah, gossip mags," Sanjeev said.

"*Yeeeeeah*," she stretched out the word, glaring at him. "And the books that everyone raves about. You know…before I found God. This one isn't holy enough." She couldn't keep the smirk off her face.

"Well, we can't ask Olivia," Cody said. "She's…not well."

"You mean she's gone crazy."

"Haven't we all?"

Michelle nodded, and Sanjeev concurred.

Cody looked to Sarah.

She plucked the invitation from his hands, repeating, "'The first death was her reputation. Enigmas never survived.'"

FIFTY-ONE

The sigh came from the other side of the room, and Sanjeev called, "What? What did you find?"

There was no response.

He'd been squatting, pilfering through Ro's toiletries, looking for a hidden compartment. It seemed like the kind of thing Rowena Dashwood would have. She'd done a whole tour for Architectural Digest showing off the bookshelf that transformed into a door if you pulled the right lever, leading you into her wine cellar. He didn't know what he wanted to find, just that he wanted to be the one to find it. To prove that he could. To everyone. But mostly, if he was honest, to Sarah.

"What have you…what are you doing?" a familiar voice asked the group.

Sanjeev's stomach dropped, and he exited the bathroom still holding the second toiletry bag, an embossed, monogrammed bag from a now-defunct luxury travel company that he'd refused to collaborate with.

"We're inspecting," Sarah snapped first. She plucked the invitation they'd cast aside onto the bed and strode across the room, past Sanjeev, and practically threw the crimson letter in Ro's face. "What does this mean?"

"I–what?" Ro caught the letter, pulling it back, her gaze darting all around the room, no doubt taking in the overturned shelves and even more bedding that dotted the floor.

A small, minuscule part of Sanjeev almost felt bad for her. The confused pain in her eyes seemed so real. But then he remembered her lies and how righteous she acted.

Some people thought Sarah had mastered that, but it was Ro she studied.

Not a single moment in the time since he'd met Rowena Dashwood did he ever think she enjoyed being in anyone's presence other than her own.

"You didn't want to tell us what it said," Sanjeev said, taking a step forward, blocking off the worst of what they'd done and hopefully refocusing Ro's attention. "On the plane. Remember? And then you lied about wearing the hoodie. It seems like you've lied about more."

"I didn't lie," she said. "I just didn't tell you what it said. That's not a crime."

"And we're not a jury," Michelle added from behind. "You're not being persecuted for a crime, only for being a bitch."

Sarah snorted next to him.

"Just tell us what it means. Please, Ro," Cody said.

"I–I don't know. I got the invitation and the gifts and was told that they wanted me to write my next book here. I wanted a vacation, so it seemed perfect. The quote doesn't mean anything–" she shrugged, and Sanjeev almost believed her "–I just assumed they were fans."

"So why didn't you tell us that on the plane?"

He could see the gears turning, but it only took her half a second to say, "Well since people already think I'm a bitch, should I add to it that Excelsior are mega fans of me while some of you are just struggling to get by?"

"Why are you up here?" Sarah asked, cocking a hip.

"It's my room," Ro argued, relenting only from seeming exhaustion. "Plus, the food is ready."

Nothing like real cooking to bring together enemies. Sarah shoved her way past Ro before she could step aside. Sanjeev felt himself kind enough to wait as she exited into the hallway, Michelle and Cody following behind, none of them saying another word to Ro.

"Should we wake up Olivia?" Michelle asked.

"We should at least check on her," Cody agreed.

It wasn't until they'd descended the stairs and Sanjeev glanced to his left, toward the kitchen, and one other room, that he realized they were missing someone else. "I hate to ask, but what about Nick?"

"Nose goes," Michelle said, bringing a finger up to tap her nose. Sanjeev copied quickly, Ro following even though they would have ignored her regardless.

Cody was last. Almost.

Sarah had clearly been too taken with the food, already spread across the table. "Huh?" She asked, her question nasally and hick, as she flipped her hair over her shoulder. "Do I have something on my face?"

Still with his finger to his nose, Sanjeev answered, "You're it. Go wake up Nick."

"Hell no," she said. "Someone else can."

The group looked around, all of them dropping their hands.

"Honestly, who cares?" Michelle asked, already crossing the other way, striding toward Olivia's room.

Cody followed her, and Ro took a few steps after them, then paused, as if unsure where she'd feel like she belonged.

Sanjeev shook his head. Michelle was right. Who cared? Honestly, this might be better. The asshole could chow down on his food later, continuing his pattern of not thanking Dylan and completely harshing whatever vibe they'd managed to salvage. Sanjeev pulled out a chair next to Sarah, who started serving him the same wine she'd opened. A bubbling rosé.

"Cheers to surviving this shit show," she said, tapping her glass against his. He drank, maintaining eye contact with her until they both swallowed. He looked away only as the voices came from down the hall. Ro, standing halfway in the dining area, halfway in the hall, looked a bit like a neglected Sim from his old gameplay streams, finally following the crowd of Michelle, Olivia, and Cody. The three took their new spots at the table.

Cody across from Ro.

Olivia sat at one crown end, and Michelle at the other.

The entire other side was nearly empty.

Three seats each for Ivy, Ian, and Lauren.

Two additional for Dylan and Nick.

"Eat, eat!" Dylan's voice came from afar, her steps echoing a little later, until she finally crossed into the dining area, carrying a final plate of what looked like fancy deviled eggs. "It's better when it's fresh. Please, enjoy."

"We were waiting for you," Cody said, although the rest dove in.

Dylan took her usual spot, several seats over from him, the gap on the other side closing. But the empty chairs were glaring. Sanjeev waited until she poured herself a glass of wine before he then joined in the chorus of scraping forks and appreciative moans.

After only a single bite, Sarah started, "We have something you might find interesting."

She crumpled Ro's scarlet invitation and tossed it over the table to Dylan, whose face somehow managed to drop. Exactly how Sanjeev felt.

Dylan set her glass down and wiped her mouth with the back of her hand. Even from here, Sanjeev could see the bits of food caked underneath her nails, and he shivered. Poor girl. The only one of them truly working.

Working *without* quotes. Because filming was "working." Always having to be "on" was "working."

No doubt Sarah would say that uncovering the mystery–snooping on Ro–was "working."

Dylan's haggard fingers worked to unravel the invitation, and they all watched as her eyes scanned.

Sanjeev shifted his gaze to Ro, who simply rolled her eyes.

"I'm literally right here," she said. "You could've just asked."

"Like you'd tell the truth," Sarah shot down.

Ro had no response.

Dylan sighed as her arm flopped down onto the table, invitation still in hand. She reached for her wine with her other hand and waved the crumpled crimson envelope in the air. "I don't know what this means." She tried to throw it back to Sarah, but it barely crossed halfway over the table, like a paper airplane created by a toddler.

"It's just a quote," Ro said, "from my first book. I already told you guys everything."

There was a tinge of desperation Sanjeev had never heard from her before, an exhaustion about to express itself through tears. He glanced to the side, confirming his suspicion.

Her eyes welled. She dropped her gaze back to her food. "I can't say I'm sorry enough, alright? I wasn't trying to scare anyone. But I'm not hiding anything from you. Not anymore. I swear."

Sarah scoffed to his left, her disbelief clear.

He reached out and patted her leg, but she shooed his hand away as if it were a fly.

"Of course you'd say that. What else are you going to say? 'I'm sorry, you're right, you caught me.' No!"

"Sarah," Sanjeev said.

A light warning. The kind he could get away with. More a faux chastising. As if anyone–least of all her–believed he'd do anything about it.

"Okay, okay," Cody said, in a way that commanded attention. He'd clearly taken over the role of "man at the table" and seemed to enjoy it immensely. Trying to protect Olivia, trying to go out and be the first to get help. "Can we just...push pause on this? While we eat?"

"Hear, hear." Michelle raised her glass. "I'd much rather chat about the first thing we do when we get back. I'm going to take the longest, nicest bath. And then I'm going to move out of my flat."

"Where are you moving to?" Dylan asked.

"Don't know yet," she said. "Somewhere warm, maybe. Somewhere like here, except with no one dying."

"Have you ever been to Thailand?" Sanjeev volunteered.

Michelle shook her head.

"It's really beautiful–"

"And really cheap," Sarah added.

"That's what I need," Michelle said. Then, with a sly grin, "You know, before all the survivor money starts rolling in."

Sarah squawked. "As if we're on a TV show! This is kind of like *Survivor*. You know someone offered me to go on *Ex on the Beach* once?"

"Ew," Sanjeev said, "with Jeremiah?"

"No, Paul Posey."

"You two didn't even date."

"Yeah, but everyone thought we did." She tapped her forehead. "That's all anyone needs. Smoke and mirrors, just enough of those to get on TV."

"That's the dream," Cody agreed. "The most I've done is a few interviews. Red carpets. Only have a couple of Getty Images to my name, though."

"It's not enough," Sarah nodded. "You need a show. Prime-time." She glanced over at Olivia, and they all followed.

The poor actress didn't chime in. Maybe she didn't even notice them.

Sarah rolled her eyes. "Although I've heard royalties are nonexistent now. We missed that train."

"But hit the influencer one dead on," Sanjeev noted.

"Eh, some of you did." Michelle shrugged. "I was early."

"You could pivot."

"Honey, haven't you seen me trying?"

Sanjeev could only drink his wine.

"Although I've had some success with Missives. It's new," she explained, likely from everyone's confused faces. It was hard to keep up with sites nowadays. "Sometimes you just need to be an early adopter."

"True," Sarah pointed her wine toward her, a bit dribbling over the lip from where she'd overfilled. Red streaks stained her wrist.

Dylan had long been quiet, only an occasional nod or "Mhmm" coming out. In terms of competition–in terms of number of followers–she was the closest to Sanjeev now.

Of course, numbers weren't everything. Her platform was short form exclusively. Incredibly large numbers, but less influencing power.

Compared to someone like Sarah. Smaller numbers, but a cult-like (or, perhaps literal) following. They'd spend hundreds–thousands–on her.

Not that every follower needed to be quantified that way. But that's how they were paid.

It was awful, if Sanjeev chose to think about it for too long. Coming from a time when he once genuinely believed in connection, when he once answered every comment, gave personalized responses on how to achieve specific looks, felt like he knew the people that came back to his livestreams again and again.

Now...

Sanjeev gulped down the rest of his rosé and accepted a new red from Sarah, which she happily poured and poured and poured, almost to the brim. They still had several bottles to get through, no doubt. And only a few more days–

No. *One* more.

He set his glass down and racked his brain. "Dylan, when's the next shipment–the supplies or whatever–supposed to come in? Tomorrow, right?"

"I'm not sure," she shook her head. "Did Lauren–" she hesitated on the name. "Did they say tomorrow? Or the next day?"

"We could ask Nick," Sarah suggested.

No one volunteered to grab him. Sanjeev wouldn't either. He brought the glass to his lips and chugged his wine.

Besides Sarah's initial accusation, they'd actually had...a nice dinner.

Not a great one. The food was good, but had nothing on Lauren's elaborate feasts. But it was homey and something he didn't have to make himself. The conversation was stale and mostly work-focused, the kinds of things they might have talked about during a normal trip before quickly moving on. But still...it was fine. Nice, even.

Almost enough to make him forget. But still not enough to keep him from hoping that tomorrow they'd be saved.

"If it is tomorrow," Michelle said, also finishing the last of her drink. "Then should we get more content? Sunset should be soon."

Sarah had already pulled out her phone, angling it to take a wide shot of the table, of people still eating and drinking. Ro followed suit, and soon Sanjeev felt the pressure, too. He wouldn't want to be the only one to not have captured it. To have to rely on someone else to send him footage he knew they never would.

"Shit," Michelle swore. "My phone's dead." She held it close to her face, trying to use it as a mirror and picking at something between her teeth. "Can we wait for a second?" But she had to have known it was useless. Her chair scraped the floor as she tossed her phone onto her now-empty chair behind her and quickly rushed to the nearby bathroom.

Sanjeev pulled out his own phone as the bathroom door squealed open, doing what Michelle had to run away for. He checked his teeth–fine. He pinched his cheeks–rosier now. And he smoothed out a single wayward brow. So much for his brow gel. He'd have to send feedback to the team. But the setting spray worked a charm and, awful as it was, he found himself channeling his inner Sarah to sell it.

This setting spray survived multiple deaths, tears, sweating, and still looked fucking good.

He glanced to his right, Ro setting down her phone, slowly raising to a stand. He followed her gaze to the bathroom, where Michelle inched back, like a cat wary of an attack.

"What?" He asked, gaze flipping back and forth between the women.

"Are you okay?" Ro called, a shocking amount of concern in her voice, something he didn't know she was able to pull except for herself. Maybe that's why she and Sarah butted heads so much.

They were too alike in that regard.

She stepped forward, and only then did he really realize the gravity of the situation.

That, and Michelle hadn't responded. Strange for her, too.

He also stood up, slower than Cody, who rushed over, his own jaw dropping, and Dylan, who wasn't far behind.

Sarah remained seated, but her curiosity was piqued.

And, for the first time, Olivia seemed to have snapped out of whatever trance she'd been put under.

"What is it?" Sanjeev asked. But none of them answered. Adrenaline spiked, mixing with all the alcohol as he staggered forward, needing to see with his own eyes what had captivated them–horrified them so.

He wished he hadn't. He wished he'd waited.

Even without the bathroom light turned on, there was no mistaking the shadow of a body hanging from the shower rod.

And there was only one of them unaccounted for.

Nick was dead.

THE DISCOVERY

FIFTY-TWO

The group stood as if frozen in time and space, not yet existing where reality met the villa.

Nick was dead. Nick had...hung himself?

Michelle had been staring at the scene the longest. She'd had the most time to recover. As if her brain snapped and zapped, she jolted forward, stepping farther into the bathroom than she had before, and switched on the light.

Someone gagged behind her.

They didn't show that in the movies. Not on *SVU*. The way the blood had constricted and pooled into his head, the awful purple color.

She'd learned a lot this trip about how the movies weren't reality. So often, reality wasn't reality either. What did they have to rely on?

She dared take another step, her gaze focusing on a note tucked into the pocket of Nick's jeans. Haphazardly, almost like an afterthought. As if it begged to be discovered.

With a hand she didn't realize was trembling until she missed the paper, she reached out, steadying herself with a breath, and tried again. Finger and thumb met page. She pulled, and it ripped. She cursed.

"What is it?" a voice from behind asked.

"It's a..." she didn't want to confirm. Not yet. But she had a hunch. She reached, keeping the rest of her body angled as far away from the body as possible, as she stretched and stretched, gently prying the half-torn page, the entire note freeing itself inch by inch. Finally, she exhaled.

Unfolding it, her suspicions were confirmed. "It's a suicide letter." Her eyes scanned the page as she turned around. Dropping it, she met Cody's gaze first. "And a confession."

"Go ahead, Michelle," Cody insisted.

He continued his role as "the leader," standing next to her, reading over her shoulder. Funny how it took her so long to see that he was just like the rest of them. Hungry for attention. Starved for it. The man wanted to be the leader only because it made him the center.

If he wanted the spotlight so much, he could just do it himself. But no, there was some element for show. A part that thought it better to look altruistic, to give her the chance to share. All for the single camera remaining...her own.

Or so she thought. As her eyes drifted over the note, she spotted Sarah and Sanjeev both adjusting their phones. Neither angled well. But really, who cared now? They'd get the details. The dirt.

The evidence.

Michelle cursed herself for letting her phone die. She glanced waywardly at where it still sat on her chair from when she'd tossed it earlier, another life–another death–ago. She could use the extra angle.

Michelle cleared her throat and began to read, "'I'm sorry–'" She stopped, dropping the page. "No, I'm sorry. I can't believe this man has the audacity to apologize once in his life and it's only after he's dead. How fucking selfish can he be?"

Dylan raised her glass and then chugged the remaining contents.

Sarah tutted from the other side of the table. “God won’t take kindly to that.” There was a lot her God wouldn’t take kindly to about this trip.

“Keep going,” Cody urged, even daring so far as to reach down and lift her hand up.

“You read it then,” she said, shoving the page into his hand and slumping into the empty seat, tossing her dead phone onto the table. “I’m tired.”

And thirsty. She poured herself another concoction as Cody continued, “‘I’m sorry. Lauren’s death is my fault. I take full responsibility for the way I treated her. She wasn’t well, and I encouraged her–’ He crossed through this a couple of times, like he was trying to find the right word,” Cody said, waving the page in the air.

“I’m not sure what he settled on,” he continued. “It’s hard to see, but then he goes, ‘I drove her to the edge. And I was there on the beach with her. She said she just wanted to swim. I’m sorry. I’m sorry.’” Cody turned the page over to the other side with a flourish and kept reading silently. “Umm,” he said. “This says something about abuse. He abused her? No. He’s saying it was–can you help?”

Michelle rolled her eyes as he offered the page back to her. She squinted. “Umm, ‘She said I abused her, and maybe she was right.’”

Across the table, Olivia hissed as she tore at the skin on her finger. Between not speaking and gnawing at her hand, that’s all she’d contributed. She paused, only for a moment, before switching to the next finger.

Sanjeev wrapped himself in a robe, then a blanket, then dragged his comforter around him, as if he could make an impenetrable barrier.

Michelle tapped her fingers against the table, waiting for Cody to continue, watching as Ro anxiously picked at the remaining bits of snack foods.

Sarah kept her eyes closed, hands pressed together, muttering a prayer.

Cody cleared his throat again. "'She said I abused her, and maybe she was right. It's my fault. All my fault. Lauren didn't deserve what I did to her. No one did.'"

"I knew it!" Sarah banged on the table, startling Olivia, the only one who hadn't looked up once.

"All these other deaths," Ro muttered. "It's the perfect cover. People would think this one was another accident."

"But then why kill himself?" Sanjeev asked, shaking his head. "It just...he doesn't seem the type."

"What do you know of his type?" Michelle asked.

"I mean, he is–*was*–so egotistical. The man was delusional, but–"

"Maybe he had a moment of clarity." Ro suggested, in that slow way, as if working her way through a character. "Realized what he'd done. Realized his business is nothing without her."

"So, what, he killed her in a rage, realizes what he's done, and seeking absolution, kills himself?" Michelle asked.

"That's what this says," Cody said, shifting his hands, slowly but surely reaching the bottom of the handwritten note. "'Let this be...' I can't read it. Michelle?"

She leaned over, squinted again, but then shook her head. "No idea. That whole sentence is off." She pointed at it. "'Let this be my salvation?' I didn't think he was religious."

Huffing, Dylan stomped over, "I've been reading his notes for years, let me see." Cody handed it off, but almost as soon as it was in her hands, she dropped it.

The letter floated to the ground.

"That's not–that's–" Dylan's mouth hung agape.

"Spit it out!" Sarah cried. "My God!"

Dylan scrambled to pick it up again, as if uncertain of what she was seeing. "This…this isn't Nick's handwriting."

FIFTY-THREE

It took a moment for the words to settle amongst the group.

As soon as they hit Olivia, she returned to gnawing at her finger. She'd already torn off her gel manicure and ripped at her hangnails. Fresh blood oozed out of her middle finger, but she couldn't even taste it anymore.

As ever, Sarah was the first to break the silence. "What do you mean?" For the first time, the words were slow, well enunciated, as if that could somehow make it make more sense. Or maybe her accent was slipping.

Olivia had clocked that a couple of times. She'd never had the pleasure of playing a Southern person–oh god, and now she might *never* have the chance.

What if she didn't get off this island? What if the curse was coming for her?

She peeled at a scab on her forearm, the wound not yet healed, more blood oozing out.

"This isn't his handwriting," Dylan reiterated, her voice shakier this time. She reached into her pocket and slipped out her phone. As she searched, Olivia reached across the table and grabbed one of the remaining Excelsior cans. All the beer bottles were gone. This would have to suffice. She started at the corner, the condensation making her fingers slip, her gnawed nails unable to snag the lip of the wrapper.

"See, look," Dylan said, showing her phone to Cody, to Michelle, to Sarah, who rushed over, to Sanjeev who bit his lip so hard it started to bleed before joining. Only she and Ro stayed behind, waiting, waiting, *waiting.*

"Lord help us," Sarah said. "Wait–is it Lauren's?"

"No," Dylan said. "No, it's not. And it's not mine," she rushed to add, swiping through picture after picture. Olivia could imagine the recipes. The scrawled additions of another ounce of rum or simple syrup.

"It's not mine!" Cody said, his attention shifting from the note to glare at Ro. "And we know it's not the hoodie person, either."

Michelle put both hands in the air. "Not me."

"Me neither," Sanjeev said.

Sarah and Ro rushed to proclaim their innocence, too.

Olivia heard it all, but she didn't care. She needed them to drown out the noise.

"Okay, and clearly she didn't," Michelle said.

"Maybe he changed his handwriting," Ro offered.

"Oooh, maybe," Michelle agreed. "I took a course once on penmanship, and there's a way–"

"Oh my God! Oh, Lord Jesus!" Sarah clapped, a grin stitching its way up her face. She circled around into the middle of the room, clapping once, twice, three more times. "I've got it. I've got it! It's *you.*"

She stared straight at Michelle Monroe, who paid her barely a cursory glance.

"What'd I do this time?" she asked with a roll of her eyes.

"You–this–all of it," Sarah gestured wildly around the room. "This is a prank! You're pranking us!"

"A prank?" Dylan repeated.

"Yeah!" Sarah looked around for support. "Hell, she's tried everything else! Why not a prank show?"

"And what, the rest of them are in on it?"

"Yes!" Sarah cried. "Or no. I don't know. I don't care! Maybe it went wrong, 'cause they always do, and now you're feeling bad, wondering how you're gonna get out of this and–"

"I'm offended," Michelle said, bringing a half-hearted hand to her chest, "that you'd think I'd stoop so low as to make a prank channel. How pathetic do you think I am?"

Sarah cocked out her hip. "You want me to answer that?"

"Sarah!" Sanjeev shrieked, shaking hands covering his face.

Olivia stopped her picking, so enraptured by the scene unfolding before her. But all he did was ball his hands into fists and bring them back to his sides. "Give it a rest. Okay?" Tensed, flat hands, then fists, tensed, fists, tensed. He did it in time with his breath.

Maybe she should try that, too.

"Or maybe…maybe it is a prank, and it's Nick," Dylan offered. "Did we check…I mean, did anyone check the body? To make sure it's…real?"

The silence hung in the air. Heads shifted slowly, but surely, all eventually training their way toward the table, forcing Olivia to stop her picking. But they weren't looking at her.

They were staring at Ro.

"Me?" Ro pointed to herself.

"You seemed to know the most about bodies. Wanting to study them and all." Cody's reaction was snide.

Olivia didn't like that about him, but she could understand it. Maybe she'd be like this, too, if she weren't so preoccupied. Her fingernail finally slipped from under the lip of the wrapper, and she sighed.

If the others paid an ounce of attention to her, they moved on quickly. She hadn't heard their decision, but they all left, one by one, standing and walking toward the bathroom, where they'd discovered the body. Another body. So many bodies. Too many bodies.

How could there be so *many* bodies?

She gripped the can so tightly it crinkled, the wrapper falling away from her finger. A gentle *tink, tink, tink* of her raw nub against the metal, and she had it again. She was getting closer. Closer each time.

The argument returned, now a room over. The sound rose, insults hissed. Only one thing penetrated through: the body was real. Nick was dead.

Dead.

Dead.

Dead.

Her finger snagged the wrapper, more than just the nail this time. With her thumb, she pressed down hard, pulling around, the wrapper tearing off in one, satisfying shiiirp, the can coming free. For half a second, Olivia experienced that pure bliss of a job well done, a thing well picked at, before the inevitable fall.

Usually, it was shame. The way her hands were now mangled, the way she'd eventually turn to her skin, or her hair.

Shame wasn't a single thought in her mind as a scream to rival the Wilhelm welled in the back of her throat, breaking free at a record pace as she stared down at the can in her hands.

"Oh my god, no more!" The shouts came back at her, but they couldn't shut her up.

No, the can did that.

Her surprise and fear were replaced with a much more worrying realization. She was in danger.

"Two-hundred twenty-three more days," she repeated. "Two-hundred twenty-three."

A few came out of the bathroom, shouting, "*What?*" at her.

They didn't get it.

Her hand shook as she held up the can, displaying a telltale brand they'd seen a million times, in a million advertisements, on a million shelves before.

"Oh, hey," Cody said, peeking his head out. "That's my favorite. Where'd you get it?"

They still didn't understand.

She squatted down, picking up the aluminum wrap she'd peeled. The Excelsior branding flapping gently in her hands.

Sarah turned on her heel, walked to the other downstairs bathroom, slammed the door shut, and screamed.

The others stayed, as if pinned to their spots on the floor.

Finally, Cody summed it up. "Fuck."

FIFTY-FOUR

Sarah sat on her knees and clasped her hands together, bringing them to her forehead. Eyes scrunched closed, she muttered her prayers.

To Jesus.

To Allah.

To Mother Nature.

To Buddha.

To Ishvara. To Zeus. To Odin.

To Aslan from *Narnia.*

She'd pimp her soul to the Devil himself if he'd save her.

"Please don't let me die on this stupid fucking island surrounded by these stupid fucking people. *Please.*"

FIFTY-FIVE

"I fucking knew it tasted familiar!" Cody said. He lunged toward the cooler, grabbed another Excelsior, and picked at the label. Over and over and over until he was able to yank it off. It ripped in half, but underneath was the unmistakable branding. "Fuck, fuck, fuck," he said. He tossed several cans onto the table, knocking over the last of Lauren's decorations and spilling drinks. No one tried to fix it. Instead, they too grabbed at the cans, frantically tearing.

Fake.

Fake.

Fake.

Excelsior didn't exist. *Excelsior* wasn't real.

None of it was real.

None of it.

They stared at the mountain of stripped cans they'd collected. Some had fallen to the floor, but most were piled on top of the table.

They went through every single one–all those in the kitchen, all those in storage, everything, *everywhere*–and there was only one conclusion to be had in Cody's opinion.

"But what does this mean?" Michelle asked. "Are they paying us to advertise false product? Like all those football players and crypto?"

"I never talked to any of the Excelsior–the whatever–people," Dylan said. "That was all Lauren. All Nick. Did any of you talk to them?"

"We're not getting saved, are we?" Sanjeev's question came quieter, but it shook the most.

"No, no," Sarah stood, taking over Cody's job of pacing. "We will. They'll find us. I've got an entire army that will break through walls if I go missing. If they don't hear from me at my usual sermon time next Sunday, well…someone will come."

"We just have to survive in the meantime," Cody said with a nod. He cracked his knuckles again. He was prepared to fight. He was always seconds away from ready.

"This is going to make such a good book someday," Ro laughed. She inhaled the giggle, hysterical.

Cody waited for Sarah to cut in–to ask her where her writing currently was. A harsh, "What book? We know you don't write anything!" But it didn't come. Sarah was picking at her hair. She alternated between picking and *zhuzhing*, today somehow doing the impossible–flattening her monstrosity.

"Oh my god, *New York Times* bestsellers. All of us!" The laugh erupted out of Ro again, her smile twitching up and down as she looked around. "We'll be set for life."

"Um, some of us already are, miss ma'am," Sarah said. "Some of us want to be sure we get out with our life story still to tell."

"We're not going to die!" Ro shouted.

Meanwhile Olivia muttered under her breath. "Two hundred twenty-two days, seven hours, thirty-one minutes." She rocked back and forth, back and forth. The glitter and gleam, the aura that surrounded her, had disappeared. No more bouncy, sexy curls. No shining eyes as her gaze flitted amongst the group. Red veins showed that, despite her getting the most sleep, she'd need more pills tonight. She'd need someone to protect her.

"We need to stick together," Cody realized. "All of us. Bathroom breaks. Sleeping. No one goes anywhere alone."

"Umm, I think not," Sarah said. "I trust y'all about as much as I trusted Nick, and he fucking killed someone already. And then himself. Two people! That's a level of hell I don't wanna know. Uh-uh."

"Sarah," Sanjeev scolded under his breath.

"It's weird, but I agree with Cody–"

"And I agree with Sarah," Michelle cut Dylan off. "Actually," she stood, "I agree with none of you. Look, it's fucking weird, right? But I cashed my crypto. It went through. And this fucking gem," she showed off her ring, the one they'd all been sent in their initial invitation package. "I know this is real. What if it's just a shitty, new company? They don't know what to do. How often to reach out. They think they'll be just fine sending us extra supplies in what, a day?"

Dylan shrugged.

Sanjeev bit his lip and nodded.

"A day, then. That's all we need to survive 'til tomorrow. We'll just go back with the suppliers, and we'll all be fine. Ain't no thing. And then yes," she pointed to Ro, "we'll sell the hell out of these novels."

"*Autobiographies*," Ro corrected.

"Whatever."

"Then how do you explain this?" Dylan said, waving the paper–Nick's suicide note–in the air. "How?"

"The man wasn't in his right mind," Michelle said. "That's enough to make anyone act crazy. The least strange thing is his handwriting being a bit shakier, right?"

Cody took in a deep breath. Someone needed to control this situation again. "Just…humor me, alright? We don't have to stay all together, but we can do a buddy system."

Sarah's hand immediately shot out for Sanjeev's. No surprise at all.

"I'll take care of Olivia," he offered, walking across the room and standing behind her. He reached down and rubbed at her shoulders. So tense. So small. Now wasn't the time, but later, after this trip, he'd suggest putting some meat on her bones. It would even help her look leaner.

"Dylan," Michelle said. "You gonna be with me?"

"Yeah, alright."

All heads turned to Ro. No one said anything. A small, tiny part of his heart ached for her. The thought was brief, but for a moment, he debated reaching out for her. That part of him died when he remembered how long she let him believe that stupid hooded person had been someone other than her. When he remembered how long she knew that Ivy was Whisper and never told him. When he remembered just how exhausting she was to be around.

"Someone needs to be with her," Sarah said. How very unlike Sarah to be the one to extend her hand, despite what she preached. Then she added, "So she doesn't try anything else."

He should've known better.

Still, she wasn't wrong.

His gaze slipped over Sanjeev and Sarah, to Michelle, already shaking her head. Dylan looked as torn as he felt.

Olivia's hair brushed along his forearm and he glanced down, her sad eyes now staring up at him. "She can come with us," she whispered.

Well, now he'd look like a dick.

"Yeah, alright," he said. "C'mon, Ro." He rolled his shoulders back, staring at the only camera still set up in the room.

If they did get out of this safely–if Ro was right, that this would launch them to superstardom, if he could get his own *New York Times* Bestselling Author tag–it would look great in his bio. Add an extra level of authority. Ro was the likeliest to sell. It'd be better for him to come out looking the hero, maybe even get an extra acknowledgment in her book. He wasn't sure how that worked, other than it was good. He could figure it out later.

Ro didn't say anything more. An appreciative nod. If not at him, then Olivia. The three of them could stick together.

"I have a giant bed–a circle one," he offered, as Ro rose to a stand, gathering her blank notebooks.

"That was definitely used for orgies," Sarah muttered.

He ignored her. "It's on the second floor. Harder to get to. And we can put a line of pillows between us."

That seemed to assure Olivia enough, who'd kept her head down the whole time other than to nod. The other duos made their own plans while Ro walked over and joined them.

"We'll go get whatever you girls need," he continued. "Then head upstairs. Together."

"Together," Olivia muttered, eyes on the ground.

Ro reached out and squeezed his arm. Somehow, even after the past few days, it was still reassuring. "Together."

FIFTY-SIX

Cody, Olivia, and Ro agreed to check upstairs. It required less movement from Olivia, and though her pace was slow, their search was thorough. They double-checked window locks, secured balcony doors, and only gasped at their own reflections in mirrors. Their hearts still beat in their chests–something to be grateful for–even if it felt like they were thumping a million miles an hour.

FIFTY-SEVEN

Michelle and Dylan took the downstairs area. One stood guard at the entrance to the room, while the other shouted out things they found. Dylan pushed furniture in front of doors, tied sheets around handles and knobs. Michelle gathered whatever personal effects everyone might need, especially their cameras.

They screamed once, then screamed more apologies, after they opened the bathroom door and saw Nick's body again. They slammed the door closed and marked it as checked, agreeing that anyone willing to hide inside there deserved to kill them.

FIFTY-EIGHT

Sanjeev and Sarah drew the short stick, and were forced to check the perimeter of the mansion. They each held a large butcher knife–the biggest ones they could find from the kitchen. When they reached the sand, Sarah stuffed some into her pockets without explaining, but Sanjeev knew better than to question her methods.

They turned each corner with a wild battle cry before facing nothing, seeing nothing, finding nothing. With the perimeter established, they grinned, a single high-five precipitating their shit-talking until an errant branch cracked and fell. A wild palm, large enough to take Sarah out, landed only a foot behind her.

Wide-eyed, the two raced back into the mansion, securing the final door behind them, crying out that they'd finished.

That they, too, almost died.

THE SUSPECT

FIFTY-NINE

In the blue hour of morning, still long before the sun fully crested above the ocean, Sanjeev awoke. He squinted into the soft light, illuminated only by the night lamp they'd turned on at the entrance, as a pair of feet quickly slipped out the doorway.

After their scares checking the villa, it didn't take long for the pairs to find themselves all joining in Cody's room.

Sanjeev sat up, his cashmere throw slipping down his shoulders, pooling at his waist. He glanced around the room, rubbing sleep from his eyes.

Michelle's head lay atop Olivia's chest, which rose lightly with her gentle snores. Dylan stayed curled in a ball at the foot of the bed. Cody splayed out next to her with his long limbs pointing every which direction. And Ro was cuddled up in the rocking chair, her book open and trapped between her chest and knees.

Sarah. Sarah left.

As quietly as he could, without disturbing Michelle and Olivia to his right or Dylan at his feet, Sanjeev slowly swung his legs over the side of the bed and tiptoed toward the door.

He peeked his head out, too slowly to catch where Sarah had gone.

Vaguely he remembered that first night, the horrible sleep after what had happened to Ivy. But when he woke up the next morning, he felt…fine.

Just fine.

He'd stepped out of his bedroom in the morning, guilty for feeling so fine, but otherwise enamored with the location, the opulence and glamor. He felt spoiled.

He was spoiled.

If the past three days had highlighted anything, it was that. Sanjeev didn't cook for himself. He didn't drive himself places. He hired professionals to shop for his groceries, and the farm animals were taken care of by highly trained staff that lived on-site.

The most he did was take pretty pictures and pretty videos, and that was easy when he paid professional editors to color correct and cut out all the times he stared off into space, thinking about nothing and wishing he were elsewhere.

He never knew *where* though. That thought didn't enter his mind. Just…elsewhere.

Now he was elsewhere, and it was horrible. He wanted to go home.

And for her many, many, many flaws, in some wretched, awful, twisted way, Sarah felt like home.

Sometimes, like the abusive home he'd once fled.

But still. *Home.*

People always wanted what they couldn't have. Maybe even more so when they nearly had it all.

He crept down the stairs, the barricaded sliding glass door easing his fears just enough. If there was one thing he knew about Sarah–and he knew everything about her–she'd need her caffeine.

"We were supposed to stay together," Sanjeev whispered as he entered the kitchen.

But Sarah couldn't be bothered to pretend she was sorry. "I just needed some coffee." It came out like a croak. Nothing like the clear shout of her preacher voice.

"And what if there were someone around and they took you? Or worse? We wouldn't be able to help."

"*Pfft*," she said. "Like you'd be able to do much with those noodle arms. Do you want your own mug or not?"

Sanjeev rolled his eyes and kicked off the marble island. "Sure," he said, crossing his noodle arms over his chest. He remembered the first time she'd called them that. Said they were endearing. That they made him approachable.

She'd always been quick to rationalize. The second she saw a face shift, expressions pinched together in hurt, a brow raised in surprise, she'd throw her head back and laugh softly and tell you why it was a good thing.

His thin hair meant he'd be able to sell more products someday, and people would actually believe him, unlike all those sluts with their already perfect, voluminous tresses.

His "basic, boring" brown eyes made him relatable. More people would click on his videos, wanting to know his tips for how to best highlight them.

His wonky teeth. His wispy eyebrows. His scarily thin frame. He'd heard it all. He'd heard it all from comments online, but he'd heard it all from her first.

"Tough love," she'd said, the one time he'd dared to ask her why she said that part out loud. "It's good for you. That's the only reason I do it. For you."

For him.

For *him*.

"Umm, do you want me to fucking bring the mug to your lips, too?" she asked.

Sanjeev snapped back to attention, back to the kitchen. He blinked at her, the outstretched mug in her hand.

"Thanks," he said softly, taking it as she nearly dropped it, a bit of scalding coffee splashing onto his hand. The kind that would leave a small burn, maybe a scar. Fitting for all the invisible scars she'd left on him already.

He wiped his hands on his silk pajama pants.

Sarah didn't apologize. She didn't notice.

Or she didn't care.

Sanjeev set the mug down on the island. "I think they stocked the fridge with oat milk, if you wanted some."

"Yes, please," she said in a singsong tone. "And if they have any sweetener in there, too, pull it out. You know how I like my coffee."

He did. He knew everything about her. In the time since their friendship…paused, he wondered what he'd missed. He hadn't watched her vlogs. Nor her sermons. He hadn't liked her pics on IG or Snapchat or anywhere else.

This trip taught him that she was the same. Mostly the same, only a little different. Harsher, maybe, more egotistical.

Maybe they all were.

They brought their coffees back up to the room, finishing them before anyone else awoke. And when they did, it was a matter of killing time. Olivia applied a green tea face mask, Ro curled up in her chair, continuing to read, and Cody stared out at the ocean whilst in a perfect scorpion pose. Dylan pulled her sleep mask over her eyes, and Michelle tried out a bit of Olivia's face mask on some stress pimples.

Sanjeev watched it all quietly, already tucked back into his sliver of the bed.

An hour later, Sarah shuffled out of the bathroom, her hair teased to the gods–well, her God. "What time were the shipments before, Dylan?"

She didn't care that the poor woman was trying to sleep.

Still, Dylan answered. "Mornings."

"Well, it's noon now."

The realization sank in without any more words. There was no stomach plummeting, no heart-wrenching for Sanjeev.

He had no hope left.

The group moseyed down to the kitchen and made sandwiches in silence. They carried them back to Cody's room in silence. And they ate together in silence.

The only interruptions came in the form of muttering. First Olivia, as she plucked single strands of golden blonde hair from her head, whispering numbers under her breath. Then increasingly wild theories that came from Ro alongside the whine of her pen against paper.

And the whipping of Cody's fist through the air as he shadowboxed. "This is for the person who brought us here. *Hya!*"

The first time he accidentally kicked the wall, they all jumped. By the sixth time, no one cared.

After a few more hours, Sarah said, "I'm bored."

Michelle agreed, and the two started filming together in the corner.

Their mindless chatter was Sanjeev's only entertainment. He painted his nails, then painted Dylan's. Olivia's single sane minute was up, and Ro seemed equally afflicted. Cody performed a weightless workout, filming himself without speaking as the sun began to set in the background. No doubt his editor would put words like "Mega!" or "Superset!" or some other meathead shit on screen.

"Maybe Ivy set this all up. Maybe she's not really dead." Ro tried her tenth theory of the hour.

"She's dead," Cody snapped.

"But what if she's not?" Her pen raced across the page, words turning over each other so fast, Sanjeev doubted she'd be able to reread her handwriting. "What if she organized this, summoned us all here, in the hopes of gaining more secrets? What if–"

"Give it a rest!"

"I wouldn't put it past her to fake her own death. She's so good at keeping secrets, what's another two or ten or twenty? If anyone was going to prank us all, it would–"

"*ENOUGH!*" Cody yelled, punching his fist into the wall.

A collective gasp, and then stillness, only a gentle breeze from the ocean enough to stir the mood.

But there was no rest to be had as Ro returned to her muttering, her theories spiraling, only a little quieter than before.

They took showers in shifts and at 10 p.m. Sanjeev, Michelle, and Sarah filmed a "get unready with us" video where they showed off their skincare routine. Michelle and Dylan had grabbed all the essentials from everyone's rooms the night before and chucked them in one of Michelle's suitcases, so it became a fun game of whose products were whose.

But when they wrapped up, signed off, closed out of their individual recordings, the smiles died, too. All for show. Show was all they had now.

He slipped into bed first and watched as Sarah kneeled at the circumference, resting her hands on the comforter.

Sometimes he wondered if she actually prayed. He never could tell if she drank her own syrup or if she sat there, waiting an appropriate amount of time for all eyes to have borne witness to her holiness.

Even after all these years, he still didn't know.

Moments later, she pulled the covers down–farther than she needed to, the sudden whoosh chilling him to his ankles–

and then hopped up into bed next to him, pushing his arm away with her head and snuggling into him.

He wrapped his arms around her, instinctively, remembering so many nights when they used to fall asleep like this. And soon, despite his best efforts, that's exactly what he did.

Again, he awoke to the faint sound of a door whining open. He didn't spot Sarah's disappearing feet this time, but the distinct lack of her on his shoulder, or the small space to his right, proved enough. She'd spent all night tossing and turning, waking him, then snoring herself quickly back to sleep, leaving him only with his thoughts and memories.

Two things, concerning her, that he hated more and more.

This time he didn't chase after her. Instead, he turned over, pulling the covers over his eyes. He'd speak with her later. If he gathered enough courage, maybe.

"So, this was all a fucking set-up, right? No one's coming."

"Don't say that," Sanjeev tried, reaching out to rub Sarah's back.

She accepted his comfort, but she still shook her head.

"Don't y'all remember? Lauren said there would be food re-stock halfway through. Lobster or something, right? Fresh caught. Well, where have they been? Nick said the same thing. No one's come by. This whole thing? A fucking scam."

"Sarah," he said, dropping his hand. "Please." He didn't need to hear what he already knew.

"I'm serious." Looking back at him, she tapped her shoulders. He relented with a roll of his eyes, bringing his hands up to her cold skin. He pressed his thumbs into her back, working his way down the muscles on the sides of her spine. "The fake products, the company we can't get in touch with, the deaths. You're telling me this makes sense to you?"

"None of it makes sense." He worked his way back up to her shoulders, making sure to dig his fingers in, kneading out his own anxiety, pressing, squeezing–

"Ow," she pulled away.

"Sorry," he said immediately. He dropped his hands to his lap, eyeing the others. Ro was reading–or pretending to read. Cody did push-ups with a jump at the end, working up a sweat. Michelle was filming a timelapse of the clouds from the window, and Dylan was helping Olivia fix up her hands. Music pumped from Cody's soundtrack, and for a moment, it almost seemed like no one else felt anything was odd at all.

Just him and Sarah. Like always.

This time, Sanjeev was awake when Sarah rolled out of bed. He could feel how she made no effort not to jostle him, not to wake him. He wondered, vaguely, if this was how she acted every time, or if she was upset he hadn't joined her yesterday.

Or, worse, if this was her strange payback for him shutting her down.

Sanjeev stared up at the ceiling, counting to ten as she shuffled into her shoes, then shuffled around the bed and out the door. He waited until he could no longer hear her footsteps before he got up himself and followed her, down the stairs, into the kitchen, making sure to keep his breath steady and calm all the while.

"Coffee?" she asked, without looking up from filling the machine with water.

"No thanks," he said. Instead, he waited not-so-patiently behind her after grabbing the electric kettle. "You know, you shouldn't be up right now."

"Neither should you."

He resisted the urge to explain that he was only up because she was. "Safety in numbers," he reminded her instead.

Sarah grumbled and shrugged, stepping out of his way after turning off the tap.

He rolled his eyes, turning the water back on and sliding the kettle underneath. It gushed in spurts before Sarah switched it *off* again.

The groan in his throat was guttural.

"What?" She blinked long, tinted lashes up at him.

The lump in his throat threatened to break out in a strangled cry. He waited, steadying his voice. "Is there a problem?"

"I don't know. Do you think there's one? Do you think there's a problem that no one has dropped off supplies and that Excelsior doesn't exist and that people on this fucking trip keep fucking dying?"

So, she was punishing him. Payback was a bitch, and Sarah always loved being one.

"Of course, I think it's a problem." He switched the water back on, but her hand was still there, immediately pushing the knob off again.

He swallowed his anger. "I thought you said your congregation would start looking for you?"

He posed it like a question, the uptick in his voice a common complaint in the reviews of his podcast. But this time it was a question. All the times Sarah lied–who was to say this was different?

Knowing him as well as he knew her, as if reading his mind, Sarah scowled. "Of course they're looking for me. Why wouldn't they be?"

"You really want me to answer that?"

Her jaw set, nostrils flared, and she crossed her arms over her chest. Her tilted chin dared him.

Maybe he was as affected as Ro and Olivia, because he answered, "Maybe they discovered all that 'charitable giving' was to yourself? I think Ivy might have been hinting at–"

She pushed him.

He stumbled, only a few feet.

Her next words were far more cutting. “And how do you figure Ivy found out, hmm? I always knew you submitted something–”

“I didn’t!” He swore he didn’t, risking a step forward. “I’ve covered for you. So many times. Even this past year and a half. But, c’mon, it’s not like you were ever subtle about–”

She pushed him again, the second he stepped close enough for her arms to reach. “As if I haven’t been covering for *you* all this time? What about those poisonous fucking–”

“Shut up!” he wailed.

“Oh no. No, no, no, you don’t talk like that to me.”

He dared step forward again, her accent dropping, as threats let loose from her lips. “If you so much as think about crossing me–ever–I will end you. Do you understand? I’ll drag you down with me.”

He took another step forward.

“And if you think you’ll survive at the bottom,” she continued, “you’re wrong. You’ll be ruined.”

He didn’t respond. He lifted the electric kettle back over the basin of the sink and turned the water on once more.

“I’ve seen the bottom and come back to life. I’ve survived the fall. I’ve been resurrected and I can do it again if I have to. You? Ha!”

She jabbed a finger into his arm, but he didn’t respond, and he could feel the heat, the anger, radiating off of her. How she hated his silence. How it inspired her crazy to spiral.

“I bet I could even send my people after you,” she hissed. “They adore me. They *worship* me. You think they wouldn’t find you? You think they’d believe you over me? You think they wouldn’t see you as the enemy? It would be so easy. So, so easy to ruin you. You think I couldn’t do it? That I wouldn’t?”

Still, he was silent, watching as the water gushed, as it overflowed. Gurgling, sloshing water, down the kettle, down the drain, down, down, down.

"Um, hello?" she yelled, jostling him with her shoulder before turning the water off once more.

He didn't scream. He said nothing as he whipped the full, heavy kettle from the sink and into the side of her head, the straw having broken his back long ago.

He saw nothing but red as he climbed on top of her, as his hands wrapped around her throat, as he pressed down, down, down, as her eyes widened with panic. She tried to hit him, but it was no use.

Even his "noodle arms" were stronger than her.

He didn't stop seeing red until minutes later.

She'd long since stopped convulsing under his grasp. Instead, she lay there, lifeless, and he continued pressing his arms down on her neck.

He stared into her wide, dead blue eyes. And he felt…nothing. At first.

Then he blinked the red away, and the dark blue of morning began to twinkle azure. The tile felt white-hot under his shins, even though he knew it was cold.

Her neck felt like iron in his hands, like the time he was a kid and he'd grabbed the still sizzling skillet and his grip tightened, his body unsure what to do until his dad raised his hand and slapped him.

He dropped his hands from her neck, his eyes focusing on the pressure forming where his fingers had been.

He had killed her.

He slid off her body as easily as he'd slid out of bed. He grabbed her cup of coffee off the island and dumped it into the sink. He stared, watching it *drip, drip, drip* all the way down, down, *down.*

Still, he gripped the mug, his brain short-circuiting, past clouding the present, as he stepped over Sarah's body and swung open the kitchen door.

He dropped the mug and didn't even hear it shatter.

SIXTY

Dylan blinked open her eyes, only vaguely aware that something had woken her up. But when she looked around, no one moved. There was no sound.

She lifted her head off the small throw pillow, feeling bits of sparkles imprinted on her cheek. She rubbed her skin, feeling each little divot. Only as she'd reached her chin did she notice that something was amiss.

1, 2, 3, 4...they were missing someone.

Cody lay at her feet and she accidentally on-purpose kicked at his shoulder.

He launched himself straight up at the hips. "What is it?" he asked, his voice hoarse.

"Sarah," she whispered.

Olivia woke next, reaching an arm up as she stretched, and Michelle rolled off the pillow they shared. Ro, too, pushed the footrest down on her armchair, the metal clicking and springing her forward.

Sanjeev sat upright, looking at them all. "What's going on?"

"Sarah," Dylan whispered again. "She's missing."

He yawned, covering his mouth as he said, "She's been going downstairs for coffee in the mornings."

"Oooh, coffee *does* sound good," Michelle said.

Ro nodded.

Cody agreed, "It'd be nice for a pre-workout."

Dylan reached the door first, opening it and peeking her head out. There was no one in the hall. She hadn't expected there to be, but still, she thought she'd hear the faraway rumbling of the espresso machine or the grinding of beans. There was none of that either.

Michelle followed, then Ro, then Cody.

Sanjeev lagged, as if still in a sleepy daze. He shooed Olivia out, the two bringing up the rear. He whispered something to her as he closed the door, nodding once to Dylan, and she led their train down the stairs.

Anxiety crept its way, tightening around her, as each additional step offered no noise from the kitchen. The only sound came from behind. "Sarah?" She called, surveying the downstairs. All the rooms remained as they had before when she and Michelle had completed their check. Marks on the doors, none ajar.

And then…

Her stomach dropped, anxiety twisting its way fully around her neck, confusion tinging every thought. She couldn't speak. For now, she was the only one who saw it, and she lifted her hand to point at the shattered porcelain that sprinkled the hallway, just in front of the kitchen.

Michelle bumped into her. "What is it?" she asked, hands gripping Dylan's arms, moving her gently aside. "Oh."

Oh.

Oh.

"Do you think…" Ro started but couldn't finish the sentence. Instead, she stepped forward. Once, then twice, Cody quickly behind, the two propelled by different kinds of curiosity, but the same need to know first.

Cody dodged the porcelain with his bare feet while Ro crunched over it with her house shoes, the first to reach the kitchen door. She swung it open and gasped.

Dylan looked at Michelle, who whipped her head around to look at Dylan. The two women stared, at a loss for words.

Cody's shouting echoed throughout the hall. "This is why we were supposed to stay together, dammit!"

As the shock settled, Dylan joined the others in the kitchen, staring down at Sarah Pruski's dead body. Olivia picked at her hands, undoing all of Dylan's hard work at repairing them, but she couldn't be bothered to chastise her.

Really, who cared?

Ro squatted down next to the body, doing her best to guess at what time Sarah died, spouting out facts to anyone who cared enough to listen.

Michelle somehow managed to make some tea, pouring additional cups, though no one else seemed able to drink with Sarah's body there.

Cody wrapped his arm around Olivia, and Sanjeev…

"Wait, where's Sanjeev?" Dylan asked.

Cody let go of Olivia and began yelling again, "What did I just say!" as he barged toward the door. "We have to stick together! *Sanjeev!*"

No response.

"Safety in numbers," Dylan repeated, her reminder for Cody, hoping he'd calm down.

The kinder, calmer Cody had disappeared the last few days, no number or intensity of exercises enough to steady him.

"*Fuck!*" Cody screamed, and the four women twitched. He swung the door closed with such force the wall shook.

Dylan's eyes jumped to the camera angled down at the kitchen, still swinging. "Oh my god!" she cried. "I forgot!"

"Forgot what?" Ro asked.

Dylan didn't answer as she rushed around the dead body and Ro, reaching the pantry and pulling out a stepladder. Placing it in front of the doorframe, with three quick steps up, she reached the camera. "This is–*was*–Nick's."

Despite belonging to the Mercers, she'd been the one to help affix it. Along with several other cameras scattered throughout the villa. These acted as a failsafe. More akin to security cameras. They had on-device storage for nearly a week–the exact amount of time the brand trip was supposed to last.

She followed the tiny cord, taped along the doorframe, and hidden behind an aesthetic mix of hand-thrown pots in various shades of blues and greens. She found the plug and pulled the cord. "It's battery powered. They use it…*used* it," she corrected herself, "for busy, full-day shoots."

No one seemed as excited as she was.

"We might be able to find out who did this!" she cried, nearly squealing. It wasn't excitement, not really. More delirium.

"Does anyone have their computer?"

"We can use mine!" Ro jumped to be helpful, to get back in the good graces of her remaining companions. With so few of them left, Dylan doubted she could afford enemies.

"I thought you didn't bring it." Michelle sipped her tea, the question targeted despite the innocence on her face.

"Who cares?" Dylan asked. Just another of Ro's many lies. Add it to the pile along with the bodies.

They left Sarah where she lay, everyone moving as a unit up to Ro's room. It was next to the library, a room so obviously meant only for one person on the trip–like Cody and the gym–that until now, Dylan doubted any of the others had even entered it.

"One sec," Ro said, dashing inside the room just long enough to snatch up her computer, and running back. As if she thought if she stayed too long, an invisible hand might claw her back.

They closed the door, marked it as safe as it could be, and returned to Cody's room with the large, circular bed.

Climbing aboard, the group gathered around Ro. She jiggled her finger across the trackpad. The computer lit up, and she opened it with the touch of her fingerprint against the sensor. "USB?"

Dylan handed it over, unwinding the cords and setting the video recorder down.

Without any more words, Ro plugged it in.

After clicking Accept on various requests, an image of the empty kitchen popped up, with a date and time on the bottom left of the screen. Ro clicked play, and the seconds ticked up.

No one moved.

"This is before we finished unpacking," Dylan said, pointing to sacks of groceries. "Nearly a week ago. We should probably fast-forward, but do we know...I mean, when do we think we should look?"

"Let's go to today," Ro said, hovering her mouse over the ninety percent mark of the video. "Ahh!"

They jumped as Sarah's dead body appeared.

"Okay, okay, back from there. An hour at a time?"

"I know," Ro hissed. She clicked in ten-minute increments until the body disappeared.

Then all they had left to do was watch.

It took minutes of nothing, everyone huddled together, not wanting to tear their eyes from the screen. And then suddenly, the screen lit up.

Someone had turned on a light in the kitchen.

Sarah came in, whistling, seemingly without a care in the world. She'd slipped out, away from safety, and minutes later, her body would be there to prove it.

For a bit, Sarah was alone. She messed with the coffee machine and scoured the fridge. She whipped her head around and shut the refrigerator door, clearly hearing something the camera hadn't picked up.

"Coffee?"

The fake accent sounded even stranger, thicker in the recording than it had in real life.

Ringing began in Dylan's ears. Her eyes widened as she realized how few of the ten minutes remained.

Michelle leaned across her, and Cody sat back, arms crossed, brows furrowed.

They hadn't yet pieced it together.

And still, in the present, there was no Sanjeev to be seen.

Dylan turned back to the screen, covering her mouth with her hand, wondering if there was some other way to explain this other than her conclusion.

The two best friends talked, and the minutes ticked down.

Only as the on-screen Sanjeev lunged did Michelle gasp beside her.

Olivia let out a mangled cry and threw herself off the bed, toward a corner in the room.

Ro's finger hesitated on the space bar, as if she couldn't will herself to stop watching.

"That fucker," Cody said. "That *fucker* did this! He probably did it to all of them! What the actual *fuck*?!"

He'd strangled her. With his own hands. And the video Sanjeev, the past Sanjeev, he kept holding on. Kept holding and holding and holding. More minutes passed.

"He doesn't look like he...*knows*?" Dylan said.

"He fucking knows *now*!" Cody shot off the bed, the momentum forcing the girls to the side, righting themselves. "He ran away. If he'd been fucking possessed, he wouldn't have run. Where the fuck did he go?"

"I mean, she probably deserved it. Besides, she attacked him first…" Michelle started before Cody stepped up into her face. The veins in his neck popped, his hands balled into fists.

"Cody!" Dylan shouted.

"None of us fucking deserve this. Don't you see? Don't you fucking see? He set this all up! And we're next!"

"Why would he kill us?" Dylan asked, following Cody around the room as he threw open the bathroom doors. Sanjeev couldn't be in there, she knew. He'd be a fool to hide there. "Look, what Michelle meant–I mean, she didn't mean, but–"

"Yes, I did. If I were him, I would've strangled that bitch ages ago."

"Michelle!" It was Ro who chastised her this time.

But Michelle didn't care. "I don't think he's after us. Look, we couldn't hear what he said then, but isn't it possible that he just snapped? Hell, look at you now."

Dylan got another good look at Cody.

They were all sleep-deprived.

All scared.

All verging on manic.

Maybe he wasn't verging anymore. He looked like he could kill. Like any one of them could be next.

"I'm going to tear this place apart." Cody stormed out of the bathroom and yanked open the door to the bedroom. "Do you hear that, Sanjeev?" he shouted to the silent villa. "I'm going to find you! And when I do…when I do…" The threat died on his lips. "*Shit!*" he swore, then slammed the door shut again so hard that it rattled the walls.

Olivia rocked herself back and forth, clutching her legs to her chest, muttering nonsense. She was worse than useless now. She was a liability.

Ro, too, seemed more entrenched with her desire to write down notes–real notes this time.

As if this wouldn't be scarred into their brains until the day they died.

Michelle threw herself back onto the large bed and inspected her nails.

Dylan stood, waiting, watching them all.

"He could have fled," Dylan said, keeping her voice even. It was harder than she thought, staring at a wild man double the size of her. She considered herself the second strongest of the villa, even when more of them had been alive. She'd held her own far better than Cody on their hike together.

And still…he terrified her.

Cody's chest heaved up and down. His arm shot out, and he grabbed his protein shake from the side of the bed. There was no way it was still good, and yet he pumped it up and down. The roller ball shook, rattled, and mixed the contents. He chugged until the drink was vertical, no more clumps coming out. "I'm going down to the kitchen. I need food."

"And to kill a motherfucker?" Michelle prompted.

"If I so much as get a whiff of his fucking perfume…"

THE HUNT

SIXTY-ONE

In their twisted game of hide and seek, Michelle expected they would have found Sanjeev sooner. Their party hunted him down, five against one.

Not that the odds had helped any of the others...

With each new room they entered, Cody's haunting threats forced their way forward...If she were Sanjeev, Michelle would have stayed hidden, too.

As it were, the women shrank behind him. She was beginning to see Dylan's point. The way Cody's muscles clenched, the way his neck reddened and the vein at his temple throbbed with each husky shout. Her initial cheering of an eye for an eye might give Cody a taste for blood.

And if he caught that, none of them would stand a chance.

"Sanjeev!" the man shouted. Overly dramatic, like a superhero about to chase down the villain.

"Is he gonna start banging on his chest?" Michelle whispered, but it seemed all the other women sensed the danger, too. None laughed. Louder, she said, "I think we've searched everywhere. If he's run away, let him run. We have the proof. And if he's in the house, he's in one of the rooms with the bodies. Let him suffer the stench."

Dylan mumbled under her breath.

"Huh?" Michelle asked.

She cleared her throat. "One of the bodies…it's in the kitchen. We probably want to move her."

"Yeah, yeah, good idea." Cody snapped in her direction. "I'm getting hungry."

A sad fact of life, something every woman learns eventually–how to placate a man. If they gave him food, maybe he'd swallow his monster for a bit longer.

As much as Michelle hated to admit it, her stomach was growling, too. She thought that, given all the deaths, that part would wane. Humanity's insistence on survival was admirable. "Maybe some steak?" she suggested.

"I liked that ahi tuna," Ro piped up.

"I won't be able to do it like Lauren…but yeah. We can… make…something." Dylan's voice trailed off as Cody stared her down.

It didn't seem malicious. But it did seem…crazed. Eyes too wide, too intense. As if he was seconds away from envisioning the steak she could be cooking and rapidly morphing her into one giant, human-sized steak.

Michelle stepped in front of Dylan, gaze locked on Cody. "Why don't you be the big, strong man and move Sarah?"

The gentle prod was all it took. He turned on his heel, the group disappearing from what once was Michelle's room in a shuffling, single-file line. By the time the women exited, and Michelle secured the door closed, Cody had returned to the hallway with Sarah.

He held her up high, like a sacrifice, her body limp, head flopping back, feet dangling at the sides. Michelle watched, a growing disdain pulling her face into a scowl she couldn't hide. Ro wore a similar expression, and Michelle hated Cody even more for making them allies.

He set the limp body down on the couch like an altar. It sat in front of the sliding glass doors, pushed in front to block whatever invisible assailant might come for them, and now bore the weight of Sarah's dead body as the focal point of the disheveled dining room.

Turning around, he clapped his hands together, as if wiping them clean, and asked, "Time for food?"

SIXTY-TWO

Ro hated mysteries she couldn't solve. Thrillers, cozies, even romantic suspense had always been her favorite genres to read because she loved getting to play detective. To discover alongside the characters the whodunnit, or the whydunnit, or the howdunnit.

And though there were so many mysteries on this island—Who invited them there? Why? Who was killing them? Why?—there was one that bothered her most. Where had Sanjeev gone? He'd seemingly vanished, but they'd double- and triple-checked every entrance and exit.

So, then where could he have disappeared to?

If she could solve this, maybe...maybe she could solve the rest of it.

She retraced their steps, literally, on the staircase. He'd been with them until that moment. He'd disappeared between the time it took them to follow the trail of the broken porcelain into the kitchen. It took a few minutes, at least, after the shock of discovering Sarah's body for them all to realize Sanjeev was gone.

At the time, she'd thought he'd left to cry. Or puke. Or scream somewhere. Now, of course...

She took another step down. Surely, they would have noticed if he'd fled upstairs. They would have heard his running.

No doubt he'd gone into one of the rooms near the kitchen.

Since the thought of going into Ian's room where his body decomposed made her gag, she chose Michelle's. She turned the doorknob first, letting it loose of the lock. Then, stepping back, she kicked it open, wide enough so she could duck out of the way.

No one was inside. Or no one she could yet see.

"Sanjeev?"

In the movies, murderers and ghouls and demons always hid in the closet, waiting for the unsuspecting protagonist. Either that or…

She dropped to her hands and knees and glanced under the bed.

"How much of a cliché can you be?" she hissed.

Pathetic they hadn't thought to check under the beds first.

"People are going to think I made this up."

Instead of punching him–as Cody might have done–or screaming for back-up, as Olivia might have–she simply jotted down notes in her phone. Glancing at her watch, she added a timestamp. "Do I have permission to get this on camera?"

He didn't respond. For a moment, she wondered if he was dead, too. Tears had streaked his cheeks, so many that they'd made their way past his layers of primer and foundation. When she ducked back under, he blinked.

Only dead in the eyes, then.

"I'm taking that as a yes," she said, pulling her phone out of her back pocket and standing, panning up first, then down, down, down, until it, too, saw under the bed. "This is where I found him. The murderer. Sarah's murderer. How long have you been here?"

No response.

"Do you want to come out on your own or do I need to get Cody to help you?"

For the first time, Sanjeev made a sound. An almost imperceptible exhale, a half sigh. Seemingly resigned, he pulled himself out, a little bit at a time.

All the while, she filmed. It occurred to her–only as he was nearly halfway out from under the bed, staring up at her with those dead eyes–that she could be next on his list.

"Dylan! Cody! I found him. *Cody!*" She shouted at the top of her lungs.

Sanjeev sighed again. He didn't run. He didn't stand. He sat on the ground, free from the bed, and waited for the storm of stomps to slow to a halt in front of the door.

"You *fucker*–"

"Cody–" Dylan called from behind him.

A small scramble followed for who would get to him first, which Ro watched from her phone screen, making sure she tracked every movement. She could almost imagine herself, five years from now, commentating on the documentary that used her own footage.

"Cody," a sweet voice said.

Olivia had chosen a perfect time–in view of the camera–to finally speak. She put herself between him and Sanjeev, while Dylan rushed forward, ushering the criminal to his feet.

Cody stopped charging forward.

"We need to tie him up. Question him," Dylan suggested.

Sanjeev still said nothing.

"*Huh?*" Cody said. "We're going to make you speak for yourself! Yeah! You're going to explain why the hell you brought all of us here and what the fuck you're planning."

But Sanjeev just shook his head.

Ro understood people only through lifelong study, mostly from afar, more often from the page. Rarely–as with Ivy–

up close. Personal. Even pretending that it aided her writing couldn't ease the hurt of those betrayals.

Still, something in his face, in his confusion that imperceptibly pushed through the blank nothingness, made Ro believe him. He had no idea what Cody was talking about. He didn't bring them here.

Ro dropped her phone.

But if he didn't…then who did?

SIXTY-THREE

"I don't know," Sanjeev repeated. It became his mantra. He didn't know. He really, truly, *honestly* didn't know.

One moment they were standing in the kitchen, talking. It was normal. Their normal, at least. Nothing strange, nothing out of place.

The next moment he was staring down at her face, her neck purple under his palms, his hands tight from squeezing.

He rolled off her, still not understanding. It had to have been a dream. *Right?* It had to have. Any moment he was going to wake up in that giant bed with Sarah rolling into his back. She'd ask for another massage. Or ask him to tell her the story of how they met again.

He didn't know how *that* wasn't reality.

How was he sitting in the closet of Michelle's room, tied up, his pants soiled, his stomach growling despite food being the last thing he was thinking about?

"C'mon! You do. Why? Just tell us why?"

Sanjeev shook his head. He'd already cried so much. When reality set in, pain came with it. The pain and the guilt. The guilt that finally, finally, finally...he was *free*.

"I don't know," he said.

From the other corner, Dylan whispered, "I don't think he did it."

"Shut up!" Cody burst.

"Let him at least change. What, we're now going to be known for torturing the guy? What with all this documenting going on?"

"Questioning a killer doesn't make us bad," Ro said.

Cody pointed in her direction. As if to say, "Exactly."

"I'm just saying, he couldn't have done all of this. He killed Sarah, yeah, but what about Nick? I've gone over it and over it in my head. He was with us the whole time. And Lauren? We were hiking! There's no way–"

"No, no," Ro said. "That was Nick. Nick killed Lauren and then, out of guilt, killed himself."

"That man didn't know guilt," Michelle chimed in. "Something's wrong, but I don't think it's what you're saying either."

"Can we please focus?" Cody shouted. But his yelling had clearly worn thin with the girls. They cared less for his outbursts than Sanjeev's sad, pathetic answers.

"Ivy overdosed before we even got here." Michelle held out a finger, as if checking it off. "Sad, not surprising. Then Ian..." She held out two fingers. "I mean, Ian fell. Right? Or did we decide someone pushed him after all?"

"Not me," Ro said. "The hoodie only showed up after."

Funny how she distanced herself from it now. Calling it 'the hoodie' as if it were some masked vigilante Other.

Not that Sanjeev could talk. He wouldn't talk. Nothing except, "I don't know" had come from him.

He took in a shaky breath, pulling attention. But it was for nothing. Off his lips another, "I don't know. But I promise...I didn't...hurt," he faltered on the word. They'd been throwing it around so casually. Killed. Murdered. *Unalived*..not even ironically. "I didn't hurt anyone else."

They stared at him. And stared at him.

Even Olivia, as she ripped off her freshly painted nails, the polish having not cured completely, filling the closet with a tinge of sharp acetone. The polish shavings hit the ground. One chip after another.

“Let’s see,” Dylan said. “Wait, can I have a page?”

Ro side-eyed her before ripping one out at the back of her notebook. “I’m guessing you want a pen, too?”

Dylan was too sweet when she answered, “Please.”

Ro handed it over, everyone watching as Dylan walked to the wall, set the pen to the page. She wrote down a series of names: Sarah, then Nick, then Lauren, Ian, and Ivy. With a long arrow connected to Sarah, she wrote Sanjeev.

With another arrow from Lauren, she wrote Nick.

“I don’t think he did it,” a timid voice in their group said.

Every time Olivia spoke up, it was like a hard reset for the group. No one knew quite how to respond. They all paused.

“I don’t either,” Dylan said, recovering first, using a similar placating voice to the one she’d given Ro. Maybe the one she’d dawned all trip–all her experience saying “Yes, I’ll get that for you” and “Enjoy” over and over again.

Olivia didn’t say anything more. She chipped away at the final bit of polish on her pinky instead.

“Did you kill him?” Michelle asked.

Sanjeev shifted slightly in his seat. The rope they’d found and bound him with was uncomfortably tight.

Michelle had asked the question, but she wasn’t staring at him. She was staring at Cody. Before the man could even respond, she continued. “You had some weird beef with him. Nick said he was blackmailing both of you.”

“You think I’d kill Ian?”

“I don’t know, you were threatening to kill Sanjeev.”

“Because he killed Sarah!”

"And Nick killed Lauren!"

It was amazing how quickly reasonable points transitioned to shouts and threats. It didn't matter if it was under life-altering circumstances or at that very first brand party Sanjeev was lucky enough to score an invite to. Inevitably, enough alcohol would be involved, tensions would rise, rivalries mixed poorly with the desire to pretend that no one could replace them.

Everyone was replaceable.

Especially when they were dead.

Despite the ruckus and the shouts and threats, Sanjeev could barely hear any of it over the sound of his own heartbeat pulsing in his ears. It thumped erratically, way too quickly. He'd killed her. *Why, why, why?*

He knew why.

Why, why, why?

But he answered himself the same way he did everyone else. "I don't know."

SIXTY-FOUR

"He's breathing."

Ro dropped her hand from just under Sanjeev's nose. They'd loosened his ties after he slumped over, passing out, interrupting their fight.

Well, only after Olivia started screaming her head off, assuming another one of them had died.

Not that Ro could blame her. The actress wasn't being dramatic this time. It seemed to make as much sense as any of the rest of this trip.

They each had their own theories. And the more Michelle talked, the more Cody argued. The more heat crept up his neck and to his cheeks, the more Dylan stood off and watched. The more Olivia picked at her skin–the more any of them did anything, the less Ro trusted any of them.

She could imagine their thoughts now, "Rich, coming from her. Perhaps the biggest liar of all."

Ro didn't trust Michelle. Hadn't trusted Michelle in years. Honestly, hadn't known what to make of her. She shifted with the wind, chasing trends instead of setting them.

Cody's hotheadedness could no longer be extinguished. She'd rarely seen that side of him, even in the old days, but he often talked about how he'd experienced it before when he'd been juicing.

She never trusted the silent types, so Dylan was out as well.

And Olivia…well Olivia had become just the type of crazy to strangle someone and not realize what she'd done. She could be the next one.

"We should get him some water," Dylan said, not moving.

"Someone should," Michelle agreed.

It took a beat for Dylan's head to turn, catching the meaning. She looked toward Cody, though he was the last one willing to help Sanjeev.

Ro would be the brave one to say the quiet part out loud. "I'm not sure I trust you," she said. "I'm not sure I trust *any* of you, actually."

She gave Cody a little shrug, noncommittal. As much to signify that she didn't mean it for him as to keep him on her good side. Of the people to kill, hopefully he'd go for one of the others first. Ro knew she wasn't as fast as Dylan, but she could probably outrun Olivia and maybe Michelle.

"None of us?" Dylan asked.

"I can't believe I'm saying this," Michelle began, "but I agree with Ro."

Cody shrugged. Clearly, he felt no one else here was a danger to him.

Olivia gnawed the side of her thumb.

"Fine," Dylan said. "Fine, I'll go by myself."

"So, we're free to leave? We can all go do…whatever we want?" Michelle asked.

"Just don't open the blockades."

Michelle nodded her agreement. Ro waited for the others. They gave it.

"If we're lucky, we've got enough people looking for us that we'll still have food by the time we're discovered," Ro said.

"We may not have received a shipment for lobster, but we've got plenty of food," Dylan said. "That you're all going to have to make for yourselves. If we're not a team anymore..."

Of course, the good girl would give them one last chance.

"I can make my own grilled cheese," Ro said.

"Fine," said Dylan.

"Fine," said Ro.

"Fine," said Michelle.

"Fine," said Cody.

Olivia gnawed some more.

THE FIGHT

SIXTY-FIVE

They'd been on the island for eight days.

Dylan paced inside their villa, peeking her head out windows every so often, confirming that nothing had changed other than another random, fallen branch.

The plane remained stagnant in the distance. The tide continued to roll. And Lauren's body remained where they pulled her from the beach.

Dylan found herself picking at the polish she'd applied, copying Olivia's movements, worrying how soon she'd be muttering instructions to herself.

The days seemed to grow longer. And yet it felt like time was running out.

SIXTY-SIX

Cody knew it was just a matter of hours now, maybe days, maximum a week. So, he continued to film. He spent most of his time in the gym. When not in the gym, he walked through to the kitchen, greeting Dylan only with a nod, and stuffed his face with whatever cold cuts he could find.

Then he returned, pounding his own protein shake mix, chugging the fake Excelsior. He always told his viewers, his subscribers, his adoring fans who came out and supported him at each triathlon, every lifting meet, that nothing should ever get in the way of training.

Now he was living proof of that.

SIXTY-SEVEN

The back of Olivia's hands bled as she dug into her skin and tore it off in strips. It's the only thing she could do besides curl over, clutching her stomach, the days passing through chants of time.

218 days, 14 hours, and 3 minutes to go.

SIXTY-EIGHT

Ro spent her time the way she had before: filming solo shots of her pretending to write. Videos were more about the representation of action than the reality of it. It would look pretty in the eventual documentary. That's what mattered.

Only when she'd finished filming on her bed did she think to go to the library, the perfect next spot.

SIXTY-NINE

Sanjeev remained tied and bound, eating only when Dylan deigned to greet him with leftovers. He tried begging for his freedom, but she never said anything. Just spoon-fed him meals, then would leave.

It was strange how quickly his fears had morphed. The discovery first was an immediate threat. That passed, and then the sinking realization, the one that ached in his very bones. It had been harder to process, going through the stages of grief. Grieving the friend he thought he once had. Grieving the friend he'd murdered.

He could think of the word now. *Murder.* With his own hands. They told him they'd caught it all on camera. But even as his own memories returned, it was as if he were watching himself from above, not a thought entering his mind.

His new worries were about what would happen after they were rescued. Or if. *If* they were rescued, what would happen to him? He could plead insanity. Anyone could see that this island–this brand trip–had driven him mad. Temporarily.

Maybe permanently.

SEVENTY

Michelle quickly grew bored. She'd filmed. She'd posed. She'd waited for each and every device to charge. She even took the time to edit her footage now, all the different horizontal and vertical videos she could.

Then she waited for everything to charge again.

She spoke to anyone she saw, but none of them gave much back. They'd all spent more than enough time together at this point. And still they had a bit more time to go…

SEVENTY-ONE

Dylan stopped when she heard the squeak. She glanced down, hands sudsy, fingers pruning, cleaning the same glass for a fourth time. She sighed, staring out the window toward the beach. The rolling waves. Again. Receding. Again. Coming in. Again.

She turned on the faucet, rinsed off the glass, her hands, and wiped them on her linen pants. Who cared anymore?

Glancing around the domain she'd inherited, she'd turned over the kitchen, restoring it to its former glory. As if it were unchanged by what happened this week.

It was the only thing unchanged.

She took another deep breath. She needed to get out of here, needed all of this to hurry up.

Dylan gave herself a silent pep talk. The door swung shut behind her, and she hurried before the momentum could swirl the stench from Ian's room toward her. She turned up the stairs as her stomach roiled.

"Hey," she said, knocking on the open gym door with the back of her knuckles. Here the horse mats carried a faint, old leather scent, along with whatever disinfectant spray Cody once used when he pretended he would share the space.

Cody waited to respond until he finished his chest press. His "Hey" coming with a gasp of exertion. "What's up?"

Now she needed a reason to talk. As if they'd all staked claims on spaces and were unwelcome invaders. Her eyes scanned the room–his multi-camera set-up still in action, positioned all around the gym, reflecting off the mirrors.

In the corner sat Cody's shirt, about twenty water bottles–half empty–and an equal number of cans of fake Excelsior. His own protein powder sat beside it, unlabeled, but with the familiar imprint on the top.

"I'm thinking of leaving–of trying again. Climbing to the top of that hill, checking out the house."

Cody responded with more heavy breathing. He put his hands on either side of his hips, his chest moving up and down as he stared at her in silence.

"Do you want to..."

"Why, Dylan?"

"Don't you want to get out of here?"

"Help is coming," he said.

She mimicked him, hands on her hips. "How do you know? Did you get reception?"

"It's been past the time we were meant to return. And people love us. They'll be looking for us."

He didn't say who, exactly, loved them. Instead, he walked over to one of his cameras and turned it off. "Timelapse," he said, by way of explanation, but Dylan didn't care.

"And what if they can't find us?"

"We're not in a fucking cave," he said, reaching down and picking up his shake. He scooped another spoonful of protein powder and poured the energy drink on top.

Dylan eyed him warily, barely able to imagine the texture–not to mention the taste.

"New flavor?" she asked, watching his grimace.

"Yeah," he said. Then, looking directly into the mirror–a camera shooting at its reflection–he said, "It tastes incredible. Best yet. You can't even tell that it's protein powder. It tastes more like a birthday cake, you know?" He pumped his drink back and forth, the shaker ball working overtime to destroy the clumps Dylan could see still caking the bottom. "My favorite so far."

"Not a high bar."

"You don't have to be a bitch," he said.

"I'm not being one," she stood up straight, dropping her arms. "Sorry. Look, I'm just…I'm nervous."

"Want a sip?" Cody said, clearly ignoring her feelings. He stepped close–too close–and Dylan took a half step back.

"Has it been FDA cleared?"

"Officially?"

"Cody."

"Dylan, c'mon. You're being a little bitch. Take a sip."

"I don't want a sip."

"Do it–for the camera. C'mon."

"No," she said, taking another step back, crossing her arms over her chest. She was only a few steps away from the exit, the waft from Ian's room and the thought of the clumpy protein powder curdling the breakfast in her stomach.

"Dammit, Dylan!" He said, throwing the shake against the wall to the side of her.

She could feel her blood run cold.

His own eyes seemed to register what he'd done, too late, as his chest heaved.

They stared at each other. And stared.

"What are you," she began, her voice quivering despite her best efforts, "'roiding out right now?"

"Don't you dare accuse me of that," he said, but the venom from before wasn't there.

She could see the mental calculations he was doing. How he'd either have to delete this or own up to it. How he was measuring what she might do.

"But it's true, isn't it?"

"Shut up," he said, walking away, retreating to his weights.

She could see his carefully manufactured facade fracturing just as all the rest of theirs had. There was no way a man could look like him without using *something*. "Why don't you–"

"Just leave, okay?" He said, his chest rapidly rising and falling, rising and falling. He blinked at her a few times, shaking his head, bringing a hand up to massage his pec. "I'm not going with you."

"Fine," she said, keeping one eye on him as she retreated the final steps to the door. A red flush had crept up his chest and to his neck, up his face, almost a literal representation of the red he'd seen just moments before. Though in the light she could've sworn it was taking on an almost purplish tinge. She hesitated a moment, then took the additional step out, leaving the room and the sound of another angry clatter of something thrown or dropped or kicked behind.

She'd ask someone else.

THE FAVOR

SEVENTY-TWO

Michelle kept her camera slung around her arm. She'd taken enough B-roll to last her a lifetime. If she couldn't get a voiceover done in the next couple of hours, she wasn't good at her job anymore.

There'd been a slight question if she ever had been.

Or if she just got lucky.

Right place, right time, right look.

But wasn't that true for all of them? That luck played a bigger factor in their meteoric rise than anything else.

Sure, they had to be personable. And pretty. You could get away with making certain aesthetic choices, but only if you were still, under it all, classically good-looking. You had to have some kind of idea of what people wanted to watch, and enough camera know-how to make that happen.

But those skills were small in the grand scheme.

And she still had all of those. And more. She was more skilled now–at so many more things, and it didn't seem to matter. It didn't translate into more views, more subscribers, more money.

She'd nose-dived off the cliff, only managing to see a minuscule peak after all the valleys. The algorithm gods would still sometimes bestow success upon her, but never at the same height. She understood they never would again. Although–she thought, as she closed the door to her room–she still knew one man at the top of his game. Someone who hadn't yet seen the basin, it seemed.

Though maybe he was feeling that now. That it would be all downhill from here.

An interesting plight from someone who'd not yet experienced it. She had so many questions for him, but that would have to wait. She set up her tripod in front of her portrait, extending it high enough so that she could stand, the oil replica of her face nearly at the same height as her. She screwed in her DSLR and flipped the viewfinder, making sure she had the framing right and it wasn't lopsided.

She took a step back. "Alright, it's Day 9 here and I'm starting to go a little stir crazy. For the future philosophers who are wondering..." she paused, trying to think of where she wanted to go with this. "Scratch that. For the documentarians, we're bored as hell. I didn't know I could feel bored after everything that's happened. But I'm bored. I'm waiting. When the hell is anyone else going to show up and find us? I'm starting to have conversations with myself," she threw a thumb in the direction of the portrait. "Best company here. But even that's starting to bore me. *I'm* starting to bore me!"

She sighed dramatically. "At this point, I'm halfway to doing what Sarah–may she rest exactly where she belongs–accused me of. I'm gonna start pranking people. Sneaking up on them. Something! Should we go check on them?" She turned to look at her portrait and pretended to nod in response. "Alright, yeah, let's do that. Let's go check on the Isle de Cairn survivors," she stepped forward, pulling her hand back like a wound toy, a string forcing it to spring forward to cover the camera's view.

The lens smothered in darkness, she used her other hand to click the recording off. An old habit from a forgotten time when everyone did it. When it was novel and fun. When she had been too.

She slipped the DSLR's strap around her shoulder and went on the search for Olivia.

Michelle didn't bother knocking on the door. Only because she was certain Olivia would be in the same place as last time. And she was right. The actress lay in bed, clutching her stomach, muttering to herself, with her eyes closed.

"Need more pain meds?"

Olivia nodded, the muttering pausing only long enough for her to sit up, grab the water by her bedside, and wait for help.

Michelle plopped onto the bed, dumping out half the contents of her tote bag. Extra camera batteries, another, smaller camera, some charging cords, and a couple of pill bottles.

"This one," Michelle said, pushing the white container toward her. "Ibuprofen. The other's birth control."

But Olivia didn't take the pills immediately, her eyes drawn to something else. Michelle looked down at the pile, to the side, to the gleaming knife that stuck halfway out of her bag.

"Protection," Michelle explained with a wave of her hand. "Not that I think Sanjeev is going to get free or anything or that Cody's going to go into a rage again or some masked menace is gonna show up, but you never know, right?"

Olivia's eyes widened, as if one of those three possibilities hadn't been something she'd imagined before. Her arm shot out as she grabbed the pills and dumped four into her hand, swallowed and washed them down with water, then returned to her muttering.

Michelle wasn't sure what the right question was to get her lucid again.

Sometimes it seemed random, a sudden spurring.

"What's that mean?" Michelle asked.

But Olivia just continued her countdown. "Two-hundred seventeen days, seven hours, four minutes."

SEVENTY-THREE

"What are you most excited to do off the island?" Michelle asked. Her seventh or eighth question.

But Olivia couldn't even think of that yet. They weren't saved. She wasn't safe. She only had 217 days, 6 hours, and 58 minutes. She needed to make it. The longer they stayed here, the less sure she was she'd see her twenty-eighth year.

"Do you prefer oranges or grapes?"

Both too easy to choke on.

"I'm thinking of shaving my hair off, but I'm worried my head is weirdly shaped. I did the big chop ages ago, but kinda want to see it bald now, you know?"

Olivia tilted her head to the side, trying to imagine it. Michelle was so beautiful, she could pull it off. Something not everyone was lucky to say. Olivia could get alopecia or cancer and only find out later that she too had a weirdly shaped head. Alopecia wouldn't kill her. Cancer. Cancer would kill her. It would strip her of her hair and so many other things. What if she had it now? Could she wait 217 days, 6 hours, and 57 minutes until then? Would she have to have chemo first?

"When did you first move to L.A.?" Michelle asked.

A different number. A different time. "Eight years ago."

"Oh wow, you've been out there a while."

Olivia shrugged, digging her nails further into her stomach. It took so long for the medicine to work. Maybe she was making it worse. Her mind was playing tricks on her. The mind and body were connected so powerfully, she was thinking herself sick. But she couldn't stop. Could she think herself into an early death too?

217 days, 6 hours, 56 minutes.

"You know, Ivy once told me a rumor..." Michelle stopped, then shook her head.

"Tell me," Olivia said.

"Well, it's about you."

"About me?"

Michelle nodded.

Olivia studied her face, at the wide-eyed look, everything else blank. What she wouldn't give to be able to master that. The way Michelle gave nothing away. Maybe there were no thoughts moving in that pretty head, the thing people so often accused Olivia of.

"What did Ivy say?"

"Something about when you first came to L.A.," Michelle shrugged. "Something about helping other girls or bringing other girls or..." she trailed off, tilting her head to the side, as if she were trying to remember.

Olivia's mind trailed off too, circling back around, to the place it always ended up. "Two-hundred seventeen days, six hours, fifty-four minutes."

"Actually, I think it's two minutes and twenty seconds."

Olivia looked at her, feeling the effects of her Botox wearing off, her brows pinching together. "Huh?"

"My cousin's friend came to L.A. around the same time as you. Just a couple of months after. Her name was Cindy."

Olivia waited to hear more.

"Do you know her? Cindy Reynolds? Ran in similar circles as you."

Olivia shook her head, shrugging a little. She'd never been good with names. Even when memorizing lines, it was the part that tripped her up. Numbers, dates–she was good with those. But names eluded her.

Michelle sat up a little, crossing her legs. "Cindy," she repeated. "She was really pretty. Had big dreams of being a star. I used to live in L.A., you know. Way back when. I told her she could crash on my couch. The paychecks and ad revenue had just started becoming a regular thing, something I could rely on, and I was able to buy a nice place–well, nice at the time." She sighed. "Cindy refused, though. Wanted to make it out on her own. Told me she had a great idea to make it happen. A girl she knew was going to help her get into acting. Said her name was Gemma Inge."

Olivia didn't dare move a muscle, her attention rapt for the first time in days.

Michelle cleared her throat, shifting again, leaning her arm and weight against her bag. "So, my cousin's friend–*my* friend, too–Cindy, she meets up with this girl, Gemma. And that girl takes care of her. Or that's what Cindy thinks. Gets her a hook-up with a music executive, promises she can be a video girl, that kinda thing. Only they want more from Cindy than that, you know? Apparently, they wanted her to 'prove her worth.' That meant doing some stuff for free. Showing her skills. Said she felt alright about it cause the girl was there, too." She paused and glanced at Olivia. "You heard anything about this?"

A lump formed in Olivia's throat, one she couldn't quite swallow. As if the pills had come back up, stagnating there.

"All that…it ruined her. Cindy. I watched her…I watched her disappear. She was in L.A., you know, but she wasn't? She never told me what happened. Never confided in me, but the light was gone. I can only assume…" She trailed off. Then her gaze sharpened. "Well, unless you got something you wanna tell me?"

Olivia shook her head, the foreboding sense of dread returning with a vengeance.

"Nothing? Nothing at all? How 'bout when you changed your name?"

Olivia just kept shaking her head and shaking her head and shaking her head, only stopping as she spotted the gleaming knife hurtling toward her a second too late.

Michelle shifted, her hand wrapped around the hilt, and Olivia knew, as the blade impaled through her neck, that there would be no more days, or hours, or minutes.

Her time was up.

THE VENDETTA

SEVENTY-FOUR

Dylan passed room after room. Empty, empty, empty. Some because their inhabitants were dead. Others–like Ro–must be elsewhere.

She stopped her search at the edge of the library, a spot she hadn't been since before the other influencers showed up. Pages turned quickly in the distance, as if ruffled by the breeze from the open window. Dylan could almost imagine Ro pretending to read instead of write.

"Hey," she said, stepping into the library. A faint slam–maybe a closing of another book–came from the other side of the room, hidden by aisles and aisles of shelves. But where Dylan expected to see Ro, there was no one. Only comfy-looking chairs, the large, open window, and a circular table. On top it sat a stack of books, each penned by Rowena Dashwood: three novels and two nonfiction, self-help books filled with interviews and inspirational quotes and general life advice, which Dylan found absurd given the Ro she knew, the way she talked, thought, acted, and generally lived her life.

She'd known Ro for years. Served her for most of them. With lots of celebrities–influencers, included–that she met, they started out humble. A few started out awful and got better, after the voracious need to prove themselves waned.

But most that were horrible, in her experience, didn't start that way. Not at the brand events Lauren and Nick catered. Those people were nice until the next event, when they managed to get just that little bit more popular, an extra touch of fame seeming to impact their ego first, their wallet next.

Ro was one of those. The "alright" turned "terrible" with every new dinner, every new launch, every premiere and party and panel. Dismissive and rude, condescending and vitriolic. To the people who deserved it least. Those trying to help. Those hired to.

"Hello?" Dylan tried again.

No response. Only minor shuffling and she could almost believe it was her imagination were this not exactly what Ro had done before. Snuck around, hiding for no obvious reason.

"Whatever," she muttered under her breath. She sank into one of the chairs, staring out at the ocean in the distance. At the hill even farther in the distance. At the roof of the house in the far-off distance. Hours and hours away. Her saving grace.

She sighed and looked back, steadying herself for the hike. Only then did she notice the invitation.

Or mock invitation.

It looked just like the ones Excelsior had sent all the others, only this scarlet note was smaller, thinner. More like a bookmark instead of a letter.

She leaned over and picked it up, twirling it in her hands.

The first death was her reputation. Enigmas never survived.

Dylan glanced at the stack of books. Rowena's first publication was missing. The one that contained the iconic quote, said by the protagonist, a barely tweaked caricature of Ivy.

She always wondered if that was when Ivy's Whisper started. If she built up her secret legacy, her reputation, in order to gain credibility when she said Ro copied and stole from others.

Maybe that motivation morphed over time, as all good intentions were wont to do when fame followed.

Dylan stood, bookmark invitation in hand, as she strolled along the aisles of books until she found the row labeled *D - G*. Her eyes scanned over fiction and nonfiction, genre and literary, everything in between until she arrived at the missing stack where all of Ro's books should have been. The one based, however inappropriately, on Ivy's own life and Ro's other friends, was missing, too.

She stared at the books until all the spines seemed to blur together. She blinked back to focus, before walking over to where the *S*'s would be. With her finger, she traced past Sachar, Sambury, Shakespeare, and Stiefvater until she reached where Ivy Strohl might have been.

And there sat Rowena Dashwood's first book.

A creak sounded on the floor.

Dylan shifted her weight, looking behind her, not sure where it had come from. It hadn't been her. "Hello?"

Nothing. No response. And yet, Dylan couldn't shake the feeling that Ro was there, hiding, crouching amongst the shelves, waiting for…something. Was Ro studying her? Inspecting up close, like she had Ian's dead body? Did she enjoy putting people on edge? Seeing them squirm?

Dylan turned back to the books, repeating under her breath the quote on the invitation. "The first death was her reputation. Enigmas never survived." Dylan never bothered reading the book. She'd briefly scanned Goodreads at the time. The ass-kissing, and somehow worse critiques for the sake of being contrarian, had filled the reviews so fully that she closed out of it within a minute.

She still had time left. She couldn't leave just yet. Reaching up and grabbing the book, she encountered a bit of resistance, as if the library had been packed too tightly.

Tugging harder, the book came free, but so did another object–a heavy string, almost a rope–that came with it.

She jumped out of the way of the teetering shelves seconds before the thundering crash of hundreds of books cascaded to the ground. Shelving falling onto more shelving, falling, falling, falling, a cacophony of chaos.

And then, a whine. Almost like an exhale. Just one.

Jaw dropped, Dylan inched forward slowly, surveying the damage with wide eyes. Each step got her closer to that final sound, almost a ghostly groan.

Underneath the flood of books and heavy shelving were a few tendrils of jet-black hair.

SEVENTY-FIVE

Sanjeev's head shot up, a crash rumbling the ceiling, the closet's chandelier shaking and jingling. What was above here? Was it an earthquake? Were there earthquakes on the island? A volcano? A terrible storm?

Nothing more. The multi-second racket gave way to silence. Sanjeev wrenched his arms against the rope, his wrists and forearms slick with anxious worry. Sweat rolled down but did nothing to help loosen the bindings. He shouted for help, but all that came out was mumbling, even to his own ears.

More sweat–or tears, maybe–trickled down his cheeks. His heart pounded against his chest.

A door outside the closet swung open. He couldn't breathe.

A screech and a blinding light, the darkness that swallowed him whole gave way to a figure. He blinked rapidly, Michelle slowly coming into view.

He sighed out, his head lolling back.

"What was that?" He tried to ask.

More mumbling.

"Okay, okay," she said. "I believe you. It's not you. You didn't do this. You didn't do that." She pointed up above her. She was whispering as she crouched inside the closet, turning the light on and slowly, silently closing the door. She tossed the bag from her shoulder to the side. "Should we investigate?"

He mumbled back.

"Oh, right, sorry," she said, stepping forward. "Count of two." On one, she ripped off the duct tape.

He yowled, and she slapped a hand over his mouth. He tried to swallow the pain.

"Sorry," she said again. "Look, I don't know how much time we have, but I think we need to get out of here."

Light glinted, blinding him as he realized that she wielded a kitchen knife. "Oh, thank god," he said, turning his head to follow her until she knelt behind him, working the blade like a saw through the rope at his feet. "Where will we go? What's the plan?"

"You'll change first," she said. "No offense."

Sanjeev's laugh felt more like a cry. "None taken."

"Then we'll…I don't know. I don't know." She stopped for a second, taking a breath. "This is going to take a while."

"That's okay," Sanjeev insisted. It didn't matter how long it took. One minute, one hour. He was going to be free. Of all the outcomes he'd managed to dream up, of all the possibilities, this hadn't been one.

"Distract me," she said, sitting back on her feet, coming into view for him. She was panting a little and wiped at her forehead.

"With what?"

She paused for a second, then her eyes settled back on the ropes below him, and she took in a deep breath. "Why you did it?" She prompted before getting back to work. "I think I deserve to hear that story, at least. Since I'm freeing you and all."

Were he not already so glued to one spot, Sanjeev would have frozen. He should have expected the question. As it was, he realized how he needed to view this. *Practice.*

He'd gone over and over and over it in his head. He'd had all the time in the world, since that was about all he could do. Think up what he'd tell his family. Her family. His friends. His community.

The eventual jury.

Or if he'd never say anything. In some scenarios, he fled. He somehow escaped this prison and ran. He'd have to look up which countries didn't allow extradition, but he could do it. He could leave and never come back.

A relief, in some ways.

But those scenarios eventually ended because it was only a relief if he could continue as he lived now. Would he be able to access his money? Once they realized what he'd done–they'd freeze his accounts. He'd make no more. Could a murderer–even one who'd been driven to it by temporary insanity–be *allowed* to keep working?

People had done worse and survived. But they'd been movie stars. Those deaths had been "accidental." Those rapes had been covered up. Could he afford to pay off the others to never say anything?

There were so few of them now, maybe he could get away with it.

"C'mon, Sanjeev," Michelle sat back, panting again. "I'm dying here. I need you to give me something."

"Sorry," he said, voice scratchy. "It's been a while since I've…talked to anyone."

"Why'd you do it? Why'd you kill her?" Michelle's big brown eyes bore into his. He turned away, breaking the gaze. This would be easier if she weren't looking at him.

"She was threatening me. My business. My livelihood. My *life*. And I think…" he began. "I just couldn't take it anymore. All these years of nitpicking, all the times she undermined me, all the episodes that were 'not her fault' and I defended her, rallied for her, rode for her. She never did it back, you know? And then...I don't know. I don't know," he shook his head. This wasn't how he'd practiced.

"Pent up rage?" She asked. He nodded. "I understand. I really do."

She leaned over so she could see his face. He dared look back, awaiting the judgment. But her gaze looked...pitying instead. Maybe he was projecting.

"And honestly? I'm surprised you didn't do it before."

He almost laughed.

"Seriously. I'm not trying to blow smoke up your ass. She was awful."

"Yeah," he said, but somehow, he couldn't fully agree. She was awful. But she could be wonderful, too. Sometimes. Occasionally. In rare, glittering moments.

"You know, this whole thing is so funny in some ways."

He looked down at her, and she shrugged.

"Not ha-ha funny," she corrected, shifting off her feet and onto her knees, slumping to the floor. "Did I ever tell you how much my mother loved you?"

Sanjeev glanced to his other side, the sawing continuing now. He rolled his wrists a little bit, tried to wiggle his ankles, but felt no freer than before.

How much time did they have?

Clearly, Michelle was going through it if she thought any of this was funny.

"No," he said. "That's very sweet, though. I'd love to meet her." He said it without really thinking. The same way he said it to every fan that came up to him, rehearsed once, regurgitated without meaning.

Once upon a time, the encounters meant something, but their importance dwindled. He still remembered the first. Now he was on the ten thousandth, and it was here, as he was tied up, with another influencer who'd come far before his time. And she was helping to free him.

Maybe Michelle was right. There was something a little funny there.

"Ah, well," she said. "She's buried in a grave, so that might be difficult."

"Oh." Sanjeev twisted again, trying to get a better look at her. "I'm so sorry."

"Yeah...yeah, we used to watch you together all the time. She couldn't really afford much when she was growing up. Couldn't really afford much when I was growing up, either. But by the time I hit it big, she'd advanced far enough and was willing to spend just a little, you know?" She smiled, as if remembering something. "And you were so great. Accessible makeup for those of us with deeper tones. Hard to find. Especially from influencers."

"Yeah," Sanjeev nodded, remembering the time himself.

All the brands would send him shit he couldn't use. He'd never say a bad word, but he would swatch it on his skin and let that do the talking.

"She even bought some of your old destashes." Michelle laughed a little. "Do you remember those?"

Sanjeev nodded, then added, "Yeah, yeah," in case she couldn't see. "Hey, do you need help? Do you want to try my wrists first, and then maybe I can take a turn?"

"No, I'm almost done here," she said. "Anyways, it was so strange when she started getting sick. None of the doctors could figure it out. All the tests would come back negative, but she just kept getting worse."

A pause. "But she'd still be smiling when I picked her up for her next appointment. Full face of glam, chatting it up with the nurses. They'd ask how she looked so good, and she'd say genetics and 'Skin by Sanjeev.'" She looked up from where she was working to look him in the eye. "When was the last time you used your powders? From that first launch?"

"Umm." Pounding returned to his ears, drowning out the sound of his own voice. "A while ago. Ages ago."

"Yeah, that makes sense," she said cooly. "It was old. Old and *toxic*."

A small crack echoed through the closet, the sound reverberating as the chair plunged forward. For half a second, Sanjeev caught himself with his foot, as one of the chair's wooden legs snapped. His balance off, unable to hold himself any longer, he fell to the ground. His head smacked against the cool marble, disorienting him enough that he almost thought–could almost have believed–that he saw knife marks through the wood.

He groaned, the pain coming only now.

"Oops," Michelle said.

A chill ran down Sanjeev's spine. Not from the cool marble that pressed against his cheek and neck, nor the pain that radiated through his temple, but from the way she'd said that "oops."

He sensed where her story was going. He knew he wouldn't like the ending.

"I actually have some of it. I brought it with me. The powders," she clarified. She sat in front of him, crossing her legs and setting the knife behind her. She reached over to her bag and pulled out the trays and tubs he remembered, and even a few he didn't.

"We would watch your videos," she continued, "as my mother became bedridden. As she was hooked up to tubes in the hospital. As she began the slow walk to the light. It was the one thing that brought her joy."

"I'm sorry."

Michelle gave a quiet *hmph* of acknowledgment.

"You know, the reports had already come out by then. I didn't realize that, though. You helped keep them real quiet. How'd you do that?"

The floor was slick now with his tears. The realization. All those hours he'd spent brainstorming. *Useless.* "I'm so, so sorry." It was all he could say. All he could try to do.

"Yeah," Michelle said. "You should be. The plus side," she reached into her bag and pulled out what looked like a gas mask, "is that if the reports were wrong–as you claimed–then you have nothing to worry about."

The sob choked him, unable to beg for his life one last time.

Michelle ripped one of her scarves off its hanger and dipped it into the powder before forcing the scarf into his open mouth. The tape roller screeched as she wrapped the adhesive around his head.

Sanjeev coughed and gagged, closing his eyes as she took his face powders and her knife and began cutting her way through the palette, sprinkling the product over his head, wafting it into his eyes, up his nose. Sanjeev's throat constricted–not yet from the poisons in the powder–but from how it caught in his sinuses, unable to breathe. He wouldn't die. Not immediately. Not yet.

"Is anyone here?!" The shout came, along with quick stomps, rattling the ceiling above.

He yelled for all he was worth, the sound muffled but enough that the stomps hurried, coming closer. Powder coated the floors, and Michelle tossed the plastic tubs behind him. She hooked her bag over her shoulder.

The knife she grabbed last. Reaching down onto the floor, she turned to look at Sanjeev. It scraped across the tile as she picked it up. With her other hand, she brought her finger to her mouth, placing it over where her lips might have been had the mask not covered them, silently shushing him.

He screamed again. Or tried.

The footsteps came closer. The door flew open.

He cried.

"Ro is dead!" Dylan shouted. "The bookshelves, they fell, they crushed–" she faltered. Her eyes widened, shifting back and forth from Michelle to him, him to Michelle.

"Help!" He shouted, though it came out as a panicked "*Hrmph!*" through the scarf over his mouth.

Dylan was frozen.

"Help, help, run!" he tried to say, to no avail.

The knife gleamed one final time before Michelle reached out and flicked off the closet light. Dylan stepped back as Michelle stepped forward. They repeated the dance–advancing and retreating–as the closet door closed behind them.

Darkness swallowed him whole.

THE BLOODBATH

SEVENTY-SIX

It was just the two of them.

Michelle ripped off her mask and tossed it to the side. "Ro's dead?"

Dylan nodded slowly. Sanjeev's shouts were muffled by the closet door and whatever Michelle had wrapped around his mouth. Dylan had last seen him at breakfast, looking terrible. On the floor, moments ago, he looked worse. *Much* worse.

From behind Michelle's back, she brandished a knife.

Dylan raised her hands up to her chest. "Michelle…" she started, but the weapon slashed through the air.

She kept her hands up, guarding her face, the blade splitting across her open palm. Dylan hissed, pulling back, staring down at the blood oozing out of her. "Shit," she cursed, stepping back, pulling her hand to her chest. She stared at Michelle, the seconds thumping in her ears. Waiting.

Waiting.

Michelle stepped forward, extending the knife out again. This time, she moved slowly.

Sanjeev was as good as dead.

Ro, too. Dylan had seen her. Skull crushed.

How fragile the human body was.

There was no doubt that Olivia, too, was gone. Maybe Cody. Sarah, and Nick, and Lauren, and Ian, and Ivy.

All dead.

Dead.

Dead.

Dead.

Michelle stepped forward once more. Light red tinged the edge of the once-clean blade. She pointed it at Dylan. Then, she flipped the blade around and held it out like an offering. "Your turn."

Dylan balled her wounded hand in a fist, reaching out for the handle with the other. "You didn't have to be so dramatic."

"I really, really did," Michelle argued. "Okay, what are you thinking? Over here, maybe?" She walked to the other side of the bathroom wall, where her towels hung to dry from days before. "Shallow. Like we practiced. A little spray."

"I know what to do," Dylan snapped. Then, at Michelle's cocked hip, she added, "Sorry, sorry. The stress of it all. It's getting to me."

"You can breathe. We're done, Dylan."

"Almost."

"Almost," Michelle agreed. "You ready?"

The knife–not unlike so many she'd used before–felt heavy in her hand. Like all the hours, days, weeks, months of planning were held within its hilt.

She took a deep breath and Michelle held her arm out, away from her body, and closed her eyes.

"One," Dylan counted. "Two. Three!"

She slashed up and to the right, finishing the stroke like a tennis shot. The blood sprayed in an arc, a little splashing onto the bathroom wall.

Michelle swallowed her pain and looked around. "Good," she said with a nod. "Good. I have some bandages in my bag."

"Should we do a little more first?"

"That depends. Is Cody dead?"

"He was pretty purple when I left," Dylan answered. "Short of breath. Honestly, I'm not even sure I needed to spike his protein powder. With how much he was drinking, all that creatine, *and* those energy drinks, it's amazing his heart didn't stop sooner."

Michelle stopped wrapping the bandage around Dylan's hand. "But is he six feet under, gone to meet his maker, swimming with the other fucking sharks? Is he *dead* dead?"

Dylan traced the room with her eyes. This room–and every single other–she'd helped to arrange an entire week before their esteemed guests descended upon the long-vacant property. Once belonging to some oligarch or another, it hadn't been touched in years. She cleaned it all. Hung the commissioned portraits. Displayed decorations and obtained the lavish requests as needed. Then Michelle flew her back to Miami, she took the next plane to LAX, and made the long trip again, this time in tow with Lauren and Nick. Ian was responsible for flying them to the island, and they'd all been impressed when they arrived at how well "Excelsior" had set them up, even though contact had been sparse.

Everything–save a rogue Sanjeev–had gone according to plan. If not Plan A, then B, or C, or D.

Now was the hardest part.

Dylan bit her lip, answering Michelle's question only by finding a spray bottle of chemical cleaner and nodding. They'd have to check.

Sanjeev's muffled cries faded into the background as they tiptoed out of the room. By the time they reached the end of the hall, only their own breathing could be heard.

"You go first, spray him, aim for the eyes, and then I'll jump out with the knife. Element of surprise."

"Speaking of surprise," Dylan crept up the stairs, keeping her voice to a whisper. "Ivy first?"

"Yeaaaaah," Michelle began. "What can I say? I was nervous. And she just made it too easy." A step creaked underfoot. "And Ro? She lasted ages. *Way* too long."

Dylan covered her mouth and plugged her nose to keep from snorting. Then, still whispering, "I can't believe I had to go pull the book to trigger it myself. I laid out *so* many clues."

It was ridiculous. All so *ridiculous*.

And yet, it had been what they'd subsisted on for the better part of a year and a half. Earlier even, if she counted the first time they truly talked, when Michelle stumbled into the Cancun kitchen and they'd spent all night chatting.

Funny in life how quickly you could connect with someone. How so many of them connected over the internet, over the versions of themselves they presented for consumption. Even "influencers" could fall victim to parasocial relationships.

And how quickly the velvet curtain could fall, mystery revealed, everyone somehow even more awful than they initially seemed.

At every subsequent event, they'd find each other. And they found their true selves.

When Dylan rose to her own fame and it was nothing like she'd hoped, when Michelle lost her friend, and her mom, when Ian crashed the plane with Dylan's cousin on board, when Cody hulked out and cornered Michelle in the bathroom, when Ro pillaged their personal lives for her own gain, sharing through character what Ivy hadn't shared in real life, when Sarah stole the last bit of hope Michelle's mom had.

Michelle joked about being the only ones left. Dylan joked that they could spike everyone's drinks. And during each event, the jokes morphed, changed, as they morphed and changed, and soon, the jokes weren't so funny.

They were serious.

They were real.

And their plan was formed.

If finding the perfect place took the longest, then writing the invitations had been the quickest. Dylan didn't know why Ro struggled so much. Coming up with calculated phrases to guarantee everyone would come had been the fun part.

"Dylan," Michelle whispered, after the two had been standing just outside the gym door for a moment too long. "You can do this."

"I can do this," she repeated. With a gulp and a wild battle cry, she launched into the room, fingers on the bottle's trigger.

There was no need to spray.

Cody Planks lay splayed on the floor of the room, eyes still open, as dead as Michelle desired.

They'd done it.

Ivy's spiked drink, silencing her–and Whisper–forever.

Ian as soon as he was no longer useful. Dylan had invited him up to the balcony and it took barely a nudge. She'd planned for far worse, far more, but he'd died instantly. A single, graceless fall.

The two of them had lured Lauren together, in the short interim between their hike and the group laying the chef to rest. Dylan and Michelle made sure that rest was forever, coaxing her to the beach, then submerging her under the water, Dylan at her shoulders, Michelle at her feet. Unspeaking, they returned to the villa, changed, and met the others with plenty of time to spare.

Nick had been an easy fall guy, planned from the beginning. Easier when Michelle wrote the letter and Dylan stashed it. No one paid attention to "the help," everyone happy to leave all the work in her hands. When she summoned him to the bathroom, he asked if she wanted to "get frisky," and it took everything in Dylan's power not to throw up before she could knock him unconscious.

Sarah had been right about one thing. Soon, they'd be discovered. No doubt their continued silence online meant people were already beginning to wonder, to investigate, to search. Sarah and Sanjeev's post had specified a *week*, and that was past. They'd needed to speed up the process.

So, they had.

Ro and Jesse and Gemma and Sanjeev.

They'd really *done* it.

A sharp, clattering behind her, and Dylan turned just in time to see Michelle raise the 10lb free weight into the air and scream as she smashed it against Cody's head.

Bits of brain matter exploded outward, littering the gym floor. His face and skull sunk inward, indistinguishable.

"That's for trying to fuck with me." Then, with another bash, more brain matter splattering, "And *that's* for all the other women you treated far worse."

Dylan looked at the only partner in any aspect of life she'd ever truly known, covered in blood and brains and gunk and sweat and grime.

She grinned.

They'd really fucking done it.

SEVENTY-SEVEN

"Looks like all my investments paid off," Michelle said, eyes locked on the rapidly decaying body of Sarah Pruski. She'd never recoup the hours or dollars or prayers her mom spent on this woman and her phony church, in the final, desperate year of her mother's life, but this would have to suffice.

She tried to burn the image into her memory.

Louder, Michelle spoke over her shoulder, still staring at the rotton preacher. "I'm only a little upset that one of us didn't get to kill her."

"Watching Sanjeev do it was better though." Dylan's reply came from a room away.

Michelle turned only as a crash echoed throughout the downstairs bathroom. When Dylan emerged, she was holding the knife and two strands of thick rope.

"What was the hardest part for you?" Michelle asked.

"Lifting him." Dylan panted. "So heavy."

"He'd been a dead weight long before that was literal." Dylan's smirk told her that whatever spell the Mercers had on her over the past week had lifted with their deaths. "Lauren?"

"Lauren was..." Dylan trailed off. Words never could explain the depths of an abusive relationship.

Michelle nodded. "I know." She clapped Dylan on the shoulder. "Now let's sow some chaos."

Dylan offered her the knife, and Michelle did the honors, slicing into her own skin then cutting off a chunk of Dylan's hair. They littered the floor with half-ripped, branded clothing, stained by their own blood, left smudged, red handprints along the walls, as if they were struggling, as if they were running away. They dripped blood through the main dining hall, the long hallway, back to Michelle's room, through the backdoor and across the tiled surface of the wrap-around pool and halfway to the ocean.

And then, they exhaled in relief.

Dylan sank into the sand, knees first, and fell onto her back. The earth cradled her. Moments passed, long enough for the clouds overhead to disappear onto the horizon, replaced by a new sky.

"C'mon." Kindness propelled Michelle now. They were so close. She offered her hand and, after a couple blinks, Dylan accepted. "Only a little more left to do."

They swept the outside first, trudging over sand and boardwalks as they removed all evidence of the Mercers' cameras. The bedrooms were next, where they took phones and DSLRs and GoPro's and deleted footage on a whim, skipping bits at a time. To keep anything from being recovered, they recorded over it, aiming them at the blank white wall opposite Sarah's body. Twenty cameras trained in the same direction, not a single thing of note in frame, counting the seconds until they outran their memory cards.

They deleted the recording of Sanjeev killing Sarah off Ro's computer. "No need to make a martyr of a miscreant."

"Just what her church would want."

And with their digital footprint erased from existence, all that remained was the physical. They destroyed each room even more, taking turns throwing lava lamps and handheld fans and even random cameras at the commissioned oil portraits. Some they tossed off balconies, others they floated in the pool, one they crashed over Ro's exposed foot, confirming the fallen books killed her.

Dead. Dead. *Dead.*

They were all dead.

Long may they rot.

As night fell and the sky cleared, giving way to a large gibbous moon and more stars than they could count, the two survivors and co-conspirators built a giant bonfire. As it roared to life, they threw in objects of the dead and damned, a last, cathartic goodbye.

They watched in silence, as flames licked at evidence, crackling and popping, until they melted into ash. With gloves on, they grabbed the remaining Excelsior and emptied the fake energy drink on top, dousing the fire and tossing the half-ripped cans aside.

They left everything else behind, hiking the five hours up the hilltop under light of the moon and stashed flashlights, where they had extra clothes, hair dye, scissors, glasses, two fake passports, and keys to another small boat to take them to another island.

After a lifetime spent making themselves over for the right audience, now they had to do it just one final time.

EPILOGUE

Lily Carroll was so close. *Achingly* close. The follower count ticked up, a new person for every second she livestreamed. Nearly 1,000,000. An echelon, a pinnacle. The number taunted her.

But she couldn't beg. Begging would be too obvious.

She bit her lip, reading the comments as they flew by, even with her subscriber-only chat mode turned on. 43,296 waiting for the update.

"Alright, alright, now that there's an entire stadium of y'all, I won't make you wait. It's been six months since the infamous Influencer Island murders, and there's been a new development. Settle in, Slaughter Stans, we're going to jump right in."

The trick was convincing nearly 1,000,000 people to care about her investigation into a new case. When the developments on this one slowed, would they follow her to the next?

"Turns out, we've got further evidence that Cody Platt–changed to Planks, I guess 'cause he was a gymbro asshat–*did* assault another former assistant. That makes two for him alone, so count 'em up and that's five, six, seven, eight, nine felonies spread between the lot of them, and I'm sure more will be uncovered."

The true-crime market was already so saturated, she needed to stand out. Be different. Be *better*.

"SolverSquad222–what up, SolverSquad? love the name–asks if I've heard anything about the supposed sighting of Michelle Monroe and Dylan Goddard in Montenegro. You know what? I did hear about that. And I heard..."

She paused. Dramatic effect. The comments soared. More comments meant better placement in the algorithm, which meant more eyes, which meant more money.

More, more, *more*.

She couldn't wait any longer. "Well, I'm going to be on Sam and Antoni's *Two Polish Bros and a Cold Case File*, and we'll for sure answer that then. But since y'all are my favorite people, I'll tell you here first. I don't believe the sighting."

It wasn't a lie. After weeks verging on months of nonstop research, Lily felt certain–Michelle and Dylan were dead. It took far too long for investigators to locate the exact island meant for their oasis. If, like Sanjeev, they'd been tied up somewhere, yet to be discovered, without food or water, then they still would have been four days too late. According to the autopsies, his was the final, official death.

But that wasn't *fun*. With half the other true crime influencers insisting they'd survived, she needed to make her own theory just as interesting, to keep the focus on *her*, to keep people coming back.

"And no, before you can ask–*before* you can ask, because I can see y'all asking in the chat–it's not just because JackTheTracker is the one who made the claim. Yes, we have beef, but I simply don't believe it. Their blood was found all over the fucking place, all their stuff was still at the villa, and we know at least Lauren's body was drowned. No doubt the other two were as well, and they'll wash up. Maybe soon, maybe never. No doubt in my mind. The question is still–who? Who did it? Was it a crazed stalker? Count those up, because that was what, four or five amongst them? Or was it a wayward Good Samaritan, if the felony count is anything to go by? A shared hysteria, a mass psychogenic illness? No, no, y'all know I don't believe that."

Time to pivot. Time to close out. Time to make bank off the backs of the deceased. Curiosity was a killer, and Lily was all too aware of that truth, even when she was only a fanatic and follower. When her voracious appetite could no longer be satisfied, when she'd devoured every true crime podcast and documentary and book, she became a content creator herself. To investigate. To learn. It had started so innocently.

"But if you can't get enough of the Influencer Island murders, and hey, who amongst us can? There's going to be so many of your favorite homicide heads going on a trip together." She clapped excitedly. "That's right! *Murder on the Orient Express* style. Not only will we be solving an actual mystery during the 72-hour trip across the country, courtesy of our friends, Sam and Antoni, we'll also be trying to solve as many cold cases as we can. Together."

Her follower count teetered on the edge of 999,987. She'd made thousands on this stream alone, on four hours of work, most of which she spent reading the Wikipedia of the crime aloud. But the money didn't matter. Not anymore. She needed something else.

"And yes, JackTheTracker will be there, too. So, if you want to see us make-up, or make-out, or maybe slice each other's throats, you know where to go. Link in the description, my Carollers, get your virtual tickets now!"

The dopamine flowed through as her followers surged to 1,000,098. No doubt Lauren and Nick, Sanjeev and Sarah, Ro, Cody, Olivia, Ivy and Ian, and even Michelle and Dylan–wherever they truly were–would be proud of her.

"That's gonna be it for this stream. I'm Lily Carroll, signing off. Until next time, thanks for watching!"

PRINT EXCLUSIVE BONUS CHAPTER

2 YEARS EARLIER

Phantom thumping pulsed between Michelle's ears, long after the intensity of the bass died. Overhead lights glared down as brand ambassadors waited for the influencers to get their final shots of the night–cute, if over-saturated, with half-empty tequila bottles propped in hand. The music festival was over, the party meandering elsewhere, already raging in bars along 6th Street.

She'd had a lot to drink. To enjoy what she could. To numb the pain. To move with a group whilst feeling so incredibly, utterly alone.

The music was the only thing keeping her from checking her phone. From seeing if there was an update from the coroner about her mother's strange illness. From the *silence.*

During her mom's decline, she'd stopped posting, stopped streaming, and–apparently–stopped mattering. To her fans, to her peers. Out of sight, out of mind. Now, no one surrounded her, clambering for a photo or promise of a potential collab.

Only one part of these events brought her comfort anymore. Michelle's eyes traced over the exclusive lounge, groups of influencers mixing and mingling, sharing trade secrets, trading shared secrets. Cody Planks bent down, whispering something in a young, up-and-coming lifestyle influencer's ear. The girl laughed, a little too loud, the tequila bottle in her hand far emptier than anyone else's.

Michelle spotted her favorite bartender finishing her closing shots with their brand ambassador, toasting her mixed beverage featuring the tequila company.

"That's a wrap. Perfect," the night's director said, and Michelle slunk away from the barrier where she'd been skulking. She kept a wide berth away from Cody Planks and away from the haughty laughter of Sarah Pruski and Sanjeev Singh.

They had a group surrounding them, hanging onto their every word.

Everyone was famous here. Or "internet famous." But Sanjeev had just attended his first Met Gala, and he was spilling the tea.

Michelle doubted any of it was real.

"Hey," she said, taking Dylan's extended hand and scaling the large step up to the bar-slash-DJ booth. The overhead speakers still warbled some pre-determined soundtrack, the noise masking their words, muffling those around them. "You done for the night?"

"Done!" Her friend exhaled out her exhaustion.

The phone attracted Dylan's hand as if it were a magnet, some unstoppable force, and the screen lit her face.

She cursed, blowing her bangs out of her eyes as the phone jingled, text after text after text coming through.

"The Mercers," Dylan said, the breathy excitement from before leaving her voice entirely. Only anxiety remained. "I think they're mad."

"Put your phone away," Michelle said, reaching out to take it, but Dylan stepped back.

"I can't. My cousin's supposed to be flying out here tonight on a redeye."

"Well, check your cousin's texts and then–"

Dylan's eyes grew wide. "Oh my god. Ian Fujii is her pilot."

"What?"

"Just announced. That'll be so fun."

Michelle missed that vigor. She tried to summon excitement for her friend–or her friend's cousin–but could only fall to a slump on the floor, resting her back and her head against the makeshift bar.

"Sorry, sorry," Dylan said as she crouched down, the frown back on her face. Even still, she couldn't put her phone away.

"Girl, don't apologize to me," Michelle said. "You should be apologizing to yourself."

"Sor–I know. I should. I just…fuck."

"Fuck?"

"Fuck!"

The bright screen flashed in front of Michelle's face, and she recognized that background, that font, that account, within half a second. Maybe a millisecond. *Whisper.*

"Those malicious, merciless, misogynistic *motherfuckers,*" she hissed.

The Mercers–in tandem–had decided to lean into a rumor about Dylan stealing their spot at the music festival. They complained in multiple comments online, not so subtly, and Whisper had picked it up, corralled all the vaguebooking and subtweeting, everything *but* tagging Dylan.

"Look at all these hate comments," Dylan said, her thumb scrolling through her mentions, the page never-ending, until a squeal of laughter and a wayward leg kicked the phone from her hands.

"Oops!" The poor new girl said, her hand holding her too-short dress down, as Cody Planks carried her, the two scattering away with half an apology and Cody's double-take in Michelle's direction.

Michelle rolled her eyes. "That's the only good thing he's ever done."

Dylan mimicked her pose, flopping fully onto the floor, her head against the bar. "Have you still been having that dream?"

Michelle narrowed her eyes, following Cody as he whisked the girl behind a column decorated with twinkling lights. "The one where I murder him? Yeah. Last night it was with one of his stupid exercise balls."

"Those rubber ones? They rebound!"

"Not in my dream," Michelle snorted.

"Okay, okay, what about with those lights? You could strangle him."

"I could learn judo just to put him in a chokehold."

They saw the shadow of Sarah Pruski before the woman herself, wandering over to the edge of the railing, looking into her phone instead of the glamor of the city. Over the music and chatter, they could just make out her repeating a Bible verse to the camera.

"I pray for her downfall." The disgust in Dylan's voice matched Michelle's own revulsion.

"I pray she falls down. Down, down, down. Over that railing. Or a mountain. With only cacti at the bottom. Like in a cartoon."

Dylan snorted. "Hopefully, she doesn't inflate herself back to life."

"She's already so full of hot air…"

The phone illuminated once more, and Dylan met Michelle's gaze, brows raising, until the pull became too strong. On hands and knees, Dylan crawled forward, just enough to see who was calling. "Lauren," she muttered, not bothering to answer, not even bothering to pick up the phone.

"Those two are going to be the death of you," Michelle said.

"Not if I kill them first…"

Michelle's eyes locked on Dylan's. They ignored the shouts from the brand ambassadors and event coordinators and the shuffling of everyone else as they maneuvered toward the exit.

"You're not really serious..." Michelle started. Dylan continued to hold her gaze, as if the two were locked in a game of conspirator chicken.

Michelle didn't dare lose.

Dylan refused to back down.

"Unless?"

PUBLIC RADIO NETWORK

The Dark Side of Internet Fame: Examining the Pressures That Led to Isle de Cairn

Lakshmi Nguyen

The recent tragedy on Isle de Cairn has reignited public attention and conversation regarding the influencer marketplace, which features a unique coalescence of secrecy, responsibility, and competition.

The world of influencer marketing thrives in murky territory. Content creators are often paid in 'cost per mille' (dollars per one thousand views) or by a benchmark of followers, encouraging the use of bots. Akin to the more standard freelancing model, but with fewer benefits, influencers often shoulder the burden of being the "face" of a product without any power over its creation. Companies utilize cheaper influencer marketing by targeting rising content creators, exploiting their fanbase, and shifting blame or ownership without the need to pay standard advertising costs.

To garner more creative control, many influencers become small-business owners. With their greater access and ease of communication, they're often more in touch with consumer needs. This growth can be quick and often requires the hiring of additional workers, positioning the influencer as no longer a single person with many jobs, but one person on whom many people rely for a job.

This exclusive field can cause loneliness, forcing content creators to cling to the few others in their position. Parasocial relationships can form not just between fan and artist, but also between influencers. In a role that requires perfection, rewards relatability, and encourages "real-time posting" — where influencers share their current location, often at branded events to drum up excitement — content creators are often left in a perilous place without a safety net.

Many brands have reported that they'll be hosting brand trips differently in the wake of this tragedy. Several more have pledged to increase transparency regarding payment of their influencers and some have even encouraged their followers to donate to causes important to the Isle de Cairn influencers.

ACKNOWLEDGMENTS

First and foremost, thank you for picking up this book. Thank you for spending your hours diving into this world with my characters. I hope you had as much fun reading it as I did writing it.

Thank you, Zara, for taking a chance on this very silly story. Your commitment, diligence, and professionalism are so admirable. It's been a joy to work together.

Thank you to the entire Inimitable Books team, to our rights agent, Biagi Literary Management, and to Simon & Schuster for their support.

Biscotti and Diddo, thank you for letting me move back into your house after I quit my corporate job to write. I feel so lucky for those extra bonus years together. And thank you for your unwavering belief that I would publish books someday.

Thank you to my brothers for marrying two incredible women and giving me the gift I've always wanted: sisters.

David, thank you for fact-checking my "injury math" and forever being my first reader.

Robert, thank you for being your unhinged self and constantly providing quotes that I shamelessly steal to put into my books.

Shout out to my bestie, Pam. I'm so glad we got lost in London together and started talking about Meg Cabot. Cheers to thirteen years of friendship and many, many more to come.

A huge internet hug to all my YouTube, Twitch, and Patreon friends. I finished so much of this book on streams, documented the entire process through vlogs and Patreon posts, and our hours spent together have meant the world to me. Thank you, thank you, thank you.

Special thanks to the Chillicothe coven–Becca, Davaisha, Jess, Katie, Lindsay, and Wallis–for your never-ending encouragement and giggles. You are all my inspiration.

Forever and always the most thankful for my husband. I'd still be working with *[brackets]* and *[insert funny quip here]* without your ability to name my characters, help brainstorm plot points and character arcs on our long walks, and fuel me with all the best foods. Thank you for giving me Auntie Ly, Aunt Kim, Mama Bao, and Nanny. Thank you for being my most ardent supporter. You are my favorite person, and I'm so glad I get to spend life with you and all our animals.

ABOUT THE AUTHOR

Perpetually curious and powered by coffee, Kate Cavanaugh is a fan of stories in all their many forms. Though she may be a "genre hopper," she particularly loves writing mystery, romance, and fantasy, especially with little twists that make her giggle.

An "AuthorTube grandma," Kate has been posting writing experiments and vlogs to her YouTube channel for over eight years. She also streams productivity sprints on Twitch, with the help of her amazing and ominous D100.

When she's not at her computer, Kate can be found watching reality TV while she crochets, surrounded by her three dogs, two cats, and one husband.

THANKS
FOR
WATCHING

CURRENT

By Patricia Simmons · November 3, 2025

What Specialists Are Sayin

8,721 Reactions 2,156 Comments

The Forum

By Aisha Patel · January 18, 2026

True Crime Expert: "This Case Will Not Be S

89.3K Reactions 31,245 Comments

S

By

E

52

BookMarked

Curated by Emily Zhang · April 21, 2026

Real Life 'And Then There Were N

34.2K Saves 12,567 Comments